TROUBLE
in Discovery

Remington Rises Up

A REMINGTON ROBERTS NOVEL

SCOTT ROSBERG

TROUBLE IN DISCOVERY
Remington Rises Up
A Remington Roberts Novel

Scott Rosberg

Print ISBN: 978-0-9961320-8-4

eBook ISBN: 978-0-9961320-9-1

Printed in the United States of America

Editing, typesetting & cover design: Denis Ouellette
Cover photo: Dean Hendrickson

SlamDunk Success
P.O. Box 2062
Livingston, Montana 59047

www.SlamDunkSuccess.com

I dedicated the first book in this series, **Ultimate Team Player,** to all the Remingtons out there trying to make their teams better, their businesses better, and their families better. I want to dedicate this book to the most important team in my life over the last twenty years.

First, my wife, Lisa: You have dedicated yourself to creating the best team possible—our family—through the years. I couldn't imagine being with anyone better than you on this journey. You have made the best experience possible for all of us. I couldn't have asked for a better co-coach through life than you. I love you!

Second, my daughter, Maggie: You'll never know how much it meant to me that you allowed this old coach to enter your/your mom's life when you were ten. I tried to instill in you at a young age the lessons I have tried to teach in these books. You took many of the lessons, applied them to your own life as you grew up, and you've grown into an incredible woman along the way!

Finally, my son, Morgan: People who know you will realize that you are the catalyst for Remington. So much of his story is your story and my story with you. While the events and characters are made up, the characteristics we see in Remington started with you. You taught me so much about selflessness, joy, and unconditional love. Our bond through basketball is strong, but our bond through the love of a father and son has always been even stronger. Thanks for all the lessons you have taught us all about being the *ultimate team player!*

Much of what I wrote in this story was informed by my own experiences or by my wishing that they were real experiences. Because authors are human beings with thoughts, feelings, experiences, and biases, no writing is completely objective. While the characters in here may have characteristics of people who I have known, observed, or heard of, none of them are based completely on any actual people. They are a combination of many people and characteristics of people I have known or that I imagined as being part of the human and athletic experience in some way. Any similarity of characteristics, behaviors, and actions to any real persons is both a possibility that it was sparked by someone you know and coincidental at the very same time.

Chapter 1

The end of the prior year's season was a whirlwind for the Sacajawea High Boys' Basketball team. While they had achieved many of their goals, they now had a new goal. Like any other team, they wanted to win a state championship. The last time that happened in Discovery was in the 1990s, and these boys wanted to be the ones to bring back the next one. The returning players made a commitment to each other that they were going to work as hard as they possibly could all off-season and come home with the ultimate hardware the next year.

On the ride home from their final game, a few of them—Remington Roberts, Nick Bertucci, Tim Nelson, and Brian Jackson—walked up to the front of the bus where the coaches were sitting and sat down. They all leaned into the aisle and told their coach, Del Brooks, they wanted to win the state championship next year. While they were a fun-loving group of boys, Del had also seen them be serious before. As they sat there talking to him, he saw and heard a determination about them that he had not seen in such an intense way before.

They spoke of how they wanted to get in the gym as much as possible beginning in another week. Kids often say that kind of thing at the end of the season, but you rarely find them anywhere near the gym for months—at least not to work. But Del saw something different in them as they sat there talking. He sensed that this group was going to be different. The best player, Remington Roberts, was a true leader. He had a way about him that made people like him. He had a mature sense of humor about him that allowed him to be at ease with adults, but he could laugh and joke with his friends as well. When it came to basketball, though, while he enjoyed the fun he had playing, there was an air about him that said, "This is business, man. Don't be screwing around out here when we are working."

Del loved that about Remington. His teammates did, too. While they didn't have the same level of ability, intensity, and passion about the game that he had, they fed off of his. The harder he worked, the harder they worked. The more he encouraged them and lifted their spirits, the more they encouraged each other. He was the ultimate team player, always picking them up and trying to make them better. Because they liked him, liked playing with him, and liked how he treated them, they didn't want to let him down. So when Remington said, "We are getting in the gym all spring, summer, and fall," they were all in.

One of the problems with Remington's idea was that a lot of his teammates played spring and fall sports. Remington himself also played soccer. He knew it was good for his basketball. He played school soccer in the fall and club soccer in the spring. Of course, the competition and the coaching he received in both soccer seasons helped him be a better athlete. The soccer teams played a tough schedule, so they were pushed hard by their opponents and by their coaches. This made him better able to handle the competitive elements and pressure that came to him during the basketball season. The footwork and conditioning aspects of soccer also had a huge impact on his development as a basketball player through the years. The more he got all of the benefits from playing soccer, the better athlete he became. The better athlete he became, the better basketball player he became.

Nick Bertucci and Tim Nelson played football and ran track. They were very good football players on a not-so-very good team. They were going to be counted on to lead the football team by putting in their share of work in the off-season. They also ran track, and while they did not have the same passion for it, their track coaches were going to want them to focus on the various events they competed in throughout the spring.

The rest of the key returning players had played other sports through the years, but they were only playing basketball now. They, too, said they were all-in for spring, summer, and fall basketball workouts. While they didn't fully comprehend the hard work that Remington had in mind, the success they just experienced during the season made them want to work harder than they had ever worked before.

As Del heard the boys speak and saw their excitement at the possibilities, he got excited, too. While he had coached players who were into improving themselves and making the team the best it could be, he had not had anyone ever outline to him what they wanted to do in the off-season to prepare themselves for next year. And he certainly had never had kids do that on the bus ride home on the last day of the season!

But this group was different. While Del had only been coaching for a few years, this group was unlike anything he had ever seen. Even in his years as a player, playing for his own dad, he hadn't seen this. He himself had it, but it was like pulling teeth to get his teammates to want to work in the off-season. There was always some excuse why his buddies couldn't make it to the gym or the playground or the weight room. While Del was there pretty much all the time, he saw different teammates on different days in different weeks, but he never saw the same ones consistently.

In Remington, he saw *a lot* of who he was when he was their age. In fact, Del thought that Remington might be *even more* dedicated than Del was when he was in high school. But he also saw in the other boys a level of excitement and interest that he had not seen before. Yet Del also knew that it was the spring, right after the season. "We'll see how long this level of interest and intensity lasts," he thought. "Anyone can talk a good game on the last day of the season. But will they walk their talk? We'll see in a few weeks who is actually showing up and putting in the work."

Ideas to Consider:

- **What did the boys do on the bus ride home from the last game that Coach Brooks hadn't seen before?**
- **What was the plan that Remington and his teammates had in mind for the off-season?**
- **What are some potential obstacles to that plan?**

Chapter 2

Two weeks later at the end-of-season banquet, Del stood before the parents and players and highlighted the season and all of the team's accomplishments. As he called out each player's name to come up to the podium to be recognized for their participation in the program, he said a few words about each of them while handing them their certificate and their varsity letter if they won one. Once all of the boys had received their letters and certificates, Del moved to the awards portion of the evening.

Del read off the various conference, state, and team awards that team members had earned. Cade Clemons and Remington Roberts had been named First Team All-Conference, with Remington garnering All-State recognition as a junior. Ricky Flynn, another senior, and Nick Bertucci, a junior, were named Second Team All-Conference players. Brian Jackson, a sophomore, was recognized as an Honorable Mention All-Conference player. Brian showed a lot of growth throughout the season, and he looked like he was going to explode in his development over the course of the next year. With Remington, Nick Bertucci, and Brian all returning, the Wolves would be heavily favored to get to the state tournament and do some damage there.

Del then shifted from speaking of the individual and team highlights of the season to looking towards the future. He talked about how promising the next year looked with all of the players they had returning with a lot of varsity experience. But he also cautioned them. "If you think that because you had some success this year, you will automatically have success next year, you would be sadly mistaken. It is going to take a whole lot more work to continue that success and go further with it. You must prepare yourselves to do so. And that won't happen if you start preparing in November. Basketball players are made between March and November. Those who try to make themselves great from November to March never achieve the greatness they seek. You must put in the time *in the off-season* to become what you want to become *in the season.*"

Del paused and looked around at the team, nodding their heads with an intensity in their expressions that showed they were ready to get to work. Del continued, "However, I have never been more confident in a group that they will do just that than I am in this group. In my years as a player and a coach, I have never seen a group of teammates as focused and committed as the group that will return next year. From returning varsity players through the JV and freshmen players, the key will be how well you translate your words and desires into action."

Del said, "I would like to close with a quote that is so appropriate right now. It comes from a basketball trainer and coach named Alan Stein Jr. He speaks all around the world to high schools, colleges, and businesses. This quote has been adopted by so many people, and it is fitting for us to consider as we begin to embark on our journey to next year. The quote is this: **"Are the HABITS you have today on par with the DREAMS you have for tomorrow?"**

Del paused and said, "Boys, you have stated your dream and what you would like to accomplish. But it will take the right daily habits to get you to that dream you seek. *Are the habits you have today on par with the dreams you have for tomorrow?* Your actions every day will determine whether or not you achieve your dream."

As Del turned back to the podium to address the crowd of parents, Remington Roberts stepped forward and said, "Coach, do you mind if I say something?"

Del looked a little startled at Remington. Del turned back to the crowd and joked, "I guess when you become an All-State player, you think you own the room, huh?"

As they all smiled and laughed, Remington had a serious look, and he stepped forward to say, "No, Coach, that's not it at all. I just want to say that your words about our off-season are the most important words you've said tonight. Yeah, we're here to celebrate the season and recognize our seniors and thank them for all they did for our program through the years. That's the main focus of the night, and it's a great thing for us to do."

Remington turned to look around at the younger players in line as he continued. "But for us younger guys, tonight is also the opening of next season. Each of us needs to put in the time this off-season to become the best we can be. We all need to get in the gym and the weight room."

Remington turned and looked out at the freshmen and JV players sitting in the crowd, too. As he spoke, he alternated from looking at the younger players in the crowd and those in the line behind him. "Don't wait until next fall. It starts tomorrow. I know a lot of us play spring sports. But we need to make the time to get our workouts in. Over at my table, I have some schedules of times for when we want to get in the gym and weight room that should work around your spring sports schedules. See me after this, and I will get you one. Guys, our state championship quest starts now!"

Remington stepped back into the line with all of the other varsity players. As he did so, players started clapping and yelling, "Yeah, Rem! We're with you, man! Absolutely! Let's go."

Del said, "Great job, Rem. Maybe I should make you assistant coach in charge of off-season scheduling!" The crowd laughed, but they could tell Remington meant business. If the boys wanted to get to the Promised Land of a State Championship, they were going to have to work harder than they had ever worked before. Del couldn't wait to see how many of the kids followed up on their words and their excitement tonight by actually getting in and starting their workouts in the next few days.

Ideas to Consider:

- **At the end-of-season banquet, Coach Brooks said, "Basketball players are made between March and November." What did he mean by that?**
- **Del reads a quote from Alan Stein, Jr. "Are the HABITS you have today on par with the DREAMS you have for tomorrow?" What does that quote mean? How is Remington already preparing to put that quote into action?**

Chapter 3

The next day after school, Remington and seven other players were in the weight room. The ones who weren't there were at their track, baseball, and tennis practices. Remington's club soccer team didn't practice until 5:00 three days a week. That meant on those days, he was able to get in the weight room and gym right after school for about an hour. On the other two days, he could be there longer.

Today was one of those non-practice days for Remington's soccer team. Therefore, his schedule was to lift with his teammates from 3:30 to 4:15. Then they would go out into the gym and do 15 minutes of ballhandling and dribbling moves around cones and against each other, and 20 minutes of shooting drills. The Montana High School Association didn't allow coaches to work with kids in the off-season until the summer, so Remington led everything.

The boys worked extremely hard, especially for a first day of off-season workouts. Their reward was playing 4-on-4 full court games afterward. This was where they put into practice what they were working on individually, as well as maintain their conditioning. However, these games can also devolve into players not working hard and developing bad habits. While coaches always struggled with this, most players rarely noticed.

But Remington wasn't like most players. He knew this was the tendency, especially after the first couple of games. He worked to combat that by constantly picking kids up, encouraging them, but also holding them accountable when they weren't taking care of business. He reminded them of the goal—a state championship. For most players, that seemed like such a long way away. Remington knew he would have to constantly remind everyone why they needed to work so hard right now.

"While I want to believe that we're the only team in the state doing what we're doing, my gut tells me that Centennial, Burlington, Longbow, and Bighorn are all in their gyms getting in workouts. How else could they always be at the state tournament? I bet they're doing the same kind of work we are. They're already good, already winning games at state and winning state championships. That means we have to work even harder than they are."

Remington looked around at the faces of his teammates. He continued, "So when you're tired and thinking about not getting your butt down into a defensive stance, or you feel like jogging down the floor instead of sprinting, just remember that those teams aren't doing that. They are getting after it as hard as they can. If we plan on beating those teams at state next year, we can't have any let-downs. Get it?"

"Got it," they responded. Some of them thought how Remington sounded like Coach Brooks. But it made sense. Remington was the son of a coach. Ever since Remington was little, Steve Roberts was delivering messages of leadership, inspiration, and commitment to him. Steve, a successful high school coach himself for many years, saw in Remington at a young age a boy who loved basketball and wanted to be great at it. So, Steve offered him the same messages that he had given to his varsity players through the years. Remington filed bits and pieces of them away throughout his young life, and he found himself saying them to his friends, teammates, and classmates as he grew up. They became ingrained in him. It was as if he was born to lead.

Each week a good number of boys were consistently working out in the weight room and getting their ball handling, dribbling, and shooting workouts in. Under Remington's leadership, guidance, and force of will, the boys worked hard. A transformation in their strength and skills was happening for those who were committed to it, and they were loving the results.

Unfortunately, not everyone was completely bought in yet. Some of the players were more sporadic in their attendance. When they worked out in the weight room, they did not always focus as much or work as hard as the others, so they weren't getting as strong as the others. At times, their attitudes would pull down the attitudes of the guys who were really into it. When certain players were in there, the entire group would not put in the same level of effort as they normally did.

Another situation presented itself that was having a negative effect on the boys. A month after the season, a new boy from Oakland, California had moved into Discovery. His name was Connor McDonald. He was a sophomore who had played on a good team in Oakland. From what he told everyone, he had been a starter last year on a team that went 20–8 and made it to the championship game of their region. Del Brooks thought that at 6'6", Connor might be the missing piece that Discovery needed to win the state championship—a big man with skills.

Connor also had a swagger about him that most kids in Discovery didn't. He was a city kid, and his attitude was different from the Discovery boys. He quickly made friends with many kids. He got especially close to some of the basketball players. He started showing up at open gyms, and right away Remington saw that he could play. Remington reached out to him and tried to bring him into the group of boys who were working out on a regular basis. Connor was grateful that he was making friends, and he enjoyed hanging out with them. He was fitting in quite well socially, something he had worried about before moving.

Connor was funny, easy-going, and likeable. As often happens at small, rural schools when a new boy shows up, everyone flocks to him. People want to get to know the new kid, especially if he has some charisma about him. Connor was a good-looking boy with light-brown hair and blue eyes. His size, good looks, and friendly, outgoing personality helped him garner a lot of attention at Sacajawea High that spring. Everyone wanted him to be their friend, and he loved all the attention. He seemed to always be surrounded by at least 4 or 5 people at his lunch table, after school, and at parties on the weekends. Connor loved his newfound celebrity.

In Oakland, Connor had gone to a school of almost 3,000. While he was a fairly popular kid and a good athlete, he had mainly just blended in. He was a good basketball player, and as a sophomore, he played a key role on the varsity. While he wasn't a leading scorer, he was a strong inside player who could also shoot. He had moments as a sophomore where people saw he could become something special if he put the work in. Some bay area reporters put him on their "rising star" list for the following year, and many projected him to be one of the better players in the area and possibly the state.

Connor's dad, Patrick, was a doctor. Patrick had grown up in Discovery, and he went to Montana State University in Bozeman for his undergraduate degree. It was during his sophomore year that he met his future wife, Debra. She was from Silverton, a small town about four hours east of Discovery. They got married after they graduated and had Connor the following year while Patrick was in medical school at Stanford. His first residency was in Oakland, and he had established himself in that community as a good doctor.

While he and Debra liked Oakland well enough and liked the people, they always wanted to move back to Montana. They were rural people at heart, and the big city just never totally fit them. They grew tired of feeling closed in and on the go and grew tired of traffic, noise, smog, and the hurried pace. They missed the open spaces, the slower pace, and the friendly vibe back home. They would escape to the mountains or the beach throughout their years in Oakland, and they found themselves longing to live that way again. When they went back to Montana to visit family and friends, it was hard to go back to Oakland.

When a general practitioner position opened up in December at the hospital in Discovery, Patrick applied for it. They were headed to Montana for a few days at Christmas, and he interviewed for the position while they were there. Two weeks later, the hospital administrator called and offered him the position. Patrick was set to start on February 1st. He and Debra decided that he would move there then, and as soon as Connor's basketball season was over and their house sold, she and Connor would move to Discovery.

Connor, though, was not excited about the move. While he wasn't from the inner-city, he was still a city kid at heart living in a large metropolitan area, and he loved it. It was all he ever knew, and all he ever wanted to know. He had good friends and was popular in his circle. He and his friends went to see his favorite team, the Golden State Warriors, two or three times a year, and he dreamed of playing in the NBA with those players one day. Like a well-worn pair of Nikes, there was a comfort to his life that he liked.

While he did okay in school, he didn't put a whole lot of effort into much of anything other than basketball. However, the effort he put into basketball was not nearly as much as it could have been either. It was enough for him to improve and develop some of his natural ability, but when his coaches told him he needed to put in more time and effort, there was usually an excuse why he couldn't do it.

Unfortunately, Connor read the articles and tweets from those bay area reporters that had him projected as a rising star. He liked how that sounded and felt. Who wouldn't? The problem was that the more he heard about how great he was, the less he did to make any of those predictions come true. The reporters were talking about his potential based on the combination of his size and skills they had seen him display.

But potential is a tricky thing. When someone is early on their journey in some endeavor, having potential means people see something in you that could develop into something better. The key to potential, though, is what you do with it. Do you do the things necessary to go out and achieve it, or do you stop working as hard as you can because being tabbed as someone with potential means you have "made it"? On the other end of the "Journey of Potential" lies what you actually have accomplished. If after all the time that you have put into something, all the minutes devoted to that craft, people are now saying that you "had" potential, it means you did not live up to what you were capable of. Ultimately, having potential means you haven't done yet what you need to do to be considered successful.

After reading those articles and tweets, Connor immediately started down a path toward mediocrity and wasted potential. In his last weeks in Oakland, he stopped going into the weight room with his teammates. As they were preparing for the move to Montana, he was a bit depressed, knowing he was leaving his friends that he had grown up with. His parents and coaches understood it was tough on him, so it was easy to cut him some slack on skipping some workouts.

However, he also had a different mindset at play. He was never the biggest go-getter in terms of working out hard and often. But he knew to compete against the caliber of players in Oakland, he had to at least put in time and get *some* work done. But now, he was going to Montana. Montana was no hotbed for basketball talent compared to California. And he wasn't even going to one of the bigger cities in Montana. Connor knew that he would not be facing the same kind of athletes in Discovery that he faced in Oakland. He figured he would show up and immediately be one of the best players, probably *the best* player, on the team.

In his first week at Sacajawea High, he met Coach Brooks. While Coach Brooks seemed like a nice guy, Connor doubted he knew too much about the game since he was just a Montana guy and hadn't played or coached anywhere else. Coach Brooks was going to have a lot of proving to do to get Connor to believe he could help Connor get to the D1 level. Then, again, Connor knew he would be getting to that level on his own anyway, so he really didn't need Coach Brooks. Still, Coach seemed like a nice guy, so Connor was friendly with him.

Coach Brooks introduced Connor to some of the members of the team while they were in the weight room that day. He couldn't help but think what a bunch of redneck cowboys they must be, so he was a bit shocked to see them all wearing baggy shorts and Nike KDs and LeBrons. In his mind, he had conjured up an image of them playing in jeans and cowboy boots. The hip-hop music blaring out of the speakers shocked him, too. He had expected that by moving to Montana he was doomed to have to listen to country music for the next two years.

Two days later, Connor went to his first after-school workout. Remington was pushing the guys through one of their workouts. Connor was not a big fan of the weight room to begin with. He was really not a fan of having to do a full-blown workout that someone else had set up and was running, especially when that someone was a fellow player. Who did this Roberts kid think he was? Why was he was telling everybody else what to do? And why were they actually doing it? Connor played along nice that day for the most part, but there was no way he was going to listen to this kid for very long.

The worst, though, was when they went out into the gym to play after they finished lifting. It was the same as in the weight room. Roberts was telling them all what to do, putting them through ballhandling, dribbling, passing, and shooting drills before they started playing games. This was too much for Connor. He did a few ballhandling drills and told them that he needed to work on his shot. No way Connor was going to let some hick from some po-dunk Montana town tell him how to practice and work on his game.

The irony was that Connor didn't really *work* on his game. He just lazily shot some jump shots without really working up any kind of a sweat. Conversely, once all the other players got to the shooting portion of their workout, there was all kinds of movement, action, and different types of shots being put up. Remington had them working on catching and shooting, shooting off the dribble, and incorporating a shot fake and then a dribble. He had them shooting from 15 feet, the 3-point line, and a foot behind the 3-point line. They did about 20 minutes of shooting work after their 15 minutes of ballhandling and dribbling work. The players' shirts were already dark with sweat in spots. Connor's shirt looked like it just came out of his dresser drawer.

Once the games started, Connor perked up. He liked to *play* basketball, not *work* basketball. Now they were finally playing. But again, this playing was different than open gyms back home. Back home each guy was able to do his own thing and show off his skills, with a lot 1-on-1 action accompanied by trash-talking. Team play, passing, and defense were more of an afterthought, and Connor liked playing that way. It was fun. He didn't have to work that hard, other than when he had the ball in his hands.

But here at Sacajawea, these guys were playing like it was the middle of the season. They were moving a lot, passing to one another, and playing real defense. Connor was stunned. This was not what open gym basketball in April was supposed to be like. This was way more intense and a lot more work than he had ever seen at this time of year. While he wanted to relax a bit, he kept getting beat off the dribble by the guy he was defending. He realized that if he didn't change his tactics, he was going to look bad against these hicks.

When he finally picked up his effort, he started to play really well. He was able to stop his man from scoring, and he was able to attack and score almost at will. The only guy he struggled to stop or to score against was Remington. While he could use his size against Remington and post him up, Remington was quick enough that he was there on every move Connor tried to make. Connor realized that this Roberts kid was the real deal, that he was a good player. Connor felt he was better than Remington, but he could see that Remington was good, maybe even *Oakland good*. They played different positions, so they weren't matched up against each other too much. The times when they were matched up against one another, though, Connor played harder, and they really pushed each other.

After the games were done, Remington immediately went up to Connor. "Nice games, Bro. Man, you were taking it to me inside there. Keep doing that, and you're going to fit in really well. You're going to make a huge difference for us, dude! I can't wait to see what we can become with you here."

Connor's first thought was that he wasn't here to "fit in," but he held his tongue and said, "Yeah that was fun. I like your game, too, man. You got some skills. You could hang with my boys back in Oakland, for sure."

Remington said, "Thanks, dude. I'd love to play there sometime. I grew up playing in Phoenix, so I know a bit what it's probably like in Oakland."

Connor said, "Cool. When did you move here?"

"Fifth grade," said Remington. "It was hard, dude. I didn't want to leave my friends there, didn't want to leave the ball there. There were some flat-out ballers down there. But when I got here, these guys were all great, and we immediately started balling, and it's been the best. You're gonna' love it here."

Connor was tired. He hadn't played in a while, and he hadn't expected to play that hard, He figured he would be able to coast and just play like he always did. He also couldn't believe how easily he got tired. Remington immediately recognized what Connor was feeling and said, "Altitude."

Connor said, "What?"

"Altitude. You have lived at sea level your whole life. You're up over 4,000 feet here. The air is thinner, so it's harder to catch your breath and to recover. It will take time, but you'll get used to it. You'll just have to work hard and push through it early on. After a couple of months, you should be fine."

"Man, I hope so," said Connor. "I never felt anything like this from playing. Back home I could ball all night and never get tired."

Remington smiled and said, "I figured that. I know how you feel. I remember feeling that way when I moved here, too. Don't worry. You'll get used to it."

Remington then turned to the rest of the guys as they were putting on their shirts, finishing getting water, and grabbing their backpacks. He said, "In here, guys." They all made their way over to Remington. Connor sat in disbelief as he watched them all come together in a huddle. Not wanting to stand out in a bad way, he stood up and stepped into the huddle.

Remington said, "Hey, great work today. Loved the effort in the weight room and the drills. And the intensity level in the games was great." He turned towards Connor and said, "Good to have you here, Connor, and raising that intensity level up in our games. That's exactly what we need to do every time we play. We're looking forward to getting things going with you as part of this." Connor didn't know what to do, so he just nodded his head.

Remington turned back to the rest of the guys. "Boys, we are on our way towards that state championship. This is exciting. With Connor, we just added the size and inside presence we've been missing. If we keep working like this throughout the year, nobody in the state can stop us. We start real practice in just seven months and the state tournament is in about ten months. That doesn't sound like a long way away to me. We have to keep working like this every week if we are going to win state. Get it?"

They all responded, "Got it!"

"All right," said Remington. "Great job." He then put his hands into the middle of the group and said, "Wolves on three—1, 2, 3," and the players all said "Wolves" and broke their huddle.

Connor couldn't believe what he was seeing and hearing. What was this place? Who was this Roberts kid? He had never seen kids in an open gym setting act like this. You would think it was the middle of the season. "It's not supposed to be like this," he thought. "Open gyms are supposed to be way more chill than this. I don't know how much of this I can take."

But Connor didn't say a word about his thoughts. He just high-fived and fist-bumped guys as they came over to him to say things like, "Nice job, dude," and "Glad you're here, man." While he liked how nice they were, he was not used to how they acted.

Ideas to Consider:

- **How is Remington leading the boys as they begin their off-season?**
- **How is Connor struggling with his move to Discovery? How could he help the Wolves this year? What will he need to do in order to do so?**
- **What kinds of potential problems can you already see developing?**

Chapter 4

Jenny Jones had been Remington's best friend since 5th grade when his family moved to Discovery. They lived just around the block from one another, and their bond was almost instant. While most boys that age want nothing to do with girls, Remington didn't think that way. He had a big sister of his own, and girls were just other people to have as friends.

Not long after he moved to Discovery, he met Jenny when he went to play basketball at a park he had found in their neighborhood. She was with a couple of friends who were swinging on the swings. As he walked onto the court with his basketball under his arm, Remington said, "Hi," in the direction of all of them. Jenny was the only one to return a "Hi" to Remington. A few minutes later when a he missed a shot, Remington's basketball rolled near Jenny. Before he could get to it, she picked it up and tossed it to him. He said, "Thanks."

She said, "You're welcome."

He asked her what her name was, and pretty soon they were in a conversation about who they each were, where he was from, and where they lived. He invited her to join him shooting baskets while they talked, and she did so. While they were shooting, she told him she was a soccer player, not a basketball player.

Remington said, "Why not play both? I do. I used to only play basketball, but this year I started playing both. Each one helps me play the other better."

"Really?" said Jenny. "How could soccer help you with basketball? You can't use your hands in soccer."

Remington said, "Yeah, but all the footwork and running and playing with your eyes up while dribbling and passing in soccer helps with those same things in basketball. My PE teacher down in Phoenix and my dad both told me that. He's a basketball coach, and he was right. I'm better at both sports now."

Jenny said, "I guess that makes sense."

Remington said, "Yeah, I think so." He paused and said, "I plan on coming down here most days around this time to work on my game. If you want to join me, I'll show you some things to help you play basketball."

Jenny said, "That would be nice. Thanks."

And that was it. They started meeting at the park most days that summer. While Remington would have rather shot alone and gotten a good workout in, he liked Jenny's company. He also liked helping her play, and she was athletic enough that she started getting good at basketball pretty quickly. He started going to the court about a half-hour early, so he could get some of his own dribbling and shooting workouts in first.

She liked Remington. He was a nice boy who was easy to talk to. Most boys didn't talk to her very much, but Remington was different. The more time they spent together, the closer their friendship grew, and as they continued to grow up through the years, their relationship got even stronger.

Last year, during their junior year, they were both feeling things about each other that they had not ever felt before. Finally, at the start of the summer, after he had gotten a letter from Coach K at Duke, Remington asked Jenny out to the movies as a way to celebrate. As he was asking her to go to the movie, he realized he was asking her out on a date. He had wanted to do that for some time, and when he finally did, they both talked about how much both of them had been wanting that for quite a while. They were each stunned to learn that the other had developed stronger feelings for the other one. "Really?" Jenny had said. "You mean you've liked me that way all year?"

Remington responded, "Well, I don't know exactly when I started feeling this way, but I know last summer when I was away at my basketball camps, I was missing you a lot and thinking about you that way."

Jenny said, "That's so wild. I started feeling the same way about you while you were gone during the summer."

They laughed and got excited about going on their first date together. They settled on the new *Avengers* movie that was out at the time. They had a nice time at the movies, and afterward they went to Romano's for pizza. When Remington drove her home, he walked her to her front door. Neither of them wanted the night to end, as they were having such a great time with each other. They both said that while they always had a good time together, this newfound realization that they were each attracted to each other as more than just friends added a whole new element to the fun they were having.

Remington repeated an idea the two of them had discussed earlier in the day when he asked her out. "Too bad we didn't know sooner that we both felt like this, huh?"

But Jenny said, "No, it's probably for the better, Rem. Who knows if our relationship was different what it might have done to your season? I mean, you guys played so well, and you made All-State, and you've got all those colleges interested in you. If we were dating, you might not have been as focused, and it might have affected your play."

Remington couldn't believe how cool Jenny was. Here they were on her front porch expressing to one another that they liked each other as more than just friends, but her first thought was how that could have negatively affected his basketball. She knew how important basketball was to him, and she didn't want to do anything that would get in the way of it.

Remington said, "Maybe. But I also know that with how strong our relationship already is, I don't think it would have been that much different. I think I would have handled it just fine." He smiled at her and then said, "I'm ready to see now how it affects me. I hope you are, too."

She looked up at him and smiled. He reached his hand up and brushed a few strands of her long brown hair away from her cheek. He smiled and said, "I just wanted to see your whole face." Before he knew it, his hands slid down, and he was holding her around her waist. She lifted her hands and placed them on his shoulders. He leaned down and kissed her for the very first time. It felt incredible.

While he had kissed a few girls that he had gone out on dates with through his high school years, he was just not all that into girls. He always said, "Basketball is my girlfriend." He even had a t-shirt with that printed on it. And while some guys said that kind of thing, Remington lived it. So he had not ever developed a lasting relationship with any of those girls. But he had always had a relationship with Jenny, and he loved it. He loved how they were when they were together. She was so much fun, and she always made him feel good. And now with his lips on hers, she was making him feel good in a whole new way.

Jenny was feeling the same way as Remington. As they were kissing, she couldn't help but feel, "I've been thinking of this for a long time, and it's finally happening." She loved the feel of his lips on hers. She was at first a little shocked when it happened, but the shock quickly became a desire for more. She loved what she was feeling right now.

While she didn't want it to end, she also didn't want it to go any further than this. After a few seconds of kissing like this, she pulled her mouth off of his, looked into his blue eyes, and said, "That was nice."

Remington smiled and said, "I know. I've been wanting to do that for a long time."

She smiled and said, "Me, too." She paused and said, "But Rem, I want to take things slowly, okay. This is kind of new territory for me." While she, too, had dates with some boys through the last couple of years, she could tell right away that those boys were after one thing, and it wasn't a steady relationship. She wasn't into that, so she quickly ended those evenings, so they didn't progress far at all.

While her feelings for Remington were much different than what she felt for any of those other boys, she also wanted to be smart and take things slowly. She didn't want to jump into doing things that she might end up regretting later. They had both talked about how much they loved each other as friends and how they didn't want to ruin that.

But when relationships start to add a physically intimate component to them, the relationship can suffer. Neither of them wanted that, and when Jenny told Remington she wanted to take things slowly, he responded, "Okay. Me, too."

Jenny said, "Thanks for understanding, Rem. Besides, it just gives us more to look forward to down the road, huh?"

He said, "Absolutely," and smiled. He then said, "All right, I've got to get home. Can I see you tomorrow?"

She said, "Sure. I'd love that."

He smiled an even bigger smile, leaned down, and gave her another kiss. Neither of them wanted to let go of the other's lips, but this time Remington pulled away and said, "Okay, I better go right now, or we're going to take what we just said and throw it out the window!"

Jenny said, "You're right. Thanks, Rem. I had a great time tonight."

Remington said, "Me too, Jen." He took his hands off of her waist as she pulled hers from around his neck. He turned away, started down her porch steps, and said, "I'll see you tomorrow."

"Can't wait," said Jenny.

Ideas to Consider:

- **What does Remington tell Jenny about playing both soccer and basketball? Do you play or coach multiple sports? Do you find one helping you in the other?**

- **As they start to get intimate, both of them feel it is best not to move too quickly. Why is this a smart thing to do for them (and for any teenage couple)?**

Chapter 5

The summer season started with a tournament in Billings. Due to high school association rules, coaches couldn't coach their kids from the end of the winter season until June 1st. The tournament was scheduled for June 2nd and 3rd, so Coach Brooks had one day to put in some things for the boys to play in the tournament. However, every other school at the tournament would be in the same situation, so he was not too concerned.

Besides, the spring open gyms and workouts had seen the best attendance in all of Del's years coaching and playing at Sacajawea. He was confident that the boys were at least in decent shape to be able to get up and down the court and compete. He also knew that summer tournaments are a lot less about running set plays and winning all the games and more about developing players individually and as a team. He also liked to try out new things in the summer, so he would start putting some of those things in the following week. This weekend was more about getting as many players playing time, working to incorporate skill development into their games, trying different combinations of players, and building team chemistry.

The Wolves' first game of the tournament was going to be against Buckley, a team from over near the Montana/North Dakota border. Buckley played in the Eastern A League that fed into the larger end-of-season Eastern Divisional Tournament with the Mid-State A League that Sacajawea played in. Buckley had been an average team in the east for years. They were consistently a middle-of-the-pack team in a very good division. They just couldn't get over the hump against the really strong eastern teams, like Burlington, Bighorn, and last year's state champion, the Longbow Bulldogs.

Sacajawea started out strong against Buckley. The combination of Remington on the outside and Connor on the inside was working well. The two of them were a match-up nightmare for teams because they could not double-team off of either of them. Combined with the scoring of Nick, Tim, Brian and Mike, Sacajawea was rolling right out of the gate. Sacajawea already had an 18-point lead about 12 minutes into the first 20-minute half when Del subbed two players in for Remington and Connor.

As they came off the floor, Remington high-fived Del. As Del reached to high-five Connor as well, Connor didn't raise his hand up to receive it. He simply asked, "Why are you taking me out, Coach? I'm just heating up."

Del was a bit shocked at this. He had just been snubbed by a player who he was trying to high-five. He was also being questioned by the player about his playing time and substitution. Del stopped him and said, "You're new here, so I'll cut you some slack this one time."

Connor looked confused as Del continued. "First of all, don't ever snub me again when I reach to give you a high-five, fist-bump, handshake or whatever. Second, we have ten guys here who are going to play. It's the summer. We need everyone to get reps. Everyone here has the right to play as much as anyone else in the summer. It is the only way they will improve. I treat summer as a chance to get everyone time, so I can see what they can do. I want to see different combinations of guys. You're going to get a lot of minutes this summer. So is everyone else."

Connor nodded his head in understanding and said, "Sorry, Coach. I just thought I was playing really well."

Del said, "You were. It's why we have an 18-point lead. You and Remington have been a force that they can't stop. I am so excited to see what we can do with you two this year, and we're only 12 minutes into the summer season. But there are a lot more guys on this team than just the two of you, and we need to get them up to speed, too."

"All right, Coach, I get it," said Connor, and he took a seat on the bench next to Remington, who told him how much fun the year was going to be with the two of them playing together like that. Remington stuck his fist out and Connor smacked knuckles with him.

The rest of the game saw more of the same with Remington and Connor dominating the entire game. This also led to a lot of good, open looks for the rest of the Wolves, and they were loving how much easier it was to get good shots off. Sacajawea ended up beating Buckley by 35 points, and it could have been a lot worse if Del had played Remington and Connor more.

After the game, Del addressed the team out on the lawn in front of the school. "Boys, that's a good start to the summer. You really took it to those guys. Rem, nice job of setting your teammates up, while also attacking and shooting your own shots. Connor, it's nice to have you with us. If you keep playing hard and pushing yourself to be the best you can be, you are going to have success here. There aren't too many players around with your combination of size and skills."

Del pointed out many of the other boys' contributions, as well. He then said, "Let's keep in mind that Buckley is not the same caliber as the really good teams, so this was not necessarily a true indication of how good we are. But it is an indication of what we can be if we play the way we're capable of playing. We face a much tougher team this afternoon. Bighorn will be really good, and we will have our work cut out for us. But with how hard you have all been working this spring, and with the combinations we now have, I like our chances against anybody."

The boys went in and got something to eat and drink. They watched some of the other games while they waited two hours for their game against Bighorn. Connor sat off by himself watching the other teams. He thought how none of them could hang with the Oakland teams that he played against. While he saw that there were some good players in the games he was watching, none looked like they were as strong inside as him. He was going to have a field day playing in this state. This was going to be easy.

Ideas to Consider:

- **Why does Coach Brooks play all of his guys a fairly equal amount of time in the summer when he knows they have a better chance of winning if the better players play more? Is his philosophy about summer play a good one for coaches to have? Why or why not?**

Chapter 6

The second game against Bighorn was just how Coach Brooks had said it would be. Bighorn was solid, with good athletes at every position. While they weren't the same athletes that Connor played against back in Oakland, they were still really good, and they could ball. They had one player named Taylor Allan who was as good a shooter as Connor had ever seen.

The game went back and forth the whole way, with neither team ever leading by more than 8 points. However, Del kept to his mantra of playing everybody and getting them all good minutes. While there were numerous moments when he wanted to just play his best five players, he knew that winning the second game of a summer tournament was not the main focus for summer. The focus was on getting all the kids minutes, so they could all have a chance to improve for when it mattered most—the winter season. He hoped that playing those players against really good competition when the outcome of the game was not nearly as important would pay dividends next season, especially in the post-season tournaments.

With Bighorn up by two with 8:00 left, Del subbed out Connor and Nick. Bighorn's coach, Jim Stilwell, was not operating under the same mindset as Del. He was playing to win right from the start. He had 11 kids on the team for this game. Six of them played a lot of minutes, two of them played sparingly, and three of them hadn't even gotten into the game yet. Del made a mental note of that for his post-game talk and for his preparation for the divisional and state tournaments, should they end up facing Bighorn then.

As Connor came off the floor, he once again started to protest to Del. Del put his hand up to stop him from continuing and said, "Connor, sit down next to me for a minute." They both sat down and Del continued. "I told you before what I'm doing. Everyone is going to get their minutes. Let me ask you something. Which of the guys on our team today haven't been at the open gyms and weight room sessions?"

Connor looked at the guys on the bench and then out on the floor. He said, "None of them. They've all been there."

Del said, "Exactly. And they were also there for three weeks before you showed up at Sacajawea. So which ones shouldn't be playing? Who doesn't deserve to be out there based on all the time and effort they've been putting in?"

"None of them. They all deserve it."

"Exactly. I'm glad you see my point."

Connor said, "Coach, I see your point. It's just that we are right there with this team, and they're only playing their studs. Some of their guys haven't even played. No offense to some of our guys, but they can't compete with their studs. If we don't have the right guys out there, we won't be able to win."

Del said, "That *may* be true. But today is June 2nd. Who the heck cares what the outcome of a game on June 2nd is? There are no standings, no newspaper clippings, no seeding for state tournaments here. The team that wins this tournament gets a plaque. So do the second and third place teams. How many times have you been to another school or even your own school in Oakland and cared about a trophy for a summer tournament? Let's start with never. Nobody cares about records in the summer."

Del paused and then said, "Yes, I want to win the game, and I will coach to win the game, and you need to play to win the game. But I also want *all* of these players as ready as possible to compete during the season, so we give ourselves the best chance at winning when it matters most. I like that their coach isn't playing his weaker players. They will not be prepared to play when we face them in the divisional or state tournament. I like that even with him only playing his studs and us playing everybody, we are ..." Del looked at the scoreboard and continued, "only down by 4 points with 7:00 left in the game. It shows me that we are going to be really good this year because we are going to have a strong bench. I'm really excited about the possibilities for our season."

Connor hung his head, but Del tapped him on the knee. "I'm especially excited about the season because you showed up. I knew we were going to be really good this year already. But now with you—holy crap, are we going to be good! I have not seen a player with your combination of size and skills the last two years. Sure, you've got work to do, and work is the key word. If you put in the time and effort, you could become one of the better players in the state."

Connor was thinking, "No duh! Of course, I can. I can be the best. There isn't anyone like me in this state." But he kept his thoughts to himself and just looked at Del and nodded.

"You and Remington together will be the best 1-2 punch in the state. No team has two guys like you two. It is going to be so much fun watching the two of you this year. But you two are a given. We know you're going to be good, along with our other key guys. But a team needs *everybody* to play well to be successful. So today and the rest of the summer is about us trying to get everybody as many minutes as they can get. Does that make sense now?"

Connor nodded his head. "Yeah, I get it, Coach. Sorry I didn't see it that way before."

Del said, "No apology necessary. Go get a drink, and at the 4:00-mark, report back in for Jimmy."

Unfortunately, by the time the 4:00-mark hit, the Wolves were down by 12. Without Connor or Nick on the floor for the last few minutes, Bighorn had pulled away. While Connor's and Nick's re-insertion into the lineup sparked the Wolves, they could never overtake Bighorn, and they ended up losing by four.

Del pulled the boys out to the same spot on the lawn where they spoke after the first game against Buckley. He could tell they were dejected and tired. Playing two and three games in a day led to tired legs, tired bodies, and tired minds. But that was a good thing, as it was teaching the players to reach inside themselves to find the toughness to persevere through the difficulty. Del said, "Boys, I'm really proud of the effort you gave out there. It's one of the things I love so much about coaching you. You never give up, and you always give 100% effort. That will serve us well in the regular season and tournaments. I know it's hard when you play a game, rest for two hours, and then play another game against a really strong team. But it's so important that you go through these kinds of trials to help you learn to push through.

"I don't know how many of you noticed, but Bighorn never played three of their players, and two of them played for maybe ten minutes. They have all their guys here this weekend, so what you saw today was their team that will supposedly be vying for a divisional and state championship this year. Don't get me wrong. They're good, and they certainly could win it all this year. But we played *all* of our guys, and you all played a lot of minutes."

Del paused to see their reactions. Most were nodding their heads. Del looked at Jimmy Thompson. "Jimmy, when's the last time you played that many minutes against some of the best varsity competition in the state?"

"I haven't. This is the first varsity experience I've had."

Del turned to Bob Bickford, another sophomore playing with the varsity this weekend. Del felt that he and Jimmy could become key contributors this year. "How about you, Bob? Have you played a lot against those kinds of players?"

Bob responded, "When I went to the MSU camp last summer there were some good players, a couple of those guys in fact. But I didn't play against them much because they were in the level above me. The only time I play against guys that good is in our open gyms against these guys," he said looking at his teammates.

"That's right," Del said. "These guys you play with every night are as good as or better than every one of those guys on Bighorn. And Longbow. And Centennial. And all the rest of the teams in our state." Del looked around, and he could see the recognition on the boys' faces.

"Guys, we will be playing everyone a lot of minutes this summer. I want to win as much as anybody. But my gosh, it's June 2nd. Who cares who wins on June 2nd? He paused and then said, "But on February 2nd and March 2nd, yeah, that's when I want to be winning. Well, our best chance of winning in February and March is when we have as many of our players ready to play as can be ready. The way that happens is by playing all of them as many minutes as possible in June and July. Look at the experience that Jimmy and Bob just had, that they just told you they never had before. And they did really well!" Del turned toward Jimmy and Bob and said, "I'm really excited for the two of you because I think you can be key contributors for us this year if you put in the time and effort all summer long."

Del turned back to looking from face-to-face at each of the players and said, "This is so important for all of you to get that kind of experience. I am so excited because of it. So when you're bummed out about losing a game like this—and yes, you should be bummed out any time you lose—keep in mind what the big picture is. The big picture is the divisional and state tournaments next February and March. Get it?"

The boys responded, "Got it."

Del said, "All right, we play our final game in three hours against Silverton. They're good, too. Not Bighorn good, but good. If we don't come out ready to play, they could be trouble for us. So just like before, get fluids, good food, rest, and be back here at 4:30."

They all stood up, came together in a circle, and put their hands up high together. Remington said, "Wolves on three—1, 2, 3." They all said, "Wolves."

The Silverton game did not go anywhere near the way the Bighorn game went. It became a blowout early, with Remington and Connor leading the way. All of the boys played a lot of minutes, and once again, Jimmy and Bob had good games. Their confidence grew with each minute they played. Nick, Tim, Brian, and Remington were all cheering them on and helping to build up their confidence for when they would need the two sophomores in the regular season. Mike Visteen and Cory Wilson also played a lot, and they continued to develop. In fact, those two had improved the most since last season. They had each only missed one workout in the spring, and it showed with how well they were playing. All of the boys were excited with how the summer was starting and where they thought they could go next year.

Ideas to Consider:
- **How did Coach Brooks's philosophy of playing in the summer get tested in the second game of the tournament? Did the opposing coach seem to have the same philosophy?**

Chapter 7

The rest of the summer went very well for the Wolves. They had a skill-building camp in the second week of June, with the best attendance for a camp in Del's time as the coach. They worked on their individual skills, followed by trying to incorporate those skills in games at the end of camp each day. Del was pleased with the results. They also continued to play in weekend tournaments in June and July, and they won the majority of their games. They actually took first place in their division at the tournament at Canyon High School, the school that Remington's dad had coached at for many years.

Del also took them to the University of Montana Team Camp in Missoula. He liked to take the boys on one trip to a team camp to help them spend some time together and bond. It also gave them opportunities to play against teams from other northwestern states. He felt it gave them a chance to measure themselves against good players in other states, while preparing them to play the teams in their own state during the season.

The team-bonding aspect of these trips was important. On these trips, the boys spent a lot of time hanging out with one another. Del was always able to work in some character instruction and team-building types of activities to begin creating the team-first attitude that is so important for teams to have if they are going to have any success whatsoever. With the addition of Connor, Del was even more interested in this aspect of the team camps. He felt that the more Connor could become close with his teammates the better chance this team had of being the best team he had coached and possibly one of the best teams to ever play at Sacajawea High School. Sacajawea had its share of great teams through the decades, but the last five to ten years had seen a drop-off in that high level of success.

Del felt a lot of pressure to win because of this. While nobody had ever said anything to him about his job being on the line, with each succeeding year of not getting to the state tournament, he felt more pressure. With the success they experienced last year and the expectations that people had for this year, he felt like a great weight was put on his shoulders.

He knew people would be expecting more success this year with all the good players coming back. With the young sophomores, Jimmy Thompson and Bob Bickford, coming up to the varsity next year and joining the strong returning players, many people felt that this team could win a state championship. With the addition of Connor McDonald, the expectations rose even higher. His combination of skill and size was unique in the state this year, and people could see that this kid might be the key to pushing Sacajawea over the top to a state championship.

However, Del also saw a problem developing. Connor had already become a bit of a challenge. Del had already seen Connor displaying a poor attitude, not giving all-out effort, and not being a good teammate. Del was walking a fine line, trying to establish a positive relationship with Connor, but also instilling in him the proper discipline necessary for success. Del needed to hold Connor accountable, but he also didn't want to lose him right away. So he dealt gingerly with him.

Already some of the elements of dealing with Connor reminded him of how he struggled with Cade Clemons the last four years. While Connor was different than Cade, there were some similarities. Both were *really* good players, but since they played different positions and had different kinds of games, it would be hard to compare the two of them. However, one place Del could see they were very similar was in their selfishness. Just like Cade, Connor was focused mostly on himself. He didn't care all that much about his teammates. He had been at the school for the last three months of the year, and he was now into his second month of the summer playing with them. By now, he should be caring about them a whole lot more than he did.

This was the biggest reason why Del looked forward to the summer team camp trip. This would be a great chance to get Connor bonding with his teammates. Del hoped that by being on the road together with his teammates for a few days, a lot of that bonding would occur. As he watched Connor's interactions with the rest of the boys, he could see it was happening. Del got excited each time he saw Connor laughing it up with Nick, Tim, or Brian.

He especially got excited when he saw Connor having fun with Remington. He knew that Connor could see Remington as a threat because Remington was the best player on the team. If he could get the two of them to become good teammates and even friends, it would go a long way towards creating future success. This was not a problem for Remington. He didn't seem to have a jealous bone in his body when it came to teammates' success. He just wanted to win. He was the best player that Del had coached and had seen in person at the high school level. But most amazing was that he was the best teammate Del had ever seen. He was all about getting everybody involved and creating success for each of his teammates. While he could have scored 25 points a game if he wanted, he would rather score 15 a game and hand out 10 assists. He knew that if he was dishing the ball to teammates for scores, they would be happy, and the team had a better chance at success.

If Del could get Connor to embrace Remington as a teammate and friend, good things could happen. Del did all that he could to put them together as

27

much as possible on this trip. Any chance he could get to have them communicating with one another, Del tried to create it. As Del watched Remington and Connor together, it looked like the plan was working. They were doing a lot of laughing and joking and just talking about things. That was a good sign. Del also created some team-bonding exercises for the players to do in the evenings after the day's games and activities. He set these activities up to put kids who didn't know one another all that well with each other. Younger players were with older players for the most part. This helped bring sophomores, juniors, and seniors together better.

While Connor and Remington were getting along well, and the overall team-building exercises were producing a lot of the desired results, there was one unintended consequence that Del had not considered. Connor was starting to *only* bond with Remington, Nick, Tim, and Brian. He did not make much of an effort to bond with any of the other players. Connor saw in those four players that they were the key guys. They were also three seniors and a junior. Connor respected them.

However, he did not seem to develop the same level of interest in getting to know the other players, especially Jimmy and Bob, the two sophomores. Connor didn't do anything to any of the other players that would be looked on as bad. He just didn't do anything with them at all. And when he played with them on the court, they might as well not even have been out there. He rarely passed them the ball, never acknowledged a good play by them, or never communicated with them in any way. Del never saw this. He was so excited that Connor was bonding well with Remington, Nick, Tim, and Brian, that he didn't see that Connor was actually driving a wedge between himself and the rest of his teammates.

So while the team camp was a success in terms of how well the team played and how well they started getting along and becoming a team, there was a minor crack in the cohesiveness of the team that had started on this trip. Unfortunately, Del never saw it. He was so excited by the success of the team in the games and the way that Connor was getting along with the older boys that he didn't see the groundwork being laid for a problem later that fall.

Ideas to Consider:

- **What does Coach Brooks feel taking his teams to a team camp and tournaments provides for them individually and as a team? Does it seem to have worked on their trip to U of M?**

- **How is Connor reacting to his experience so far? How is he getting along with his new teammates?**

Chapter 8

The rest of the summer went very well for Remington and Jenny. They spent even more time together than they would in a normal summer. The intensity of their relationship continued to grow. But staying true to what they had said they wanted to do, they took things quite slowly in the physical aspects of their relationship.

As difficult as it was at times, they both knew it was the right thing to do. Jenny was starting her senior year of soccer soon, and she didn't want her focus to be in the wrong place. Remington understood that concept all too well, and he didn't want to be a distraction to her. Jenny was a good soccer player, one of the top three players on the team. She had an opportunity to possibly receive some scholarship money to play at one of the small schools in the state. While her top choices for school were Stanford, University of Montana, and Montana State, places she was not good enough to play soccer, she hadn't completely ruled out going to a smaller school and playing.

Remington did not want to hurt her chances of playing in college if that's what she decided she wanted to do. He also knew that Jenny was a really good student, #1 in her class for the last three years. No matter where she ended up, she would want to have the best GPA, as well as the best ACT and SAT scores possible. The last thing Remington needed was the guilt of being the reason why any of those scores might not be where she wanted them.

Remington also knew that these were all the same kinds of things he was dealing with for his own future. A really good student himself, he knew that he needed to stay sharp and focused on his studies and his workouts if he was going to achieve the dreams and goals that he had. As much as he was really enjoying their time together and what they were exploring with each other, he also knew that if he allowed himself to get too hung up on her, it could drastically affect his season and his future.

"My future," he thought. "What will my future be like?" This was a recurring thought for Remington on an almost daily basis. While he did his best to push a lot of it aside when he would get overwhelmed by it, it was hard to do. Everyday there was a new letter from a school interested in him going there. Most were form letters or brochures sent out to seniors all across the country, whether they were athletes or not. But after the team camp, as well as tournaments he played at with the Montana Select AAU team, he started receiving more letters or text messages from coaches in the western part of the country who saw him play. They were interested in getting him to their campus. By the end of July, he had eight schools that had separated themselves for him as his top choices: University of Montana, Montana State, Gonzaga, Oregon, Colorado, Arizona State, Stanford, and Duke.

Eight schools were still way too many schools to have in mind at this point in his decision-making. But he just couldn't make up his mind. Each school provided an excitement for him. He had met a coach from each of those schools this summer, except for one—Duke. The coaches he had met were all very nice and very complimentary of his play. They all said that they liked how he played, but all but ASU said he would probably have to red-shirt for his freshman year to get his skills up. However, the ASU coaches, head coach Dave Meador and assistant coach Wylie Carson, both said they felt he might be able to play right away. Remington liked that. While he understood the concept and value of red-shirting, he had never sat out a season before. He struggled seeing himself doing that. He loved to play more than anything else, and he wondered if he would be able to handle sitting and watching and not playing for an entire season.

Remington and Wylie Carson hit it off quite well from the first time Coach Carson introduced himself. Remington felt a good vibe with him, and he looked forward to seeing Coach Carson each day at the two tournaments where he saw him. Even though he hadn't visited the ASU campus since he was a little kid living in Phoenix, Coach Carson was such a positive influence that Remington was leaning that way a bit now.

However, there were a few problems with that. First, he had not been to the campus since he was little. When Remington lived in Phoenix, they had gone to a football game there. He remembered the football stadium sitting right next to a mountain with a big "A" on it, and he remembered how much fun it was being in that large of a crowd cheering on the team. They had driven around the campus another time, too, but he didn't remember much of it. The thought had always been in the back of his mind that he might go to school there. But the further away from his days in Phoenix he got, the further away ASU was from his mind.

Second, ASU was not on Jenny's list of schools that she was interested in. As their relationship had grown stronger all summer, this became a real concern for Remington. While they had both said they shouldn't pick a school based on where the other one was going, that idea came from the rational thought part of them. Remington was so torn. He knew that he should not let Jenny affect his decision in any way, but he couldn't stand the thought of not being with her. He wanted to be with her every chance he could. The thought of her being at one college and him being at another was too hard to take. It's one of the reasons why U of M and MSU were still on his list and why Stanford was now also on it.

Finally, there was that one school on the list that Remington could not get out of his head—Duke. It was the dream, the ultimate school for him. His whole life he had dreamed of going there and playing for Coach K. While they were the one school where he had not personally met a coach, they were still on his list. Coach James, an assistant coach from Duke, had actually contacted him late in the summer, and he was at one of the western tournaments that Remington played at with his AAU team, although they never got to meet in-person. Coach James said he liked what he saw of Remington. He said he had also been in touch with Remington's AAU coach, and his coach had been quite complimentary of Remington. In fact, Coach James said, "He said you're the best player on the team, and it's not even close."

Remington was happy to hear his coach had said that about him. Coach James said he wanted to stay in touch with Remington. He said that they had two spots left for red-shirt freshmen to come in and work and hopefully develop to become key guys over the following years. He said he couldn't offer him one of those yet, but that he would be telling Coach K about Remington and there was a possibility they would offer him that spot.

While this made Remington extremely happy and excited, it also added to his confusion. What should he do? When he and Jenny went out to dinner in mid-August, a week before their soccer seasons were about to begin, Remington still had so much that was unknown and so much left to decide. They talked about the summer. She talked about how her summer soccer season had gone so well and how excited she was to get started practicing in a week.

Remington said, "A week? That's all we have? Gosh, I need more than that. I'm so tired. I don't even want to think of soccer right now."

Jenny had never heard Remington say anything like that. In Montana, the girls' and boys' soccer seasons were both in the fall. Every year for Remington's first three years of high school soccer, he was excited to get the season started. Each spring he played with the local club team in a season that ended in June. For the last few weeks of spring soccer, he had to juggle the end of that season with the beginning of summer basketball. But this year, he knew he needed to put even more time into basketball if he was going to achieve his college dreams, so he missed two of the final three weekends of spring soccer.

Now that the school soccer season was here, he should have been chomping at the bit to get going. But all he could think was that it never felt like he had a summer. He was constantly working in some fashion, mainly on his basketball game. He just wanted to rest for a while and take some time off. He said, "I'm sure in the next week, I will start to get excited for soccer, getting back hanging with Sean, Conrad, Luke, and the rest of the boys. But right now, I just want to sleep." He laid his head down on the table.

Jenny could see he was drained. She also figured the stress of his college decision was tearing him apart. She didn't know exactly what to say or do. She reached across the table to hold his hand. He looked up at her. "Rem, I'm here for you. I don't know what I can do to help, but I'll try anything if it helps you feel better."

Remington perked up. "Anything?! Really?"

Jenny knew where he was going. "Not that, Rem. You know what I mean. We've talked about that before. We both know that we need to be smart about that. The last thing we need is for me to get pregnant. Is that what you want? You think you're tired now? Imagine having a baby to take care of while you're trying to do school and basketball. The tired you're dealing with now will go away in a week. But if you have a wife and kid to deal with, it's forever."

Remington was startled. "Wife?" he asked.

"Well, yeah, Rem!" Jenny was upset. "What do you think is going to happen if we have a kid? Do you think I'm just going to do everything myself and not have you there? Seriously?! Is that how you think it would go if we ended up having a kid?"

Remington was flustered, trying to find the right words to say. "No, no, no, Jen. That's not it at all. Of course, I would be there for you. I wouldn't leave you. Heck, I don't ever want to leave you. That's part of the problem with this college decision. I don't want to leave you." He paused to see if she was understanding that he was serious. He continued, "I was just shocked to hear the word 'wife' when you were talking about you and me. That's the first time I've thought about us being married. I didn't know you had ever thought that way."

Jenny said, "Well, it's not like I think about it a lot. I mean, my God, we're 17-years-old. I don't want to be married. But in the future, I will. And it might just be you who I will want to be married to. Of course, I've thought at times about what it would be like if we were married in the future. But, no, that's not a thought I have very often." She paused and then added, "But when we're talking about if I get pregnant because we do something stupid, then yeah, you're darn right I expect that we'll be married."

Remington said, "I get it. And you're right. It would be stupid for us to throw all that we have in our future away for that. Still, it's not easy."

Jenny said, "I know. I'm struggling with it, too. But we have to be smart and strong. You're the one with all the discipline to do all your workouts and make sure that you eat right and get enough sleep. You need to have that same kind of discipline for this, okay?"

Remington said, "Great. I'm Mr. Discipline for my teams, and now I get to be Mr. Discipline for us." He smiled as he said it, and they both laughed.

Ideas to Consider:

- While it would seem to an outsider that being a great basketball player and having colleges all want you to play for them would be a good thing, how is it a difficult thing for Remington right now? Which school is he leaning towards? Why? Which one is always in the back of his mind as his dream school? Why?

- While both he and Jenny have desires to advance their relationship, they both know that it could completely alter their futures. Why is it so important that they stay disciplined and focused on their futures and not give in to their desires?

Chapter 9

The next school year at Sacajawea started out with a lot of promise for the boys. The fall sports seasons all saw their share of success for the Wolves' teams. The golf, volleyball, cross country, and football teams all had very good records and did well come playoff time. Remington's soccer season also went really well. Like he had expected, over the course of the week after his talk with Jenny, Remington got excited for soccer more and more each day. The week before practice began, he was at the soccer fields with his soccer friends, getting in skill work and playing games, and he was back in his usual "soccer mode."

As the season started, the soccer team immediately started having its share of success. Remington had been a Second-Team All-Conference player on a team that made it to the playoffs the year before, and he had high hopes and expectations for this season. Just like in basketball, he was a great distributor of the ball, handing out assists to scorers on a regular basis. To start this year, though, his coaches asked him to take on more of a scoring role, too. Remington and one of his senior teammates, Sean McKay, were the most skilled scorers on the team. After their first five games of the season, Sean was second in the state in scoring, and Remington was seventh. Remington was also third in the state in assists, with a majority of those assists coming on goals by Sean. They were a great 1-2 combination, and they enjoyed playing together.

The soccer team ended up in second place in the conference. They headed to the playoffs as a favorite to do some damage. They won their first game somewhat handily, but in the second round, they ran into, Grinnell Point, a strong team from the Northwest that was a perennial state championship contender. Sacajawea battled them hard, but eventually lost 4–2. Remington scored one of the goals and assisted to Sean on the other one. Two weeks later, Sean and Remington were both named First-Team All-Conference players.

While Remington truly enjoyed the soccer season and all that it brought, when the end came, he was ready for it to be over. While he had hoped to make it to the state championship, he knew that was a long shot. What wasn't a long shot in his mind, though, was a state championship in basketball. It was now time to set his sights and his teammates' sights on that. He could barely contain his excitement for the beginning of that quest.

Jenny's soccer season did not go as well as she had hoped. While she had success individually, the team struggled to win. A knee injury to their best player in the second week of the season all but eliminated them from any chance of getting to the playoffs. Still, she had a lot of fun with her teammates, enjoyed her final year of soccer, and garnered a Second-Team All-Conference award for her play.

But that was it; she was done with soccer. Other than possibly playing intramurals in college, her soccer experience was over, and she was fine with that. She knew that college was for her to prepare for the rest of her life. It was time to start focusing on what she was going to go to college for—to get a degree in a field she wanted to pursue for her career. The problem was, she wasn't sure what she wanted to do in life. She had so many different interests that she struggled pinpointing one thing that would bring her joy and a sense of self-worth, while at the same time providing an income that could sustain her and eventually a family.

A family. She had thought about what it would be like to be married to Remington and what it would be like raising kids with him. She always got a warm feeling thinking about that. She knew he would be a good dad because his number one focus was always on others. It's what made him such a great teammate on all of the teams he ever played on. And Jenny was sure it would be what would make him a great dad and husband.

Husband. Would Remington be her husband someday? Who knew? Right now, they each had so much ahead of them to focus on, and unfortunately, most of that didn't involve the other one. It was one of the cruelties of youth. You establish relationships with other people throughout your childhood, some very close. Then, when you graduate from high school, you leave most of them behind. It didn't happen for any specific reason. People just start down a path that leads them on to other things in life, and pretty soon they are simply memories who see each other at ten-year reunions.

Was that what she and Remington were destined to have happen? "Will he forget how he felt about me?" she wondered. "Will he forget all the things he said to me?" She paused and then thought, " Will I forget how great it feels to be with him? Will I forget how much I loved him?"

She gasped. "Oh my gosh, I said it. I mean I didn't really say it out loud, but there it is. Is it true? Do I really love him?"

She looked around the coffee shop to see if anyone nearby could hear her talking to herself. She was waiting for Remington to meet her. It was the Sunday morning before the basketball season was set to begin. While Remington was the talk of the town and expectations were high for him and the Wolves, Jenny was still trying to decide if she was going to play basketball. While she would be good enough to be a contributor to the varsity team, she wasn't all that into it anymore.

She was torn, and she wanted to talk to Remington about it. He always seemed to know how to make her feel better. They had been out on a date at the movies the night before, but they hadn't talked about it. In fact, they hadn't done much talking at all. They were okay watching the movie, as neither of them liked to show public displays of affection. Making out in a theater was a strict no-no for both of them. It grossed them out when they saw other kids do it, so they would never consider it. Besides, when you're spending $20 for a couple of movie tickets, you want to get your money's worth and watch the movie.

But afterwards they drove up Dry Creek to the trailhead parking lot. While it was cold outside, it wasn't yet so cold that they didn't want to go park. They figured it would warm up soon enough in the car. Once again, things started getting hot in a hurry between them, and they both struggled to fight off the urges they were having to go further with the physical aspects of their relationship. They were smart enough to not have sex because of all the potential consequences of that, but it was difficult. This was new territory for both of them.

In one passionate moment that night, Jenny almost blurted out "I love you." She held back, though, and she was glad of it. Now, sitting in the coffee shop, having the same thought pop into her head, she started wondering what to do about it. She decided she shouldn't tell him. "I don't want to lay that on him right now as he is getting ready for his season," she thought. "And I'm not even sure if it's true. I mean, I think I love him, but I've never loved anyone in that way before, so how would I know?"

Just then, Remington walked through the door, smiling from ear-to-ear. He surveyed the room as he walked up to her table to see who was around. The shop just had a few older couples sitting in it, so he leaned down and gave her a quick kiss on the cheek.

"What are you doing?" Jenny said, a bit startled.

"What? I can't give my girlfriend a kiss on the cheek?" he responded.

She smiled and said, "Well, yeah sure. It's just that, you know, we don't like doing that kind of stuff in public."

He said, "I know. But as great as I feel today after last night with you, I just wanted to let you know by giving you a kiss on the cheek." He sat down and said, "So what's so important that you wanted to talk about with me this early? Not that I mind being up this early, especially when it means I get to see you."

She said, "I want to talk with you about basketball."

"What about it? Greatest sport ever. I hope you aren't going to tell me that I need to quit playing it if we're going to keep going out. Cuz you know, I've always told you that basket—"

Jenny cut him off by saying, "I know. 'Basketball is my first girlfriend.' You've only told me that about 1,000 times. Don't worry. I'm not going to ask you to break up with your other girlfriend."

"Okay, good. Besides, maybe I wouldn't break up with my other girlfriend if I had to choose," Remington said in a smart-aleck way.

Jenny leaned over and punched him lightly on the arm as she said, "Remington! That's not nice."

He laughed and said, "Sorry. So, what do you want to talk about?"

"I don't think I'm going to play basketball," said Jenny.

"What?!" said Remington. "Why not? You love basketball, and you're really good at it."

"No, Rem, I don't *love* basketball; you do. And I'm not really good at it; *you* are."

"That's not true, Jen. You're a good player. You're one of the top five or six on the team. That means you're good. They need you."

Jenny said, "First of all, I'm lucky if I'm in the top eight. Second, they don't need me. The JV girls from last year will do just fine, maybe even better than I would. Mostly, though, I'm just not all that into it. I don't love it anymore. I'm not into basketball like you are. I mean, I'm into watching you play basketball 'cuz you're good, and the team is good, and you guys win, and well, I get to watch you. I love *that* basketball. But I don't love playing it anymore."

Remington sat for a few seconds, taking sips of the caramel macchiato Jenny had bought for him before he got there. He finally said, "Well then don't play. 'Cuz if you're not into it, you won't have fun, and you'll be taking a spot from someone else who is into it. Have you talked to Coach Martin?"

"No," she said. "I'm going to go talk to her after school tomorrow. But I'm scared she'll be upset with me."

Remington said, "Well if that happens, you'll just have to live with your decision. But it was your decision, and you made it in your best interest. She'll have to understand. Jen, you have to stand up for yourself at times and do what's best for you, not what's best for others."

"Oh, that's rich coming from you," Jenny said in a bit of a scolding manner. "Mr. Team Player, Mr. I Don't Want to Upset Anybody, Mr. I'll Let Cade Clemons Walk All Over Me Because I'm Afraid to Do Anything or Say Anything."

Jenny hit a nerve with Remington. While Cade had been off to college at Montana Tech in Butte for the last three months, it still sent a bit of a shiver through Remington whenever he thought of how Cade treated him the last couple of years and how he rarely stood up to Cade. He didn't say anything, and now Jenny felt bad.

"Sorry about that, Rem. I shouldn't have said that. That was uncalled for."

"No apology necessary," Remington said. "Not only was it not uncalled for, but in many ways, it may have even been called for." He paused, took another sip, and then said, "Who do I think I am saying that stuff to you when I couldn't do it myself last year?"

Jenny didn't say anything as she could see the wheels turning in Remington's head. He continued, "Now this year we have a new problem that I will probably have to address—Connor. I wonder if I might have to confront him in some way."

Jenny said, "I hope you don't have to, Rem, but I'm sure if you do, you will this year. Cade was different. He was a year older than you, and you grew up playing with him. There was always that thing between you two. But Connor is the new kid on the block. He's come to your team now. He is the one who will need to change, not you."

"Good points, every one of them," said Remington. "I hope I won't have to deal with him, but if I do, I will."

"Good," said Jenny. "Well, I'm done with my coffee. Do you want to go hang out for a while?"

"Since it's so warm," he said, "I thought it would be nice to go to the park and get some shots up. Wanna' join me?"

"Yeah, sure," she said.

They got up and headed out the door. Remington loved days like today in between seasons. While he loved both sports he played, he also liked the break between them. There were a few weeks before basketball practice would begin. He still got in his workouts, but it was on his time, not someone else's. It also gave him time to do some of the other things he liked before the grind of a season began.

He especially felt the grind coming this year. Though he loved basketball more than just about anything else, he felt so much pressure to perform well because this year would determine so much for him about his future. While most of the top 5-star prospects around the country had already signed with the big-name schools, many of the players in the next tier had not signed yet. Remington didn't know if he was in that tier of players, but according to many, he was. He was also in the discussion for the best player in Montana. But, again, that was a lot to live up to. He felt confident in his abilities, but he struggled knowing for sure how to handle all the hype. He tried not to think about it, and that's why he just wanted to go shoot baskets with Jenny. It took his mind off of all the things that he was thinking about, and he liked that.

Ideas to Consider:

- Why is it good for kids to play multiple sports instead of focusing on just one too early in life?

- Why is Jenny struggling with whether or not she should play basketball? What is Remington's advice? What do you think—should she play or shouldn't she?

Chapter 10

Brian Jackson, Mike Visteen, and Connor didn't play a fall sport. There were a few JV and freshmen players who also didn't play fall sports, but none of them were projected to be on the varsity. Brian and Mike were consistent with their fall after school workouts. They made a commitment to each other that since most of their teammates were in a fall sport working hard every day, they needed to work hard on basketball every day.

They lifted three days a week, and they did skill work and played games every day, either at an outdoor court or in the gym on days the volleyball team wasn't in there. They encouraged the other basketball players not in a fall sport to join them. A couple of the younger players worked with them, trying to show Brian and Mike that they were all-in to improve themselves for the season. The more they showed up, the more Brian and Mike encouraged them and talked to them and built relationships with them. Even though they were probably not going to be varsity players, Brian and Mike tried setting an example for those kids, so they did their best to connect with them in a positive way.

Connor was one of the players who came in to the weight room. The only problem was that he showed up on random days each week. Over the course of the eight weeks to start the year, he never made it for all three days of the week. When he did show up, he did a few sets of a few exercises at about half-intensity and headed out.

Unfortunately, some of the other younger players started following Connor's lead, showing up only on certain days and leaving early with him. This was creating a minor rift with the committed players. They saw what was happening, and they didn't like it. Here they were working hard and putting in the time necessary for success, and their buddies were blowing it off.

Two of the players following Connor's lead, Jared Tatum and Chris Davis, were a couple of the better players on the JV. The other one, Cole Gifford, was the best freshman player in the program. He was projected to swing between the frosh and the JV teams, but Brian and Mike could see that he was headed in the wrong direction. One day when Jared, Chris, and Cole were in the weight room and Connor wasn't there yet, Brian and Mike cornered them. Brian said, "Guys, you know how important this weight room is to our success and yours, right?"

They all nodded and said, "Yeah."

"Then why are you only in here one day a week? And why is it that when you are in here you aren't doing our work out?" They didn't respond.

Mike said. "Guys, we need *you* to be *your best*, so *we* can be *our best*. This whole program is all about giving everything you've got. We're not fall sport players. Our teammates in fall sports are busting their butts every day for their sports. They're in shape and will be in shape in November when we start hoops. We need to do the same thing and work our butts off, so we're as good as we can be."

Brian picked up where Mike left off. "I don't know what teams you guys will be on this year, but I know all three of you are good enough to play. You guys all got skills. But there's no way you should be pissing them away by not busting your butt in here and in that gym. We all need you to bust your butt in here and in that gym out there. And not just one day a week. Get it?"

All three said, "Got it."

Brian said, "Good. Now let's get to work."

Brian and Mike never saw those three work as hard in the weight room as they did that day. They got after it with an intensity they had not displayed before. Part of that was due to Connor never showing up, so they didn't feel the need to look cool around him. They just did what they were supposed to do. The harder they worked, the more Brian and Mike encouraged them, high-fiving them and fist-bumping them each time they saw great effort. The three younger boys' faces all lit up each time this happened.

When they headed out into the gym after their workout, the volleyball team was nowhere to be found. Brian and Mike invited everyone out to get a short ball handling and shooting workout in and then play some games. Even though the young players were tired, they were excited to play. Again, they worked hard on their skill work. They were drenched in sweat as the shooting workout finished, and again, Brian and Mike went to each of them high-fiving and fist-bumping them all.

Brian and Mike knew how it felt to receive this kind of encouragement from Remington, and they liked it. They also liked how it felt dishing it out. It felt good knowing that they were having a positive impact on these younger players. While they knew it would pay dividends for those players, it also just felt good being good teammates to one another. While the younger players might never play on the same team as Brian and Mike, they were all part of the program. This was how you built a program and a culture that was rich in tradition and success. It felt good to Brian and Mike knowing they were laying a foundation of success that would hopefully continue long after they were gone.

Unfortunately, Connor was not there for any of the workouts or the team-building that happened that day. He had stepped into the weight room while they all were stretching and warming up and said he would be right back after he dropped a friend off at home. But he never showed up. This was becoming an all-too-common occurrence.

Another common occurrence was who Connor was hanging out with. He stopped doing things socially with Remington, Nick, Tim, and Brian. He was still friendly with them and acted like he was one of "their boys," but he so rarely did anything with them, that it would be hard to call him one of their real friends. The guys he was hanging out with now, though, were trouble. They had bad reputations with regards to behavior. They were not athletes, at least not any more. A few of them had been good athletes when they were younger. But as they got into high school, they got into behaviors that kept them from continuing to be good athletes. It started with drinking beer at parties that older kids were having. It soon turned to drinking beer and some hard liquor at their own houses or up in the mountains. Eventually, they started smoking dope.

The more they did these things, the less they played or worked on their sports. The less they played sports, the less they improved. Because they were not improving at their sports, they played less. It became a cycle. Then, the less they played sports, the less they hung out with their athlete friends. Their grades also started to slip because they weren't focused like they needed to be. By the middle of their sophomore year, they were fringe players in the program, not getting very many minutes in JV games. They said that they didn't play much because the coaches were screwing them over. They weren't going to go out for the team this year. "What's the point of going out for the team if the coaches are just going to play the players they like, the brown-nosers who show up at everything and work hard all the time? No way I want to be one of those guys."

Connor heard some of the same things he was thinking. One of them said, "I don't know what's wrong with those guys. All they ever do is *work* at their games. Open gyms aren't fun. They do all that skill work and shooting work before they play games. They're practicing like it's the season, and it's only April! Who do they think they are, NBA guys?"

Connor said, "I know. Back in Oakland, we just play games and ball. That's how you get good, man. All that skill work doesn't help you nearly as much as playing games."

One of the other boys responded. "I know, dude. These guys just don't have that kind of skill, though, so they gotta' do drills. When we were balling in 7th and 8th grade, we were good. We didn't need to do all that drill work. We just played. I ain't going out next year. I'd rather just hang out and have fun. I can still play at the park and get my balling' in there. Besides, that's where the real balling happens."

"Damn straight," said Connor. "Back home, there are so many good ballers out in the playgrounds. That's where I got pushed to really have to play. Of course, I didn't go into some of the neighborhoods on my own to play. I had to go with some of my homeys from school. But when I played there, now that was some ball. And none of those guys were out there doing ball handling and dribbling and shooting drills. No offense, but you guys just don't have the kind of ballers here that we got back home. Nothing close to it."

Another boy said, "I don't know, dude. Remington Roberts is really good. I don't like all the work he puts in and he makes everyone else put in, but that guy is solid. He can flat-out ball. I bet he could hang with your boys back home."

Connor said, "Yeah, he's good. I don't know about *Oakland good*, but he's good. But that's about the only one I seen that's any good."

One of the boys said, "Brian Jackson is pretty good, and with all the work he puts in, he could get really good. Same with Nick Bertucci and Tim Nelson and Mike Visteen. They all work hard. But that's the problem, man. Where's the fun in that?"

"No kidding," said Connor. "They all gotta' work like that to be any good. I'd rather just play."

Of course, all those boys couldn't see the irony in everything they said. Unfortunately, all of them drifted further away from basketball and the basketball players. The moment the school day ended, they would head out the doors of the school, and more often than not, they were headed out to do things that they shouldn't be doing.

Remington struggled with what he was seeing and hearing about Connor. He saw the guys Connor was hanging with. They were guys who used to play with Remington back in middle school. Like Connor, they were not into working on their games; they just wanted to play. During his freshman year, Remington saw those guys start hanging out with some shady characters. He tried to bring them to the workouts and do the things necessary to become good players, but they never jumped on board with him.

He realized in the summer between his freshman and sophomore years that he wasn't going to change those guys. He decided to concentrate on the guys who wanted to be there and wanted to work hard. That was Nick, Tim, Brian, Mike, and Cory. It was a good group to build around. Remington knew they would do some damage if he could keep them all focused. Their success last year was a direct result of that attitude and effort. Remington knew that if they kept that up this year, they had a great chance to do even better. And with Connor here the chances were even greater.

However, with the way Connor was now behaving, Remington started to get a little worried. He tried talking to Connor, but that didn't seem to help. He tried getting the other guys to talk to him, too, but that didn't help either. He went to Coach Brooks and let him know his concerns. Coach Brooks thanked him for coming in and told him he would talk to Connor, but Remington still kept hearing that Connor was not showing up for workouts. Remington couldn't understand how Connor could have so much talent and just be wasting it the way he was. He hoped that Coach Brooks's talk with Connor would turn him around, but he also didn't have a lot of faith in that happening.

Ideas to Consider:

- **What problems with work ethic is Connor displaying? How are these problems affecting other younger players? How do Mike and Brian address the situation? How did the younger players respond?**

- **How have you been treated by older players? What did the way you were treated teach you about the way you should treat younger players when you are older?**

- **How are the guys Connor is hanging out with affecting him? Think about who you hang out with. Are they a positive influence on you? Are you a positive influence on them?**

Chapter 11

Del approached Connor in the hallway the day after Remington had talked with him. Connor was at his locker talking to a couple of the boys that used to play basketball. As Del walked up to them, he said, "What's happening, fellas?"

They all said, "Hey Coach."

Del said, "I haven't seen you guys at any of the workouts this year. Are you planning on coming out for the team?"

Connor immediately shot back with, "I've been to some of them. Of course, I'm coming out for the team."

Del said, "Yeah, Connor, I know *you're* coming out for the team. But you haven't been getting into the weight room or the gym much. But the rest of these guys haven't been in there at all and weren't here all summer. I was asking *them* if they're coming out for the team."

One of boys said, "I'm not sure yet, Coach. I might be getting a job. I want to get a car this year, and I need to make money." The other boy said nothing.

Del said, "I get that, but you know what? You're going to have a job for the rest of your life. You're also going to have a car for the rest of your life. But you only get so much time to play competitive basketball for your school. Once that's over, you can't ever get it back."

Del paused for a moment to let his comment sink in. He then added, "You really should consider playing ball with us this year. We'd love to have you. But if you do decide to play, you need to start getting in for workouts, okay?"

They both nodded their heads and said, "Okay, Coach." They then turned toward Connor and said, "We gotta' get to class. See you after school, man."

Connor said, "Cool. I gotta' get to class, too. See ya' later." He then turned to Del and said, "See ya' later, Coach."

Del said, "Connor, hang on for a few minutes?"

Connor said, "Coach, I gotta' get to English."

Del said, "I know. I already talked to Mrs. Hutchinson. She said it's fine if you're a few minutes late. Let's step into Mr. Watson's office. He said we could talk in there." Randy Watson was the Athletic Director at Sacajawea.

After they both sat down, Del said, "Connor, I'm going to give it to you straight. I hear you're starting to have some issues here at school already."

Connor had a somewhat confused look on his face, but he didn't say anything. Del continued. "First, I'm hearing you're not showing up at workouts, or you're only showing up one day a week. You have the potential to be one of the best players in the state over the course of the next two years. But you're going to have work your tail off to do so. As good as you are now, you have the potential to be so much better. Do you want to play in college?"

"Of course," replied Connor. "Isn't that every baller's dream?"

Del said, "Well, you would think so, but not everyone who plays the game has that as a goal. Some of them just love to play and that's it. There's nothing wrong with that either. But when you're a player who has the skill to go to the next level combined with the desire to do so, then it becomes more of a focus. I see you having both of those. However, your desire alone won't get you there. And you know what? Your skill alone won't get you there either. You have to have the work ethic and attitude to get there. Then, you have to have both to stay there. Right now, I'm not seeing it from you."

Connor put his head down and looked at the floor. He wanted to say that he didn't need to work that hard in this state, that he was good enough to get to college on his own. He wanted to say that Del was wrong, that he was working out and doing all he needed to be doing. But he knew it was a lie. Deep down, he knew Del was right.

Del said, "Your lack of commitment to your workouts is just one of the problems. When I talked with Mrs. Hutchinson, she said you have not handed in a single assignment yet. She said you are already digging yourself a hole in her class. I spoke with Mr. Cullen as well. He said that, while you seem to have a grasp of math, your homework is sloppy and rushed. And Mr. Maracek says that in science you haven't handed in the first two lab assignments."

Del paused and then said, "Connor, those are the only three teachers I have talked to so far. I'm willing to bet that when I talk to the rest of your teachers, I'm going to hear the same thing. Young man, in order to play a sport at this school, you need to be passing all of your classes. You are already on your way to being ineligible. If we were in the season right now, you would be sitting out this week. You have to start getting after it in class, or you won't be playing for us. All your teachers say that you're smart enough to do the work. You're just choosing not to. Well, that has to change."

Connor said, "Okay, Coach. Sorry. With it being a new school to me and all, I just got a little behind."

Del looked at Connor intently and said, "Really? *New school?* You were here for the last two-and-a-half months last year. You know the deal here. You know what you need to do. You're just not doing it."

Del paused as Connor dropped his head and stared at the floor. He continued. "One more thing. I'm seeing you hanging out with some guys that you probably shouldn't be hanging with. The guys you're hanging with don't have the best of reputations in this school. Your grades are a direct reflection of the kinds of grades they get, too.

"You know, Ethan and Mark who you were just talking to fit that bill, too. It's a shame. They used to be pretty good ballplayers in middle school. I thought they would come up here and become really good players. But, like you, they started hanging out with the wrong crowd, and it dragged them right down. While they are not nearly the players they were a couple of years ago, I still want them to come out for the team. Do you know why?"

Connor looked up at Del and said, "Why?"

"Because they need it. In fact, they need basketball a whole lot more than basketball needs them. They could be decent JV players this year and maybe varsity players next year. But they would have to put in a whole lot of work to get there. If they did, they would be doing good things for themselves and helping themselves in a lot of ways. They would be better for being a part of it. I'd love to see them come back out because I want to help them. But I can't help them if they're not willing to help themselves."

Connor was fixated on every word Del was saying now. Del continued. "The truth is, I'm worried you're heading down the same path as them. I'm worried that you are going to start doing the things away from school that I hear they and their friends are doing. To tell you the truth, I'm worried you're already doing them."

Del saw Connor drop his head again, a sign that Del was right in his concern. "If you are, that has to stop now. You will not be on this team if I hear you're partying. The best way to keep yourself on the right track is to hang out with others who are on the right track. You have a lot of good guys like that on the team. You need to start hanging with them more. It's been said that we are the average of the five people we hang out with the most. Think for a minute about what five people are you hanging out with the most."

Del let that sink in, let Connor process it. Connor thought about the five kids he was hanging out with the most. Del asked Connor, "Are the five guys you're hanging out with the most the kind of person you want to be?"

Del looked at Connor, but Connor just dropped his head and stared at the floor. Del said, "Only you can answer that, Connor. And your answer won't be in the form of words. It will be in your actions. I hope you choose the right ones."

Connor kept staring at the ground. After a couple of seconds Del said, "All right. I've taken up too much of your English class time. You need to turn things around in there, so I better not keep you out of there any longer. Go ahead and get to class, but remember what I said. Things need to change if you're going to play basketball with us this year. Get it?"

Connor responded the way he had heard all the players respond to this question since he got there last year. "Got it, Coach." As Connor walked out the door Del wondered if he really "got it" or if he was just saying that.

Ideas to Consider:

- **How does Coach Brooks treat the players at Connor's locker who haven't been showing up to things this year? What does he hope they will do?**

- **What does Coach mean when he says, "It's been said that we are the average of the five people we hang out with the most."? How is that possible? What is he trying to get Connor to do?**

Chapter 12

Del talked to Connor's other teachers, and each of them said some version of the same thing that the first three teachers told Del. A couple of them also expressed that Connor had a poor attitude, and he constantly talked and goofed around throughout the class period. Del knew he would need to address this, but since he had just hit Connor pretty hard with some things, he wanted to give him a little bit of time before approaching him again.

That day after school, Del stopped in to see the boys in the weight room. They were just getting finished with their stretches and warm-ups. Del was so grateful that Sacajawea hired Brent Sebastian that year to be the after-school weight room supervisor. Randy Watson and Dirk Cameron, the football coach, had written a grant the year before to try to get money to hire a paid weight room supervisor.

Brent was a Sacajawea graduate five years earlier. He then went to Montana State and studied exercise physiology for his undergraduate degree. He was now in the graduate program there, with the goal of becoming a college strength coach. Sacajawea was a perfect fit for him right now to start his apprenticeship in the field. He was knowledgeable and enthusiastic about helping kids get the strength gains they needed for their different sports. He was great with the kids, and he was totally invested in them.

The Sacajawea coaches loved having Brent there. When he was a student-athlete, he was the kind of kid they loved teaching and coaching. Now, they trusted him completely as the weight room supervisor, and he allowed them the freedom to attend to other things, without worrying about their kids being taught and monitored correctly.

Del asked Brent, "How's it going, Brent? Are my boys getting after it?"

"We're just about to get started, Coach," replied Brent. "Just finished the warm-up and it's time to hit it hard." He leaned in closer to Del and said, "I tell you what, though. It just isn't the same in here when Remington isn't around. That kid just picks everybody up. Their effort and intensity is so much different when he is here. I'm trying to push them, Coach, but when he's in here, it explodes. You must love coaching that kid."

Del smiled. "It sure makes it a whole lot more fun when you have a kid like him on your team."

Brent said, "That kid is one-of-a-kind. It's a shame when you think about it, though. How come that kind of kid is one-of-a-kind? You would think they would all see what he's like, see how good he is at playing, and then go, 'Geez, maybe if I acted like him, I might be as good as him.'"

Del chuckled. "You would think so, wouldn't you? Although I have to say that Brian, Nick, Tim, and Mike are pretty good at following his lead."

Brent said, "I'll give you that. Brian and Mike are working hard in here. I don't see Nick and Tim right now 'cuz they're in football, but they definitely lead the football team in here the same way Remington does with your guys."

"How 'bout Connor?" asked Del. "How's he doing? Do you see him much?"

Brent had a confused look on his face. "Connor? Which one is he?"

"Well, I guess that answers my question," said Del. "I kind of wondered based on things I've heard from some kids. You'd notice him if he was in here. He's the big 6'6" kid."

Brent nodded. "Oh, the kid from Oakland. No, I don't see him much at all. Quite honestly, it doesn't bother me too much either. I mean, Coach, I want to help everyone who comes in here. But when he's in here, it just sucks the energy right out of the room. The intensity level plummets. He doesn't want to work at all. The problem is he brings other guys right down with him."

This worried Del. He knew if players were starting to buy into Connor's way, it would become a real problem in the future. "Thanks for the info, Brent. I appreciate it. Sorry to take time away from you with the kids."

Brent said, "No worries, Coach. Look," and he pointed at Brian and Mike. "Those two have them whipped into shape. They have really taken on that role well without Remington in here."

Del said, "That's awesome. Thanks for all you're doing in here, Brent. Let me know if you see any changes with Connor showing up."

"Will do, Coach."

Del walked over to Brian and Mike. "How's it going boys?"

"Good, Coach," said Brian. "We kind of wish a few more guys were in here, though. Well, one in particular."

"Connor?" said Del.

Mike responded, "Yeah. We see him maybe once a week. But then he doesn't do anything. He just stands and talks with Cole, Jared, and Chris. He does a few sets of what he wants to do and then leaves, usually taking them with him."

Del replied, "Yeah, that's what I was afraid of. But they look like they're getting after it pretty hard right now."

Brian said, "We had a little chat with them about their attitudes and effort in here and out in the gym. They're starting to come on board. But if we're going to get them totally on board, we have to get Connor totally on board."

"Yeah, I know," said Del. "I'm working on him. I spoke with him earlier. I thought he would be in here today after we talked. That's really disappointing."

"Stay on him, Coach. We will too. He could be a real key to our season."

"No kidding," said Del. "All right, well you guys have a workout to get back to. Just wanted to say 'Hi' and 'Thanks' for all you're doing in here."

"You got it, Coach," said Brian. "Can't wait for November!"

It was guys like Brian, Mike, Nick, Tim, and of course, Remington that made Del love coaching. These were the guys who "got it." They would be any coach's dream to coach. Unfortunately, Connor was not falling into that category. But Del also knew, he needed Connor to help solidify their opportunity to win the state this year. Somehow, Del had to make sure that he kept Connor eligible, energized, and excited about being on the team this year. He just didn't know how he was going to do that. He also didn't know what he would do if he couldn't do that.

Ideas to Consider:

- **What do Coach Brooks and Brent Sebastian say is so hard to understand about kids not being more like Remington? Why do *you* think it's so hard for so many kids to figure that out?**

- **How does Brent say the atmosphere in the weight room is when Connor is there? Have you ever had a teammate who had that kind of an effect on a team? What did you and/or your teammates do about it? Is there something you could or should have done differently to make the situation better?**

Chapter 13

With the leaves almost completely off the trees, the days had turned gray with rain and occasionally snow. The fall sport seasons were now over, and open gyms and pre-season workouts were in full swing. Remington, fresh off of his stellar soccer season, had taken a few days off from any kind of workouts to refresh his body and rejuvenate his spirit.

Remington loved basketball as much as anything in the world, but he knew it was the longest season of all the school sports seasons. He knew that he would need to be in prime shape to be able to be his best for four months. He also knew that the grind of a season can be worse mentally than physically. Coming right out of one season and into another can be fun and exciting, but it can also lead to burnout sooner in the second season.

So Remington took a couple of days away from the school and gym right after soccer had ended. He went fishing a couple of days on one of the blue-ribbon trout streams nearby, one of his favorite hobbies to decompress a bit. More than anything, though, this year he had looked forward to a few days off to spend time with Jenny after school and in the evening. While Jenny didn't love fishing the way Remington did, she did like hiking. They were fortunate that, while the days were turning cooler and rainy, the afternoons in the week right after soccer ended were sunny. They left school and immediately headed up to Dry Creek on Monday.

While getting physical with Jenny was on Remington's mind more these days, their focus today was on getting physical in a different way. They wanted to enjoy nature spending some time hiking and hopefully seeing some wildlife. Remington didn't want to push his body too hard, as one of the main reasons he wanted to do this was to NOT tax his muscles. But a nice, light hike could be the perfect antidote for a body coming out of a sports season. They had a great hike together out in nature away from people. They even saw a moose and her baby. On their ride home, Remington said, "Just what the doctor ordered!"

Unfortunately, even though he wasn't a fall sport athlete, Connor McDonald seemed to feel that he, too, deserved a bit of time away before the season began. He was nowhere to be found the entire week after the fall sports seasons ended. His teammates and coaches couldn't believe it. Yet, in many ways they had come to expect it. Some had already grown tired of Connor.

Del stopped him in the hall after school the third day after the fall sports seasons had ended. "Hey, Connor. How's it going?"

Connor was walking with a couple of kids who Del did not know, but who he had heard were trouble. "Oh, hey, Coach," said Connor.

Del asked, "You got a second?"

Connor looked hesitant as he looked at his friends. "Uh, yeah, I guess. But only a second. I've gotta' give these guys a ride home."

"Okay," said Del. "I'll keep it short."

Connor stopped as his two friends headed out the door to the parking lot to Connor's car. He said, "What's up?"

Del said, "So are you coming to the weight room and the open gym today after you drop them off?"

Connor looked like he was searching for the right thing to say that would allow him to not have to go without feeling like he was doing the wrong thing. "Uh, well, I wasn't planning on it. I was taking this week off, you know, like Remington, Nick, Tim, and the rest of the guys."

Del's brow furrowed. "First of all, they might not be taking a full week off. They might, but they might not. That's up to them to know best what they need after their fall sports season. But do you realize why they're taking a few days off?"

Connor said, "Yeah, to rest and get ready for the season."

"Well, yes, that's partly right," said Del. "But they are resting and rejuvenating from the long grind of the football and soccer seasons. Those games and practices are taxing on the body and mind. So I'm fine with them taking a few days off. But a few days off for each of them, might just be two or three days. Most of them will probably be back here today or tomorrow, ready to go."

Connor seemed to squirm a little, but he didn't say anything. Del pressed on. "But you haven't been through a fall sports season. You haven't been to practice every single day and playing in games for the last three months. You've had open gyms and weight room workouts a few days each week, but you haven't even gone to those very much. You showed up one day a week and on the rare occasion two days a week."

Connor looked stunned. Del hadn't been there either. How could he have known how often he was there?

"I asked Brent to keep track of all the guys' workouts and how well they were doing. He said he rarely saw you in there. In fact, I had to describe to him who you were because he didn't know you at first. That's not a good sign. Some of your teammates also were concerned that you weren't showing up. They want you there, Connor. They want you to be invested in the team and be the best you can be. They think you have a chance to really help put us over the top and win a state championship. But the only way you can do that is to show up and work hard."

Connor dropped his head. Del said, "So, yeah, your team needs you to be at the workouts and open gyms starting today. We have the rest of this week, next week, and then the first couple days the following week, and then the season starts. You need to get yourself ready to go. Go take your friends home, and then we'll see you after that."

Connor said, "All right," with all the conviction of a 5-year-old telling his mom that he'll eat his peas. He turned and walked quickly out the door to his car.

Del turned and walked back into the gym towards the weight room. Remington walked in right behind him and said, "Hey, Coach."

Del turned around and said, "Hey, Rem. What are you doing here?"

"I'm ready. I can't wait, Coach!"

Del could hear the excitement in Remington's voice. Del said, "But it's only Wednesday. I figured I wouldn't see you until tomorrow, Friday, or even Monday."

"Not this year, Coach. I can't wait to get it going. This is going to be our year. With the guys we have back and now adding Connor, we are going to state and we're going to do damage there. I know it. I don't want to wait another day. I had my fun fishing and hanging with Jenny over the weekend and the last couple of days. But when I was out there, I kept thinking about being in here with the guys getting after it. I knew right then, I'm ready."

"Glad to hear it, Rem," said Del. "I'm ready, too. I can't wait to get this season started. You're right. With the guys we have back, this is going to be a lot of fun. We just need to find a way to bring Connor on board."

Remington looked upset. "Really?! Still? You're kidding. He's still not showing up? What's with that guy?"

"I don't know, Rem. All that physical talent and yet he doesn't seem to want to apply it. I just don't get it. If I had his body, combined with his skills, you'd have to drag me away from this place."

"No kidding," said Remington. "I wish I was 6'6" and built like him."

Del smiled. "If you were 6'6" and built like him, you'd be a Gatorade All-American. You still might be, mind you, but if you had his physical gifts, it would be a guarantee. But 6'6" and built like him means nothing without the right attitude and effort. And I just haven't seen that from him yet. However,

I'm hopeful that's about to change. I just had a chat with him and told him he needs to be here starting today, so he should be here in a little bit."

"I hope so, Coach, but I'll believe it when I see it."

"Unfortunately, I know what you mean," said Del. "All right, go get changed and I'll see you in the weight room."

Remington and Tim were the only fall sport athletes to show up to the workout, but that was fine with them and with Del. Every kid was different and needed to come back on his own timeline. They knew that Nick and the others would be there in the next few days.

What wasn't fine with them, though, was that Connor never showed up. Remington kept glancing over at Coach, who kept glancing up at the clock. With each passing ten minutes, it looked like Coach was getting madder and madder. As the weight workout was finishing up and the guys were headed out to the gym to do their skill work, Remington and Tim went over to Del.

Remington said, "Coach, don't worry about Connor. We'll talk with him." Remington paused for a minute. He then put his hand on Del's shoulder and said, "But also, coach, we'll be fine with or without him. Remember when we talked to you on the bus on the last day of the season last year?"

Del said, "Yeah, how could I forget?"

"When we came to talk to you, Connor wasn't part of the plan. There was just us. We knew that if we worked hard and did the right things, we would be fine. Well, every one of those guys and a lot of the young guys have worked hard and done all the right things since the season ended, so we're good. Sure, we'd be better with Connor committed to it. But if he's not, we'll be fine. So don't worry about it."

Del smiled and looked at both Remington and Tim and said, "Thanks, guys. You're right. We'll be fine no matter what happens with Connor."

Del, Remington, and Tim walked out into the gym, and Brian and Mike had already started leading the rest of the guys through the ball handling drills that Remington normally led since last spring. "Jeez, I guess you guys don't need me anymore," Remington said through a laugh to Brian and Mike.

Brian smiled and said, "Well, we figured you probably forgot how to do this, so we thought we'd show you again. You know you are getting a lot older, and they say the memory is the first thing to go."

Del said, "Wait a minute, Bri. I'm a lot older than any of you, so what does that say about me?"

Brian had a huge grin and said, "Take it however you want, Coach. But I think there's a rocking chair up on the balcony with a blanket on it if you want to go sit down and watch us work!"

Del said, "Thanks for pointing that out to me, Bri. That way I'll be able to take a nap up there since there won't be anything worth watching out here with *you* playing!"

The boys all started laughing, with Remington saying, "Oh, snap, Bri! He got you good!"

Del said, "What are you talking about Rem? When I said *you*, I meant *all of you!*" Del smiled a big smile at Remington.

Brian laughed and said, "Oh 'snap' back at ya,' Rem. He burned you good, too!"

Del loved it. It was moments like these that made him love coaching most of all. Of course, the games and the wins and the competition were all great. But the relationships he got to build with kids like this were priceless, the stuff that made a coach want to coach. It's also the stuff that made teams become teams and learn what it means to be all-in together.

The only thing that tainted this moment in Del's mind was that Connor McDonald wasn't here to be a part of it. "What do I have to do to get that kid on board?" he thought. "I know Remington thinks we'll be fine without him, but I'm not sure. The difference he made this summer was huge. We need him to help us become the team we want to be. I have to find a way to get that kid in here with us, no matter what it takes."

Ideas to Consider:

- **Why does Remington like to take a few days off of any sports between his seasons? Is this a good idea in your opinion?**

- **How important is putting in effort in your off-season, no matter what you do and no matter what your "off-season" is?**

- **What are some of the mental, emotional, and team consequences of players showing up and working hard or not showing up and working hard in the off-season?**

Chapter 14

Over the next two weeks, the open gyms and workouts went well. While Del was not allowed to do any coaching, he could sit and watch the kids work out and play. He loved seeing where they were in their development. They were much farther ahead in this pre-season than any pre-season he had experienced in his years coaching.

Connor had started showing up regularly, too. That was a good sign. While he was behind in terms of where his skills and conditioning should be, he was working his way into shape. He pushed himself hard at times, but Del would have liked to see him push himself harder and more often. He needed to get into shape, and he only had two weeks to do so.

Still, he was there and he was re-forging relationships with the guys that had been built in the summer. He laughed a lot with them and genuinely seemed to enjoy himself around them. However, each night right around 5:30, the two boys who had been with him when Del stopped him after school the week before would step inside the gym doors and watch. The moment the game that Connor was playing was over, he would high-five and fist-bump guys and say "Nice game." He would then grab his stuff, say "Gotta' go. See you guys tomorrow," and head out the door with his friends.

Del did not like what he was seeing. He had spoken to Sharon Abernathy, one of the school's two counselors, after the day in the hall with Connor and asked her about the two boys. She immediately said, "Bobby Maxwell and Tommy Garret. That's not good. Let me get their files." She started typing on her computer keyboard and a minute later said, "Okay, Bobby is new this year. He's from LA. Supposedly was a gang member down there, but who knows? He's only passing two classes right now, and he had an MIP a month ago."

"Tommy is one of our own. He has been in and out of juvenile detention through the years. Mom is a meth-head and dad is nowhere in the picture. Tommy's a known partyer, and people think he deals drugs. They think that the LA boy is helping supply him. You'll notice how nice their clothes are. They aren't buying those from working at McDonald's or Taco Bell."

Del said, "Great. I've been trying to get Connor to buy into us and all the good he can get being with the team, and he's hanging out with drug dealers."

Sharon said, "Sorry, Del. I'll keep my eyes and ears open. If I hear any more,

I'll let you know. In the meantime, I'll chat with Cindy, Bill, and Rick about talking with Connor and trying to steer him in the right direction."

Cindy, the other counselor, was actually Connor's counselor. Bill James was the assistant principal. He handled all the discipline issues at the school. Rick Bryson was the school resource officer from the Discovery police department. Del decided to talk to each of them the next day.

When he talked to Cindy the next day, she said, "Those two boys are trouble. They are not the kids you want him hanging out with."

Del said, "I was afraid of that." He switched gears and asked, "So what's your relationship with Connor like? Does he open up to you? Do you think he would be receptive to you talking with him?"

Cindy frowned a bit. "Not really. I tried to get to know him last year when he got here, but he was really closed-off. It was hard for him moving here from Oakland, and he put up walls all around himself. It's been like trying to break through them with a small hammer, and quite honestly, I haven't broken through much."

Del thanked Cindy, left her office, and walked over to Rick Bryson's office. Rick was a big man, and he commanded a presence with both his size and his uniform. He knew both of those things could work in his favor in some ways and work against him in others. While he needed to show control and receive respect in his position, he also needed to connect and build relationships with kids, especially the tough ones, the ones who seemed to always find trouble to get into. They saw the uniform and badge and immediately headed the other way, maybe not physically, but mentally and emotionally.

Rick needed to counter his physical appearance with a warmth and caring attitude that showed he wanted to help. So he was very approachable for kids. He joked with them a lot and did all that he could to get in their good graces. Kids liked him because of that, even the ones who he might be seeing on weekend nights in whole different settings doing things that they shouldn't be. But it was his demeanor with them at school that helped him diffuse situations with them out of school, and it worked really well.

Del said, "Hey, Rick. What's up?"

Rick responded, "Just fighting crime here at Sacajawea High."

Del said, "What do you know about the two kids my big post player, Connor McDonald, is hanging out with?"

Rick shook his head and furrowed his brow. "A lot, and it's not good. I don't like it, and I'm not the one trying to win a state championship."

Del sunk into a chair across from Rick's desk, as Rick continued. "Bobby Maxwell is from LA. I imagine he and Connor look at it like a California connection they have here. Bobby had a record down there. Drugs, stealing cars, things like that. Supposedly gang-affiliated, although we hear that from city kids who move here all the time. Usually, they're just blowing smoke, trying to get small-town hick kids to think they're tough gang kids. I'm not sure about this one. But he is trouble, that's for sure."

"That's what I was afraid of," said Del.

"Tommy Garrett is one of Discovery's finest," Rick said sarcastically. "I've dealt with him for the last six years. In and out of juvey all that time. Dad is nowhere to be found. Some think he's in prison. Mom's a meth-head. We're at her house a couple of times a month. That boy has grown up in such a bad atmosphere, it's a wonder he gets himself to school. The thing I don't get is if you're going to rise above your life like that and make it to school somewhat consistently, why wouldn't you then do something while you're here? But he doesn't. He's flunking most of his classes."

"Do you have any kind of relationship with either of them?"

Rick said, "Yeah, I have a decent relationship with Tommy. I've worked with him for six years, so I would hope so. But every time I seem to be making some headway getting him on the right track, he derails, so it's been tough."

"What about the LA kid? Do you know him at all?"

"He's a much tougher nut to crack. He sees me and starts walking the other way. When the two of them are together, that's about the only time I can talk with him because Tommy will come up and say 'Hi' or at least not walk away."

Del said, "What about Connor? Do you ever deal with him?"

Rick said, "Not much. He hasn't done anything wrong or at least so wrong that I've had to get involved. He says 'Hi' to me when he's with Tommy, but I haven't built a relationship with him all that much. I kind of haven't had to. But it sounds like I might be real soon, huh?"

"That's what I'm afraid of," said Del. "I hear he's getting into some bad stuff with these two, so yeah, you might be dealing with him more. Well, do me a favor and work with him a bit if you can and let me know if you find anything out, or you see him getting better... or worse."

"Will do. Sorry I couldn't be more help. I hear he's a pretty good ball player."

Del looked at him. "He's unlike anything we've seen in this place. He's unlike anything in the state right now. All that physical talent, and he's wasting it. He is a legit D1 prospect, and he's pissing it away. It's so frustrating."

Rick said, "Yeah, and probably more frustrating when you have guys like Remington, Nick, Tim, and Brian to compare him to. Those kids are special, especially Remington. Is he getting any looks?"

"Yeah, lots of them," said Del. "U of M, MSU and all the small schools around here already offered him. Gonzaga, Oregon, Colorado, and Arizona State haven't made any offers yet, but I think they will."

"Wow! Good for him. Couldn't happen to a better kid. It's funny. That's a kid I NEVER have to deal with, yet I see him all the time. He stops in and says 'Hi' and talks about things with me. Just a great kid."

"Best I ever coached," said Del. "I'm going to miss him after this year. I just wish Connor would pick up some of who he is and what he does. They could be the best 1-2 punch in the state if he would. Hell, they still might be."

"Not if Connor isn't eligible," said Rick. "Then it won't matter."

Del said, "I know. That's what I'm so worried about. I have to find a way to keep him eligible. He's too important to our success to have him not playing."

Del thanked Rick and headed across the hall to talk to Bill James, the assistant principal. Del heard the same things from Bill that he heard from Sharon, Cindy, and Rick. Del figured he needed to do something, but he didn't know what. Practice started in a few days. He needed Connor on board and all-in. But how was Del going to do that? He was as confused as he had ever been about a player. "Why can't they all be like Rem?" he thought. "Yeah, right. That'll be the day."

Ideas to Consider:

- **How are Connor's friends hurting him and potentially the team?**
- **What's harder—to be a player with great skills and abilities to perform, or to be a player with great discipline, effort, and attitude? What happens to players who are both?**

Chapter 15

With basketball season about to start, Jenny and Remington spent as much time with each other as they could. After his open gyms, Remington would either meet Jenny at the Elkhorn for hot chocolate or coffee, or they would meet at one of their houses and play video games, listen to music, talk, and laugh a whole lot.

What they didn't do was advance their relationship any further physically. They would sneak away and make out a bit, but they never took it further than that. They knew that if they did, there would be no turning back, and that both of their lives would get pretty intense. While they both wanted to advance things, they let their heads rule their hearts, knowing that the consequences for their actions could end up changing the rest of their lives. They were both just too focused on their futures to take that risk.

Remington struggled with this the most. He really wanted to be with Jenny in more ways than they were. It was difficult for him not to push things further along. The irony, of course, was that of the two of them, Remington had a bigger opportunity in front of him, and he could lose the whole thing if they weren't smart about things.

It's not that Jenny's future wasn't important, wasn't big, or wasn't something that she could afford to lose. She was a very smart young woman with a bright future, too. She wanted to pursue a career in one of the science fields. She knew that it would require a huge sacrifice of time and effort, with a lot of years of school, studying, and learning. She wanted to maximize her chances of success, and if she and Remington were not strong and had a child together, her goals would be extremely hard to pursue. So, Jenny had a lot to lose, too.

It's just that Remington's opportunity had a couple of added elements that made it even more devastating if he were not to be able to fulfill it. He not only had college in front of him and all that it would entail. He also had a future in basketball. He could achieve his lifelong dream of playing college basketball. He was already being recruited by some of the top Division 1 schools in the western part of the country. But he still had to get there. He also had to finish off his senior year.

But over the last few months with Jenny, he had felt a little crack in his discipline. He found himself thinking about her more and more. The problem was that what the thoughts of her were replacing were the thoughts of doing all that he had hoped to achieve in his senior season. From the end of last year, his number one focus was getting to the state tournament and winning the whole thing. He wanted that so badly he could taste it. He started working out harder than ever before, both on his own and with his teammates.

As the spring and summer went on however, he found himself spending more and more time with Jenny. That was not necessarily a bad thing, as they were having so much more fun together, and their relationship was advancing in incredible ways. The problem was that many of the minutes and hours he was spending with her were minutes and hours that he used to be spending working on his basketball game or in the weight room. He was sacrificing some of his important workout times to be with Jenny.

Not only was he jeopardizing his and his team's chances of winning a state championship, but he was also jeopardizing his college dreams. With the D1 schools that he had interested in him, he knew he had some great choices of schools where he could continue his career, and they would pay for his education. He had already been offered a full-ride scholarship to U of M and MSU, and some larger schools had indicated that they were going to do so, as well.

He was grateful that Jenny was smart enough and strong enough to focus on their futures. With her putting her foot down on the physical nature of their relationship, she was helping them both realize the dreams they each had. Going too far with their relationship was too much of a risk for either of them. One way Remington tried to deal with it was to not see her as much, so he wouldn't be tempted in that way. The problem was that he wanted to see her all the time. He wanted to hang out with her for all kinds of reasons, not just the physical nature of their relationship. Life was just more fun and more complete when he was with her.

He had chosen not to see her too much over the soccer season. That had helped him stay focused on soccer and on his basketball workouts. Once the soccer season was over, though, they had been seeing each other a lot more. Their hikes, meetings at the Elkhorn, or time spent at their houses were some of the most fun Remington was having. That was his dilemma. He needed to balance his time better. He needed to get into the gym and weight room, maximize his time in there with intense, focused workouts, and then go see Jenny. Prioritizing his time this way, he felt better about what he was doing and where he was headed.

Jenny agreed. She, too, felt that each of them taking three hours after school to do the things they each needed to do was the best course of action. Then, after that time, they could see each other. Of course, there was also school work to take care of, and some nights when they would see each other it was to do homework together, but that was okay. The key was that they were spending time with each other, which was what they both wanted.

And so, as basketball practices were about to begin and Remington and Jenny looked back on the previous months, they both felt good knowing that, while they had advanced their relationship to new heights in many ways, they were smart and strong enough not to advance it too far in other ways. They could see their futures out there on the horizon somewhere. They could not see clearly exactly where they were each headed, but they could at least see that the things they were after were out there and ready for them to pursue. The question was which things were they each going to pursue, where would they be pursuing them, and would they be together in their pursuits of them.

Ideas to Consider:

- **Remington and Jenny have a physical, intimate aspect to their relationship. How are they handling it? Why is it important for teenagers to hold off on advancing their relationships too far? Why do so many fail and end up completely altering their futures?**

Chapter 16

As the season was about to start, Del reflected on the past few years of his coaching career. He had been mentored by two of the best coaches one could ever ask for—his dad and Jim Turner. He had been fortunate enough to be Mason Brooks's son and to then have Jim Turner follow his dad as the head coach at Sacajawea. It was like everything fell into place for Del to become a coach of the highest caliber.

Del had always loved the messages and lessons his dad taught him. He learned so much about how to coach the right way from his dad, and Del was so glad to have had his dad in his life as his own coach and then as a mentor for his first few years of becoming a coach himself. His dad was the greatest influence on his coaching, and he never wanted to let his dad down.

When his dad died a little over two years ago, it left a huge hole in Del's life. It wasn't just the coaching either. His dad had been like his best friend. They talked about everything and did so many things together. Fishing one of the many blue-ribbon trout streams in Montana with his dad was one of Del's favorite things to do. The times in his dad's boat fishing the Madison or Jefferson Rivers were some of the most impactful learning that Del ever went through for both coaching and life in general. Even now, when Del fished those rivers with friends, when he floated through certain places, he would remember specific coaching points that his dad had told him while they were in those spots. Then in practice or in games, he would be saying those things to his team that his dad had told him, and in his mind, he was right back in that spot on the river where his dad had said them to him.

Del's coaching was a reflection of his dad's, and Del liked it that way. Del was proud to be Mason Brooks's son, and he liked continuing the culture of instilling life lessons in kids that he saw his dad work hard to create. However, Del also felt great pressure to win. He knew that people had come to believe that winning was almost a birthright here at Sacajawea. The teams had been so successful in years past that the community took it for granted that they were going to win all the time.

After Mason Brooks retired, Jim Turner took over the program. He carried on some of that success that Mason had established years before, and he did it in the same way as Mason—with a focus on character, integrity, and teaching kids lessons that they would take into the rest of their lives. Like Mason Brooks, Jim felt that if you taught kids the right way to work hard and be great teammates and people of great character, the winning would follow. And for his first few years, he was right.

However, to win at a high level, you also need talent. Unfortunately, for a couple of years, the talent level of boys coming into the Sacajawea basketball program just wasn't there. While Jim still offered camps and a "Little Dribblers" program for the young kids in the community, he saw fewer kids attending them. There were so many other things that kids could do in the new millennium that they just didn't seem to want to put in the time and effort to basketball. As those kids got older, they were a step or two behind other teams in their conference, and Sacajawea started losing to teams they had consistently beaten through the years. Jim Turner could see the writing on the wall. Kids were not receiving his messages the way they used to. He knew they needed a different voice to lead them.

Jim liked what he had seen from Del when he played, how he handled himself and led his teammates. Jim encouraged Del to apply to be the freshman coach when Del was hired as a history teacher at Sacajawea. Del applied and Jim hired him. Del was the freshmen coach for two years and the JV coach for the next two years. As Jim was deciding to step down from the job, he felt that Del would be a good candidate to take over and turn things around. Del had been a good assistant coach, and he learned a lot and gave a lot to the program.

Del had been a disciple and strong proponent of all of the methods and messages that both his dad and Jim had instilled in players and teams through the years. He was also young and enthusiastic, and he had the energy to put into the kids that they needed. He could also relate to so many of them because he had been right there in their situation not too many years before. And having played in college, he had even more credibility with the kids. It was a natural fit in Jim's mind for Del to take over as head coach.

Jim approached Del near the end of the season that year. He told him he was going to hang up his whistle and that he thought Del was ready to step in and be the head coach. Del was sad to hear that Jim was going to resign. He liked Jim a lot and had enjoyed their friendship and the mentorship that Jim gave him. He was like a second dad to Del in some ways, and he learned things from Jim that he hadn't from his dad.

Yet, while he was sad that Jim was going to step down, Del was also excited. He knew he wanted to be a head coach someday, just like his dad. He would also love to be the head coach at his own high school. If he was hired, it would be a dream come true. He would get to carry on the traditions of his dad and Jim, while also adding his own touches to the program. Del knew that his dad would be extremely proud of him. While he knew his dad was proud of him no matter what he did, he also knew that his dad had hoped that Del would one day be the head coach at Sacajawea. This would be the best situation possible in both of their eyes. Del would also be able to call upon his dad for guidance as he started leading the program.

For his first two years as head coach, Del would talk to his dad on a regular basis throughout the season, asking for tips, pointers, and suggestions on anything from how to teach a certain move to how to handle a kid who was acting a certain way. Del loved that his dad was there, and he generally did what his dad told him. His dad's focus was always that Del needed to "do the right things" in terms of running his program. He talked about teaching and instilling character first and foremost. If you took care of that first, the Xs & Os, techniques, skills, and strategies were so much easier to instill and develop.

His dad said, "It's not that skills and techniques and strategies aren't important. You aren't going to be very successful if you don't have those things down-pat. But if you don't take care of all the character pieces first, the Xs and Os won't matter. Those things won't work to the best of their abilities if your kids won't work to the best of theirs. If you can't get kids to work hard, pay attention, be great teammates, stay eligible, and all the other things that truly matter, it doesn't matter what offense or defense you run. You will not succeed."

For his first two years as head coach, that is exactly what Del focused on, and his teams were rewarded for it. While they didn't get to the state tournament those two years, they were successful in a variety of ways. They had their share of scoreboard success, but the place Del felt most successful was in carrying on the tradition of instilling the values and lessons that his dad and Jim had worked to instill in the program throughout their years of coaching.

The problem was that Del didn't feel like he was being appreciated for it. He knew the importance of instilling those elements. He knew that focusing on creating a culture of great character and developing core values in a program were far more important than winning games. However, he heard grumblings that people in the community were restless about the team not winning championships lately. Del didn't know who felt this way or if it was even true, but he got it into his head that *everyone* felt that way. Because of that, he shut people out and stopped talking to parents and community members because he felt he couldn't trust anyone. He felt that "everyone is out to get me."

He retreated into his own world where he insulated himself with only his fellow coaches and friends. In just his third year of coaching, he was letting a feeling of paranoia overtake him. The more he closed himself off, the more he felt the paranoia. Because he stopped talking to parents and community members, people actually *were* talking about him. They couldn't understand why he wouldn't talk to them.

Also, the timing of this behavior was horrible. Del's father had died of a heart attack the summer before. It was a total shock, as Mason Brooks had stayed relatively healthy his whole life, by watching what he ate and working out fairly consistently. He was not the "ideal candidate" for a heart attack at 64-years-old.

His dad's death completely rocked Del's world. While Del and his mom had a good relationship, it was his dad who Del was connected to the most. Basketball had been their link ever since Del was little. As he grew up, that bond just grew and grew. They were like best friends. What was Del to do now? Who would he talk to about coaching, sports, fishing, and life in general? While he had Jim Turner, and Jim had offered to help in any way he could, Del knew that he had his own life and family to focus on. Del didn't want to bother him too much.

During that first season without his dad, Del felt lost at times. He struggled to instill the elements in his team that had always been the cornerstones of the program—character, integrity, discipline, work habits, and sportsmanship. While he knew he needed to be teaching those elements every year, Del felt like this team needed more of the Xs and Os and strategy elements than teams of the past, so he zeroed in on those concepts instead of the character concepts.

However, his plan backfired. It was Remington's sophomore year and Cade Clemons's junior year. While Cade had more talent than anyone in the program, Del had seen the problems with Cade's attitude and behavior in his first two years in the program, especially how poorly he sometimes treated Remington. Del knew that if he didn't get a handle on Cade's selfishness and behavior, it could be a real problem for their team's chemistry. However, Del struggled to do so the entire year. He knew Cade was really good. He felt they *needed* Cade to succeed, so he allowed some things from Cade that he would never allow other players to do. Del's acceptance of Cade's poor behavior cost them dearly that year. They could have been a really good team, but because Del allowed Cade to act the way he did, by the end of the season, nobody wanted to be there.

Del knew he had blown it. In his desire to win, he had turned his focus to winning, instead of creating a great team culture. In doing so, he lost his team. He also started to lose the culture that his dad had started and Jim Turner and he had continued through the years. Del knew he had to re-focus the following year on what was most important. So, he made a more concerted effort with Cade last year in his senior season. While Del still struggled holding Cade accountable at times throughout the season, they both made strides. At the end of the season, when the problem came to a head, Del finally chose "team" instead of "Cade," and it paid off. The lessons that his dad and Jim Turner had instilled for all those years really did work.

As that year ended and Del looked ahead to this season, things were looking up even more. While Cade and a couple of other key seniors were gone, the younger players stepping up into key roles were going to be even better this year, and they would certainly be a much better *team* without Cade's behaviors. With the unexpected addition of Connor McDonald last spring, the expectations for this year were catapulted into the stratosphere. People had already felt that they could contend for a state championship with the team they had returning. With Connor's inside presence added into the mix, some people felt a state championship would be the only acceptable result.

So, while there was a lot of energy and buzz around the team this year, Del felt a huge amount of pressure. He felt that *everyone* was expecting a state championship, and he felt he needed to produce one. Anything less meant he would be deemed a failure. He figured he would be fired if they didn't win it all. The more he thought this way the more pressure he felt. The more pressure he felt, the more he thought this way. He was stuck in a cycle that was not healthy, and he needed to win in order to get out of that cycle. This was not a good place for Del Brooks to be as he headed into the new season.

Ideas to Consider:

- **What lessons did Del's father and Jim Turner teach him about coaching? What did they feel coaches should focus on most of all? Why?**

- **While we all want to win, what is the danger of getting too consumed with it? How did Del get away from his core values in the last couple of years?**

- **What problems can you see that might already be starting for Del with regards to this same concept this year?**

Chapter 17

As he stood before his team in the locker room prior to their first practice, Del felt all of what transpired over the last few years come over him like a giant wave that a surfer knows he needs to ride out before it crashes down upon him. The entire group of boys trying out for all three teams was sitting in the locker room ready to get started.

Del always liked to start the season in the locker room. It was the place that teams spend so much time together, getting ready for practices and games, talking tactics and strategies, building bonds and friendships. Del learned from his dad the idea that there was a sacredness to the locker room for teams. He wanted the boys to understand the importance of treating it like a home. He stressed respecting and taking care of it and cleaning up after themselves every time they were in there. He talked about how others might not treat it well, but that they had a duty to keep it clean and in good order. It would be an important room in their "house" over the next four months.

He then shifted his focus to taking care of each other. "Boys, these are going to be your brothers over the next four months. I know many of you think of each other like brothers all year long, but I also know that you don't look at everyone here that way. For the next four months, those of you who make the team need to treat each other like family. Yes, I know that some families are dysfunctional. Sometimes brothers argue or fight. Things won't be perfect."

Del paused to look around the room to try to gauge if his words were connecting with the boys. The returning varsity players were totally locked in on Del, nodding at each of his sentences. Connor, though, seemed to be drifting in and out as Del spoke. In some ways, Del couldn't believe what he was seeing. Here it was, the first night of this kid's new team experience for the new season, and he wasn't focused on what his coach was saying.

Del wrapped up his speech by saying, "Boys, we have a chance unlike any we have had in my years here. We have a state championship-contending team sitting here. Some people would not bring that up with their team on the first night of the season. They might feel like it's too early to do so—that it might add way too much pressure to a team. But my feeling is, why hide it? We know we are good, and we know there is a lot that is expected of us this year. Let's get it out in front of us, so we know exactly what we are dealing with."

As Del glanced around the room, he sensed that all of the boys seemed to be that much more excited about it. They knew they would be one of the teams that people would have as their favorite to win the state. To hear their coach say it just reinforced for them that expectation. There was no added pressure on their part right now—only added confidence.

Del continued, "However, with that kind of expectation comes responsibility. The only way you will live up to that responsibility is if you maximize the potential that you have. You must work harder than you have ever worked before. You might not think you have to do that because you are good. But the reason you are good is because of all the effort that you put into this. So if you want to achieve what you are here to achieve, you need to raise your effort levels." He paused and then asked, "Are you ready?"

The boys nodded, and Del now yelled, "ARE YOU READY?"

The boys jumped from the benches they were on and screamed things like, "YES! Let's go! Let's do this!" Del put his hand up in the air and all the boys joined him. He said, "Rem, get us going."

While Remington didn't know Coach Brooks would tell him to do this, he had prepared for this moment for the last eight months. He said, "Boys, this is what we have been waiting for since the end of last year. This is what we worked for all spring, summer, and fall. No excuses now! It's time to get after it. Leave it all out on the floor every night starting right now. Everybody with me. 'Champs' on three—1, 2, 3" and they all yelled, "Champs!"

As the boys headed out the locker room door towards the court, Del tapped Connor on the shoulder and said, "Connor, come here for a minute?" They walked into the coaches' office in the locker room, along with Kevin Nixon, the JV coach. As he shut the door behind him, Del said, "I need to address this right now, Connor."

He paused to make sure Connor was looking at him and then said, "I've told you before that you have the potential to be a great player. But as great as you could be, right now that is all it is—you *could* be great. You will need to work extremely hard, focus your attention on your practice habits, focus your attention in the classroom, and focus your attention when I or anyone else is speaking."

Connor dropped his head because he knew he wasn't focusing his attention while Del was speaking to the team. Del continued, "You have a chance to become one of the best players in this state. But that starts with your focus. I don't know if you heard a word I just said to the team, and that concerns me. Because if you can't be focused on the first night of the year, how are you going to be on the twenty-first, thirty-first, or any other night of the year? How can I count on you in key moments if I don't know if you're listening to me?"

Del paused to gauge Connor's reaction. This was the first time he had seen Connor squirm a bit, and Del knew he was getting through to him. "Your talent will only take you so far. If you don't have the work ethic, attitude, and focus, your talent will not take you where you want to go. You need to change things around really quickly. Do you understand?"

Connor looked up at Del and said, "Yes, Coach. Sorry. It won't happen again."

"I hope not, Connor. Not for me, but for you and for your teammates. They're counting on you to be the player we all know you can be. Don't let them down."

"Okay, Coach. I won't."

"Good. Now get out there and get warmed up," said Del.

After Connor left, Kevin Nixon said, "Feels like déjà vu all over again, just like with Cade last year in this same room on this same night."

"That's exactly what I was just thinking," said Del.

Kevin said, "Del, we can't let Connor do to this team what we let Cade do the last couple of years. Cade held everyone hostage for way too long last year, and it almost cost us dearly. With his size and ability, Connor has the potential to do more for us than Cade did, especially when he is paired up with Rem. We can't let him slide. We can't let him off the hook. We need to keep him on a much shorter leash than we did with Cade."

Del heard what Kevin was saying and was processing it. Kevin was such a good assistant, and he had become a surrogate for his own dad's coaching after his dad passed away. Between Kevin and Jim Turner, Del had two really good guys to keep alive the concepts his father had instilled in him. He also had in Kevin someone who would call him out on things without singling him out and hurting him.

Del said, "You mean *I* can't let him slide. *I* can't let him off the hook. *I* need to keep him on a shorter leash. And you're right. I'm the head coach. It's my responsibility."

"Well, yes, you are, and yes, it is ultimately your responsibility as the head coach," said Kevin. "But it is all of our responsibilities—yours, mine, Braden's, and the entire team's—to keep everyone accountable for their actions. So while *you* need to be the ultimate enforcer of that, we all need to be on the same page and doing the same thing."

Del said, "Great point." They were almost to the locker room door, and Kevin grabbed Del by the elbow. Del stopped and wheeled around.

Kevin said, "Coach, you've got this. You're a good coach. Everything you went through with Cade has prepared you for anything this kid may throw at you. You had a great mentor in your dad, and you know what he would tell you to do. You just need to do it."

Del knew exactly what Kevin was saying. He nodded without saying a word, turned, pushed the locker room door open, and stepped out into the gym. It was "go-time"!

Ideas to Consider:

- **What are some of Coach Brooks's main messages to his team in the locker room?**
- **Coach Brooks tells Connor he has great potential. What does he say is the only way for someone to ensure they live up to their potential? Do you agree?**

Chapter 18

The early season practices went well. Connor was blending in nicely, and the team was gelling. Not only was Connor playing well with his teammates, but he was also hanging out with them more. Del was so glad that was happening. If Connor would spend more time with the team, he would not be spending it with Tommy Garrett and Bobby Maxwell and getting into the kind of trouble they were prone to get into.

While Remington was the best player and a natural leader that all the kids followed, Nick and Tim were also two of the leaders that people gravitated towards. With the three of them leading, practices went smoothly, and everyone was on the same page. Even Connor stayed in line and followed their lead for the most part.

There was an obvious hierarchy of leadership on the team, and Connor seemed content being in the second tier of leadership. He and Brian Jackson were the two best juniors. They both had leadership capabilities that they exerted at times. Remington, Nick, and Tim were smart enough and mature enough to be fine with that. They knew that the two juniors were the leaders of the future, so they let them step into some leadership roles occasionally.

As the first game approached, though, the boys noticed Connor trying to exert his leadership a little more than usual and in a little different way than before. In the first two weeks of practices, he said positive, upbeat things to the team. But in the last couple of days before the first game, he changed. He started yelling at his teammates in a negative tone. He would point out their mistakes, calling guys out for things he thought they should have done differently. He was yelling, criticizing, or bullying others.

Connor had seen people in leadership roles telling others what to do, and often they were yelling when doing it. He saw coaches yelling at players and sometimes yelling loudly at them. If that's what they did to lead, it only made sense that's what he should do. He didn't realize that behaving that way is not leadership. Leadership is showing by example, picking people up, encouraging, helping, serving, and working with them, not directing and ordering them.

However, Connor's behavior was turning his teammates off in a big way. Many of them grumbled underneath their breaths when he would yell at them. He would yell, "Come on! You've got to work harder than that!"

Their first thoughts were, "Who are you to be talking to anyone about working hard? You're the laziest guy out here." The players he was doing this to at first were the younger players, the ones who weren't going to be the starters and who weren't the leaders of the team. He didn't feel any threat from them, so he let them have it.

But the night before the first game, he did it to Tim Nelson. Connor was posting up inside. He had his man on his hip and sealed off away from the basket. Tim had the ball on the wing and was looking at Connor. However, Brian, who stood three inches taller than Tim, was guarding Tim, and Tim did not have a good lane to get the pass into Connor. He swung the ball out to Remington who was open on the point. Remington swished a three-pointer. Connor immediately turned out towards Tim and barked, "Get me the ball when I'm open in here! I need the ball if we're going to win!"

Tim was a senior. He was not a guy who needed to be yelled at by anyone to get him to perform properly. He had been one of the steady performers from last year who was going to step into an even bigger role this year. His teammates loved his work ethic, attitude, and way he treated them. He usually made the right play, rarely forcing any action he shouldn't. He knew his role and his limitations, so he played within himself and rarely made mistakes. Unlike Remington who was skilled enough to push the envelope on plays, if Tim didn't feel he could make the pass, he wouldn't make it.

When Connor yelled at him, Tim immediately walked up to him and got into his chest. Tim didn't care one bit that Connor was five inches taller than him. He was stronger than Connor, but more importantly, Tim was the toughest kid in the program. He didn't back down from anybody. The look on his face had Connor scared. Tim put his right index finger into Connor's chest and said in a calm but stern voice, "Don't ever talk to me like that again. If you do, you won't like the result."

Tim stood there and stared at Connor. Del and Kevin both yelled, "All right! That's enough," and they both started walking towards them to make sure things didn't escalate. Del said, "We've got a game tomorrow night that we need to prepare for. We need everyone on the same page. That kind of stuff ends right now, get it?"

Tim calmly said, "Oh, I got it, Coach. I just wanted make sure Connor got it."

Del turned towards Connor waiting for him to respond. Connor didn't know what to do. He had just been put in his place by a teammate, and a teammate who was not nearly as skilled as he was. But he also knew that Tim was not a guy to mess with. Not only was he a tough kid and really strong, but everyone on the team liked Tim. Connor just stared at Tim as he was walking away.

Del turned towards the rest of the team and said, "Boys, we've been going at each other hard for two weeks. It's understandable that you are going to have some tensions and emotions with each other. In fact, that can be a good thing. But save it and let it build for Flint Rock tomorrow night, all right?" Everyone nodded. "All right, let's get back at it."

That was the end of the scuffle between Tim and Connor. They stayed away from each other the rest of the practice. Connor tried to save some face by acting a lot tougher after that. He talked trash with some of the younger players. They didn't really respond all that much, as they were intimidated by him. However, the other seniors and juniors were emboldened by Tim's reaction. When Connor popped off at a sophomore on the JV, Nick Bertucci said, "Leave him alone, Connor. At least he's busting his ass trying. That's more than you're doing."

Again, Connor didn't know what to do. Nick was chosen as a Team Captain along with Remington. He, too, was a football player, and if Tim wasn't the toughest kid on the team, Nick was. Nick was a very vocal leader. He also did not have the same calm demeanor that Tim had. His fuse was short, and he might just punch Connor without provocation. Connor just turned away and got back into the line without saying a word.

All of this was leading to a difficult dynamic. Connor was a very good player and was tearing it up on the court with his play. And while he had been establishing good relationships with the guys early on, he was alienating himself a bit with his words the last couple of days. At the same time, the rest of the team was bonding over it. The older guys were already sick of dealing with Connor's antics. They had gotten sick of it in the spring and summer, but they had hoped that once the season started, things would change. They liked what he brought to the team in terms of their chances to win a state championship, but they didn't like how he acted.

They had been through seasons with a bad teammate in Cade Clemons, and they didn't like it. But Cade was older than them, and he had a grip on the team because of it. They fell in line because they were underclassmen. But Connor was new, and he was younger than them. They knew what they wanted and knew what they needed to do to get it. They were not about to let some cocky, new kid with a poor attitude and work ethic get in their way. They knew they needed to deal with him early and often, and the more they did, the stronger they felt.

It's not that they wanted to gang up on Connor. It's that they wanted him to join them and become one of them. If he did that, they could be really good. But if he didn't, their attitude was, "We don't need him. We'll do it without him. We just don't want him to get in our way and screw things up."

Del did all he could to stay on top of the situation. He constantly asked the players about how things were going. He was trying to see what he needed to do to help them thrive. Of course, he talked mostly to Remington, Nick, and Tim, but he knew the importance of listening to everyone, so he asked all of the kids about their experience at various times, too. Throughout the summer and fall and now the first two weeks of the season, they all said something to the effect of, "You've got to do something about Connor."

Del was so frustrated. He had been through four years with Cade Clemons. He did not want to go through that again for the next two years with Connor McDonald. But he also felt that Connor was the key to a state championship. With him, the road to championship would be so much easier than without him. And with all the pressure Del had been feeling the last couple of years to get to the state tournament and get back to bringing home some hardware, he knew he needed to do all that he could to keep Connor in the mix.

Del tried to stay positive with Connor most of the time. The problem was that by not dealing with the worst attitude on his team, he was starting to lose the respect of all of the best attitudes on his team. The rest of the guys started thinking, "Why doesn't Coach do something about him?" And the key guys— Remington, Nick, Tim, Brian, and Mike—weren't just thinking it. They were talking about it.

Just like last year with Cade, they doubted Coach would do anything about Connor. They all liked Coach Brooks. However, they felt he talked a good game, but he didn't follow through on holding good players accountable for poor choices. Of course, they all saw this the last few years with Cade, but they had also seen it with other players, even themselves at times. It was like he didn't want to rock the boat and make waves with the players he knew would help them win. But they all knew that those players needed to be held accountable for their actions if they were going to grow and succeed. If they knew that as kids, why didn't he know it as an adult? And if he did know it, why didn't he do it?

With Connor, though, they had had enough. It was time to step up and do something. This was *their* team. For the seniors, this was their final season. They didn't want it to end in disappointment and frustration. They knew how good they could be with or without Connor. They didn't want anything—or anybody—getting in their way.

Ideas to Consider:

- **How does Connor start acting? How do the rest of the guys react? How does Coach Brooks react?**

- **What are the boys starting to feel about Coach Brooks... again? Why is this a potentially dangerous situation?**

Chapter 19

The Butte Tip-Off Tournament was an all-day tournament on Friday and Saturday. The Wolves were scheduled to play at 12:30 on Friday. The night before the tournament, Remington was at Jenny's house doing schoolwork. They had papers and books spread out all over Jenny's kitchen table. They were both trying to finish up homework to hand in before school the next morning. Even though Jenny wasn't playing, she was going to take the day off of school and go watch Remington play.

"I'm glad you're going to be there," he said to her. "I'm so nervous, I might just go up and sit in the bleachers with you."

"Really?" she asked. "Why? What are you so nervous about, Rem?"

"What am I so nervous about? Are you kidding? This is it. This is what I've been thinking about every day for the last eight months."

"Rem," she said. "You haven't just been *thinking about* this day for eight months. You've been *working* for this day for eight months. You've got nothing to be nervous about. This is exactly what you've been getting ready for." She paused, set her pencil down, and reached across the table, and cradled his hand in hers. "Rem, there is nobody in the state more ready for tomorrow than you are. While I know I have been part of your thoughts for the last eight months, NOTHING has been bigger in your mind than this game tomorrow. You are *so ready* for this. You have nothing to be nervous about."

Remington squeezed her hand and said, "You're right. I am ready for this. We're all ready for this. We've put in so much work to get here. At the end of last season, I had ideas on what I hoped we would all do to get ready for this. Quite honestly, we did so much more and worked so much harder than I hoped we would that I know we're ready. And then by adding Connor, we're that much better than we could have even hoped for at that time."

"Really?" Jenny asked. "Are you really that much better with him?"

"Are you kidding?" he asked. "He's great. He makes us a complete team."

Jenny said, "Does he really? I mean does he really make you a complete *team*? Or is he just a really talented big, strong kid who plays well?"

Remington smiled and said, "Listen to you! Who do you think you are—Dickie V?"

"Who's Dickie V?" she asked.

"Dick Vitale. The college basketball announcer." Remington imitated Dick Vitale's voice and one of his famous lines, "'He's AWESOME, Baby, with a capital A.' You've never heard that guy on the games when we watch Duke?"

Jenny smiled and said, "Oh yeah, I've heard that guy. I just didn't know that was his name. Anyway, maybe I'm not Dickie V, but I do know that everything you say about Connor and the problems you guys have been having with him make it sound like he is not helping you be a better TEAM. He may be a really good player, but that doesn't mean he's helping you be a better team."

"You're absolutely right, Jen. He is really good. But he also kind of hurts all the good things we're trying to do as a team."

Jenny said, "Gee, kind of sounds like someone I remember from last year."

Remington said, "No kidding. I can't tell you how many times since Connor started playing with us in the summer I thought, 'He acts just like Cade.'"

"And how did that work out last year?" she asked.

"Not great, but not too bad either," said Remington.

Jenny said, "Sure, but is that what you want to happen with Connor? Go through the whole year and having it end up being 'not great, but not too bad either'?"

Remington said, "No. There's no way I want to go through that again. I've got to do something about him, that's for sure."

Jenny said, "Rem, *you* shouldn't have to do anything. It should be Coach Brooks who does something."

"Yes, you're right," said Remington. "But you're wrong, too. I mean, Coach Brooks needs to deal with Connor, for sure. But this is my senior year. I've been elected a team captain again. Connor is a junior. I need to step up and do what needs to be done to keep him in line."

"Rem, you're not the only senior, you know. Nick and Tim are right there with you. All three of you need to do something about him."

Remington nodded and said, "Absolutely. In fact, tonight at practice, Connor was popping off, but he finally popped off to the wrong guy—Tim."

"Ooh, I bet that didn't go too well," said Jenny. "What happened?"

"Connor yelled at Tim to get him the ball. Tim walked over to him, got in his face, thumped him one in his chest, and said, 'Don't ever talk to me like that again.' That was it. Connor kind of wilted right there in front of us. Of course, later he had to act tough with the young kids, but he didn't say a word to the rest of us the rest of practice."

"Good," said Jenny. "That's what he needs. He needs you guys to put him in his place."

Remington looked at the table and said, "The problem is that I'm the leader of the team. It starts with me. I need to be the one who steps up when Connor acts like an idiot."

"Rem, I get it. You're the leader, so you need to lead. But you're not the only one who needs to lead. Nick and Tim are also good leaders. It's not all on your shoulders."

"I know," said Remington. "But so far, I haven't actually stepped up to him. I've tried to bring him along, bring him into the fold and be with us. I feel like if I can get him to join us, that will help him and help us that much more."

Jenny said, "Okay, that's good. That's leadership, too. Leading isn't only getting on guys. My gosh, Rem, you're the first guy to say that all the time. So, if that's the way you want to lead, then that's how you should lead."

"Yeah, I know," he said. Jenny could tell he was struggling with something when he said, "Can I let you in on a little secret?"

"Sure," she said.

"You can't tell any of the guys this, okay?"

"Okay," said Jenny.

Remington fumbled for the right words. "It's just that there is a part of me that's afraid to step up the way that Tim did, the way that Nick would. I just don't like confrontation like that. I'm not a tough guy, not a fighter. I don't do that kind of thing well. I didn't do it in all my time with Cade. Now here I have a younger guy acting in a way he shouldn't, and I'm still struggling with it."

Jenny smiled and said, "Rem, it's okay. It's not your personality to be that way. You're not comfortable with that...yet. But when the time comes, if you need to, you'll stand up to him. It was different with Cade. You grew up with him, and he was older than you. He always had to show everyone he was the best. When you came along and threatened that, he didn't like it."

She paused to see if her words were sinking in. Then she said, "But Connor is different. He doesn't know you. He has respect for you because you're older, you're a great player, and all of the other guys like you and listen to you. You said he wilted when Tim stood up to him, right?"

Remington nodded his head. Jenny said, "He'll do the same thing with you. I guarantee it. But you might not ever have to do that either, and that's okay. Lead the way *you* lead. Don't try to be anyone else. In fact, maybe it's better that you leave the tough guy stuff to Nick and Tim, and you be the guy who is there trying to bring Connor along. He'll need to know one of you seniors likes him. Plus, with you two being the two best players, you guys need to play well together. The more you work with him and try to bring him into being a good teammate with everyone, the better he will be."

Remington looked at Jenny with a bit of disbelief. "Gosh, first you're Dickie V. and now you're Coach K. That's awesome, Jen. Have you ever thought about becoming a coach in the future?"

Jenny couldn't tell if he was serious. She said, "Well, no, not really. But playing soccer all those years and then hanging out with you all this time, I guess some ideas have just stuck with me." She paused and looked off towards the kitchen cabinets. "But, no, I never thought about being a coach. I just look at situations on my teams and on yours and think about them, that's all."

"Well, I'm serious," said Remington. "You should think about coaching someday. You'd be good at it."

She squeezed his hand and said, "Thanks, Rem. I've had a good mentor in thinking that way."

Remington smiled and said, "Well, I don't know about that." He looked at the kitchen clock and said, "But I do know that I need to get home. I need to get a good night's sleep before tomorrow's game. Although I wonder if I will be able to sleep at all."

Jenny smiled and said, "Rem, I told you, you have nothing to worry about. You're ready for this. Go home and get some sleep."

He got up and put all of his schoolwork in his backpack. Jenny stood up, hugged him, kissed him, and said, "See you tomorrow."

He hugged her back and said, "See you tomorrow. And thanks for everything tonight. I needed that."

"No problem," she said. "Your bill will be in the mail tomorrow. My counseling sessions aren't cheap, you know." They both laughed as Remington walked out the door.

The next day, at the Butte Tip-Off Tournament, playing against Flint Rock, a team from the west side of the state, just west of Missoula, Jenny's words were borne out. Sacajawea came out focused and on fire. They jumped out to a double-digit lead with two minutes left in the first quarter. The inside-out combination of Remington and Connor proved unstoppable, and Flint Rock didn't have an answer for them. When they double-teamed Remington, he found either Connor inside for easy lay-ups and alley oops or one of the wings on the perimeter for open jump shots.

Flint Rock was so focused on Remington and Connor that Brian, Nick, Tim, and Mike were all getting great looks from the perimeter and on cuts to the basket. By the end of the first half, Sacajawea was up by 21 points, and Del had already gotten everyone into the game. In the second half it was more of the same, and Sacajawea won by 29, even with none of the starters playing in the fourth quarter.

While Flint Rock was not a very strong team, the next night's opponent, Bitterroot from the Bitterroot Valley south of Missoula, was a perennial state tournament participant, and they had almost everyone back from last year. Del knew that Sacajawea would need to play their "A" game to beat Bitterroot, and he made that clear beforehand in the locker room. "This won't be like last night," he said. "This team is good, one of the best teams on the west side. It will not be easy."

However, the boys came out focused and on top of their game again. Bitterroot didn't know what hit them. While Del was right that it wasn't easy, it wasn't nearly as difficult as he thought it would be. Again, Remington and Connor were the "Dynamic Duo" as *The Montana Standard* newspaper called them in their Sunday Sports section. Remington led the way with 18 points and 11 assists. Connor had 17 points and 14 rebounds. He was an absolute beast inside, and Bitterroot had no answers for him. The others all had a very balanced, solid scoring game as well, and the Wolves beat Bitterroot, 71–59.

The state was served notice about Sacajawea on the first weekend of the year, and it felt good for the Wolves. They knew they were going to be good; it was just a matter of finding out how good. With Connor, everything was that much better. Defenses couldn't concentrate on Remington like they thought they would be able to this year. While he would have found any of his open teammates due to his skills and his unselfishness, with Connor added into the mix, he was finding a strong post player who could finish well around the basket. The scoring percentages were going to go up.

Connor's behavior on the court was good. Once in the first game on a dead ball situation, he barked at Bob Bickford when Bob hadn't gotten him the ball on the previous play. Del yelled out, "Connor!" and that was all it took. Connor immediately recognized what he had done, went over to Bob and said, "Sorry, dude. I know that would have been a tough pass to get in to me. You did the right thing. My bad." He high-fived Bob and hustled back to his spot. That was the only time Del saw Connor yell at somebody, and Del felt really good about things. He couldn't have asked for a better start to the season.

Ideas to Consider:

- **How is Remington feeling the night before the first game? Why? How does Jenny help him through what he is feeling?**

- **What is the "little secret" that he tells Jenny? Do you think this is actually pretty common for players to feel this way? What can they do to work on that?**

Chapter 20

Officer Rick Bryson had been filling in for another police officer on Saturday night. At around 9:30, they got a call about a party at Evan Turnbull's house, a junior whose family lived up in the foothills of the Tobacco Root Mountains. By 10:30, the police officers had processed paperwork on all of the underaged kids who were there, and they were waiting for all the parents to come take them home. Rick Bryson was outside while the rest of the officers were inside dealing with the kids who were there.

As a car pulled up into the driveway, Officer Bryson realized that it was Ethan Wilcox's car, and he saw Ethan driving. He shined his flashlight at Ethan and waved for him to stop as he came around the circular driveway. Officer Bryson could tell that Ethan was trying to get out of there without having to stop, but because of all the cars lined up along the driveway, he could only follow the circle around and stop when Officer Bryson stood in his way.

As Ethan rolled down his window, Officer Bryson shined his flashlight into the car. He saw Mark Gallagher in the front passenger seat and Connor McDonald in the back seat. Connor was pressed up into the corner, trying not to be seen by Officer Bryson.

"What's going on, boys?" asked Officer Bryson.

"Nothing," said Ethan. "Just coming out to Evan's house to play video games." Ethan, Mark, and Evan were some of the former basketball players who had played when they were younger and had some skills, but didn't like all the work that they were asked to do to improve. They didn't go out for the team their sophomore year, and they started partying a lot. This past fall, they went to the open gyms, and Del talked to them about turning themselves around and working to improve if they wanted to make the team. Once again, they wanted no part of all the work, so they didn't try out this year either.

Officer Bryson shined the flashlight into the back seat. "How 'bout you, Connor? How is it that you're here? I thought you guys were playing in the Tip-Off Tournament in Butte."

Connor said, "Oh yeah, we did. We just got home about an hour ago. We grabbed some Taco Bell and headed up here to play some Fortnite with Evan."

"How did you guys do?" asked Officer Bryson.

"We won both games," said Connor. "We played really good."

Officer Bryson asked, "How did *you* do?"

"Pretty good."

Officer Bryson nodded his head and said, "Well, that's good. It's gonna' be fun to watch you guys because you guys could be really good! As long as everyone stays eligible and out of trouble."

All Connor could say was, "Yeah," because he didn't want to hear about being in trouble.

Officer Bryson said, "I bet you guys know why I'm here."

They all said, "No, why?"

Officer Bryson responded. "About an hour ago, we got a call about a party here. When we got here there were about 30 students and former students here. Sure enough, they were partying with some pretty hard stuff. Something tells me that's what you were coming here for, not some video games."

Connor immediately responded, "Officer, I was texting Ethan on the ride home, and he was telling me that he and Mark were going to Evan's to play video games. I said that would be cool, so when I got off the bus, Ethan picked me up. We headed to Taco Bell, and then headed up here." He lifted up his bag of tacos and his cup from Taco Bell for Officer Bryson to see and said, "See?"

"Oh, I see," said Officer Bryson. "I also see three high school boys driving up to a house with 30 kids drinking and smoking dope, and I know what my eyes tell me when that happens, too."

Connor said, "I swear I knew nothing about a party here. I thought we were coming here to play Fortnite with Evan." Ethan and Mark just nodded their heads.

A silver Land Rover pulled up, and Officer Bryson saw one of the girls from the party being escorted out to the car by another officer. As the officer spoke with the girl's parents, Officer Bryson leaned back into the car and said, "Well, I gotta' go and help with getting these kids picked up. You three are awfully lucky that your timing worked out the way it did, so nothing is going to happen to you, at least not with regards to the police."

Officer Bryson leaned in a bit more, looked into the backseat and said, "However, I don't know what your coach will do to you, Connor. I know what I would do if I were coaching you, and I know you wouldn't like it." He paused to see what Connor's reaction was. Connor didn't make a move or any kind of face at all.

Officer Bryson continued, "Young man, you have a lot of skill on the basketball court, and that skill could take you somewhere in the future. But you won't go anywhere if you're not on the court because you're making bad choices. You better think twice about the people you're hanging out with." He pointed at the house as he said it.

Then he nodded at Ethan and Mark as he added, "Otherwise, you're going to blow it, and end up like so many kids who we've had come through here with talent who don't want to work and do the things asked of them to be their best and help their teams be their best. Then those guys just drift away, and I see them on the streets or in the bars or in the meth houses here in town, talking about how great they were as players, but their coaches screwed them over. Don't become that guy, Connor. Start making better decisions."

Connor didn't say anything.

Officer Bryson looked at Ethan and said, "You two guys, as well. I'm sick of hearing your names from people talking about kids who are partying. You two used to be good ballplayers when you were freshmen. You should think about playing again. But if you do, this kind of stuff has to stop. You guys need to start making better decisions. Get it?"

All three of them replied, "Got it," almost instinctively from being in Coach Brooks's basketball program.

Officer Bryson said, "All right, get out of here."

Connor half-raised his hand to wave good-bye to Officer Bryson as Ethan drove away.

Ideas to Consider:

- **Do you think Connor, Ethan, and Mark were going to Evan's house to play video games or to party? Why do you think that way?**

- **Have you or any of your teammates ever been at a party that got broken up by the police? If so, what was the outcome of the situation? Were you or your teammates punished in some fashion through the school, the athletic code, or the team's set of standards?**

- **Why do you think schools have rules like that, governing behaviors away from the team? Is it fair for them to do that? Why or why not?**

Chapter 21

On Monday morning, Bill James, the assistant principal, walked into Del's room before first period and told him what had happened with Connor on Saturday night. Del couldn't believe what he was hearing. Here the kid was, two games into his season and playing well, and he was already jeopardizing his season. While he had not been caught *at* the party, and there was nothing the school could do to punish him based on the athletic code, a part of Del still felt like he needed to do something. He just didn't know what.

Del asked Bill James, "So, how do we handle this?"

"Well, from the school's perspective, there is nothing to do. He was not on school property, and he technically didn't do anything wrong or violate the athletic code, so it is not a school issue. However, he certainly violated your trust and put himself in a bad position. You probably need to do something."

Del breathed a deep sigh. "It just never ends does it? Never gets easy?"

"Nope," replied Bill. "But no one ever said it was going to be easy. We deal with 14 through 18-year-old kids navigating their way through life. They make all kinds of decisions every day. Some of them are bad decisions. It's up to us to help them learn from those, even if it isn't easy."

Del worried about what he was going to have to do. Coaching could be the greatest, most rewarding profession in the world. It could also suck the life out of someone. Right now, it was sucking the life out of Del. Here he had just experienced the best weekend a team of his had ever had to start off the year. He was excited about where the season could go. Now this hit him. Four years into his head coaching journey, he was already questioning if he had the desire to keep going.

Del walked out of his classroom and headed down to Rick Bryson's office to hear more about the situation. "How bad is it, Rick?" asked Del.

"Well, it could have been a whole lot worse," said Rick. "We broke up the party a little after 10:00. I was outside waiting for parents to pick their kids up, when Ethan, Mark, and Connor drive up. I told them there was a party there, that they were lucky they showed up when they did, or they would have been in a whole lot of trouble, and that they needed to get out of there."

Del nodded, and Rick said, "I also talked to all three boys about making the right choices and the consequences if they don't. I doubt that anything I said sunk in, but I tried."

"Thanks for doing that, Rick," said Del. "How many times are we going to have to give those kinds of messages to this kid before he figures it out?"

Rick said, "It's hard to say. He might never get it. But it doesn't mean we stop trying. Kids are bombarded with all kinds of messages from all kinds of sources every day. It's up to us to make sure we are constantly offering positive messages of potential and consequences for actions so that maybe they learn something from some of them."

"Absolutely," said Del. "So, I assume that nothing was done to them from your end."

"There was nothing to do," said Rick. "They drove up to the house after everything was over. I didn't smell any booze or dope in the car, so I didn't have any reason to test them. They were clean. They were lucky. Had they gotten there a half-hour or so earlier, it would have been a different story."

"Okay, thanks," said Del.

Del started to walk out of the office, but Rick's words stopped him. "So what are you gonna' do about it?"

"You just said there really isn't anything we could do," said Del.

Rick said, "No. I said there wasn't anything *we* could do. I didn't say you couldn't do anything. You could hold him out for part of a game. You could make him run. You could do a lot of things. I mean, let's face it. The kid wasn't going up there to play video games. He knew *exactly* what was going on there. You could certainly hold him accountable in some way."

Del dropped his head, thinking about what Rick had said. He then responded, "Yeah, you're right. I'm going to head down to Randy's office and see what he thinks."

"Good idea," said Rick. "Good luck with all of it."

Del walked out of Rick's office and walked into Randy Watson's. Randy had been the athletic director at Sacajawea since Del had been a student there. Del knew Randy would have some ideas for him on how to handle it. Randy said, "Well, this is a fun way to start off a Monday morning."

"Unbelievable, huh?" said Del.

"Is it really all that unbelievable with this kid?" asked Randy. "He's given us signs pretty much from the time he got here that this would not be all that unbelievable. So what do you think you're going to do?"

Del said, "I'm not sure. That's why I wanted to talk to you. Any ideas?"

"Some," said Randy, "but none that I absolutely love. It's a hard one. While you and I both know he went up there to party, he didn't party because of the timing, so technically, he did nothing wrong. He didn't violate the athletic code. Heck, he didn't even violate your team's standards... *technically*. He just went with some friends to a house to play video games."

"Yeah, I know," said Del. "That's what makes it so hard. If I come down on him in any way, I am attacking him for something that he didn't do," Del made air quotes with his fingers and said, "*technically*."

"Right," said Randy. "I don't think you can punish him, but I think you should talk to him, ask him what happened. What was he doing there? Did he know about the party? I would act from the side that you trust that he is telling the truth. Then I would lay out for him how serious the consequence would have been if he had actually been at that party when the police got there. You want to help him learn to make the right decisions. By outlining what would have happened to him, maybe he makes a better decision next time."

Del looked at Randy with a sideways glance and said, "Do you really think this kid is going to be deterred by that?"

Randy admitted, "I doubt it. He's shown too many signs already that he's just going to do what he wants. But this is a way for you to strengthen your relationship with him *and* talk about making the right decisions. Hopefully, one of these times, he'll get it."

"Hopefully," said Del. "But I gotta' admit, I'm not too hopeful about much with this kid."

"I know," said Randy. "He's a frustrating one, that's for sure. All that ability and not much character and discipline to channel that ability in a positive direction. That's why he needs you. You become his barometer of discipline to help him learn the proper ways to behave."

"Isn't that his parents' job?" asked Del.

"Of course, it is. But either they've not done it or given up or he hasn't listened to them. So now it's your turn."

"Great," said Del sarcastically. "I get to be his parent."

"Well, not just you. All of us need to be—you, me, your assistants, his teachers, the administrators. Every adult in his life needs to be a part of it. But it's not just him. It's every kid. While it's the parents first and foremost who must teach and instill in kids the lessons of life, it's up to the rest of us, too." Randy paused and then said, "And it's a never-ending job. But it's one of the most important jobs ever in the world."

Del nodded and said, "Okay. Thanks for your help, Randy. I appreciate it."

Randy said, "That's what I'm here for. Let me know how it goes."

Ideas to Consider:
- **What is the dilemma that Coach Brooks is facing with Connor?**
- **What do you think Coach Brooks should do?**

Chapter 22

Del found Connor at his locker prior to heading into lunch. Del said, "Hey, Connor," in a fairly upbeat way. He didn't want to have the conversation head south right away.

Connor smiled and said, "Hey, Coach."

Del said, "Can I talk to you for a minute before you head into lunch?"

"Sure," said Connor.

"Let's walk and talk," said Del. As they turned away from Connor's locker, Del said, "I heard you had a little incident after we got home on Saturday night."

Connor looked stunned. He said, "Coach, I didn't do anything wrong!"

Del put his hand up to stop Connor from continuing and said, "I know you didn't. Officer Bryson told me the whole story. You weren't at the party. I get it. The problem is you were about to be if the police hadn't been there."

"Coach, we were going up there to play video games. I swear it. I had no idea they were having a party."

"I know," said Del. "That's what Officer Bryson told me you told him. You got caught in a tough spot. You weren't at the party, so technically, you did nothing wrong. The problem is this—think about how it looks to Officer Bryson, to me, to your teammates, to anyone who hears about it. It looks like you were headed up there to a party. Now I know you say you didn't know there was a party, and I'm going to take your word for it. I'm going to believe you. I'm not going to punish you because technically you did nothing wrong."

Connor looked relieved. But Del continued before Connor could say anything. "But this is it, Connor. This is a wake-up call for you. Look who you've been hanging out with. Look at how the things they are doing are going to drag you right down and sabotage any chance you have at the kind of future you say you want to have. Is that what you want?"

Connor said, "No."

Del said, "Connor, life is all about the choices we make. Here's a quote for you—'We make our choices, and then our choices make us.' Who you hang out with is a choice. How you behave when you hang out with them is a choice. You are constantly making choices that are determining where you are going in your life. I don't know for sure if the way you say what happened the other night actually happened that way. But you do. And if it did happen the way you said, then you got put into a bad position. But you made the choice to hang with the guys you hang with that put you in that position. That was *your* choice, nobody else's."

Del paused. He was searching to see if he was getting through to Connor, but he couldn't tell. "And if it didn't go the way you said it did and you knew there was a party there, again, that was your choice—nobody else's. Connor, you need to take a long look in the mirror and ask yourself about the choices you have been making lately. Are they the best choices you can make for yourself, your team, or your future? Are they leading you towards the person you want to become? I can't answer those questions for you. Only you can. But you need to start coming up with answers soon, before it's too late to save yourself from the choices you are making."

Connor looked at the floor and wiped his eyes. Del thought that maybe his words had done something. Or if not his words, at least Connor's own thoughts were getting to him. Connor looked up and said, "I'm sorry, Coach. You're right. I haven't made the best choices since I moved here. I know I gotta' do better. But this has been so hard. I miss Oakland and my friends so much. It's just been hard."

He stopped for a couple of seconds as Del nodded to him and said, "I know it has."

Connor then gathered himself and said, "But I swear, I didn't know there was a party at that house when I went there."

"All right, I believe you, Connor. Just keep thinking about the decisions and choices you're making *before* you make them, okay?"

"Okay," said Connor.

"All right," said Del. "Go ahead and get to lunch. I'll see you at practice." Connor turned and headed to the cafeteria. Del watched him and thought, "I hope he's telling the truth, and I hope he gets it. I need him to get it. 'Cuz if he does, he's gonna' help me get that state championship."

Ideas to Consider:

- **Do you believe Connor is telling the truth? Do you believe Coach Brooks believes him?**

- **Coach Brooks decides not to punish Connor. How do you think people will react to Coach Brooks not punishing him? Should the potential public reaction even be a part of a coach's decision-making process?**

Chapter 23

Del felt he needed to address the situation with his team before practice that day. By now, everyone would have heard that Connor had been up at Evan's house. The way rumors start and then spread, Del figured people would have thought Connor was actually at the party and got busted for it. So Del felt he needed to say something to the team about it. However, he struggled to figure out the best way to address Connor's situation in a way that would benefit both the team and Connor but also keep Connor's privacy rights intact. He also knew they would wonder what would happen to Connor.

Del wasn't sure where the whole team stood on Connor. He knew some of them, the key guys, were disgusted with how Connor behaved. At least that's what they said. But he also knew they were 16-, 17-, and 18-year-old kids. They might be doing some of the same things that Connor was doing. While Del wanted to believe they weren't, he was not naïve enough to believe that none of his kids ever did anything they shouldn't.

But Del knew this was a pretty special group of kids, extremely committed to their success. He knew they had high hopes for the season and plans for how they wanted to get there. He didn't think most of them would be willing to risk any of their goals by doing something stupid, like partying or misbehaving in any way that would jeopardize that. But of course, he didn't know for sure.

He told the team that Connor had made a decision the other night that almost affected him and the team in a bad way. He explained that due to Connor's privacy rights, Del couldn't tell them any details about it. He said that it was determined that Connor did not violate the school's athletic code based on what Officer Bryson saw, so there would be no school or athletic department punishment.

"So, he will not face any consequences because he did not actually do anything that would require consequences for his actions," said Del. "Some of you may be thinking, 'That's good. If he didn't do anything wrong, he shouldn't be punished.' Some of you may be thinking, 'Seriously? We all know what he was doing. He should be punished.' All of you have a right to think whatever way you think. But if you know something that the police and the school don't know, you have a whole different set of information on which you are basing your thoughts. We can only go on what we know. I believe Connor is telling us the truth, and the facts that we have bear that out."

He paused, looked around at each face, and then said, "Boys, this is a learning experience like so many learning experiences. I hope Connor has learned something from it. But I hope the rest of you have learned something from it, too. You saw this past weekend how special of a season this could be. Let's make sure we ALL keep our eyes on the prize and handle ourselves the right way the rest of the year. Get it?"

They all responded, "Got it!"

The team headed out the locker room door to the gym. Nick, Remington, and Tim went to one of the far baskets. Nick said to the other two, "What a crock! You know Connor was up there to party. He wasn't going there to play video games. Coach should have done something to him."

Remington said, "I agree that he was probably there to party, but the school has no proof. He hadn't even left the car yet, so the school can't do anything."

Nick said, "Well, if he's going to act like an idiot, we don't need him."

Remington said, "I don't agree. If he acts like an idiot, he needs to pay a price, sure. But I'm not so sure about 'We don't need him.' Yes, we're a good team, and we could win the whole thing without him. But you saw him at Butte. He's really good, and he helps us a lot. We are much better with him than without him."

Tim said, "Yeah, I get that. But I just can't stand the way he acts."

"I know," said Remington. "But I also want to see him stay with us. He really makes us a complete team." Remington paused and then said, "You know what. The three of us need to do a little more to reach out and bring him into our group."

"Are you kidding me?" asked Nick. "We tried to do that all summer, and he never would do anything with us. Also, I don't like the guy. He's cocky and arrogant and all about himself. I don't want to hang out with him. And look at the guys he's hanging out with. I don't want them around me either."

Remington responded, "Those are exactly the reasons why we need to bring him into our group more. I'm not saying that he has to be with us every day. But the more he hangs with us, the less he's hanging with those guys. That may just keep him clean. We'll get Brian in on this, too. He's been trying to build a bit of a relationship with him, so we can help him, and he can help us. In four months when we're holding up a state championship trophy, it will all be worth it."

Tim looked at Remington and said, "Rem, you sound like you don't think we can win it without him. Don't you think we can do this?"

"Absolutely I think we can," Remington replied. "When we were on that bus ride home last year, I believed it with all my heart, and I believe it today. I just know that with Connor added into the mix, we have an even better chance."

"You're right, I guess," said Tim. "I just don't like it, that's all."

"I don't either," said Remington. "But it's only four months, and actually, as of now it's only three months. We can deal with him for three months, can't we?"

"I sure hope so," said Nick. "But I'm not inviting him to my house. I don't trust him."

"Nobody said you have to have him over to your house," said Remington. "Let's just invite him out when we go for pizza or hang out or whatever. Let's take him out of the elements where he's going to get into trouble. Let's show him that he can have fun without that stuff."

Del blew the whistle and yelled, "Let's go. Everyone on the baseline."

As they jogged over to the other end of the gym, Nick said, "Leave it to Rem to always be thinking of ways to make us a team. Sometimes, though, you drive me nuts with that!"

Ideas to Consider:

- **Why do Nick and Tim think Connor should have been punished? Why does Remington think he shouldn't have been punished? Why does Remington want them to reach out to Connor?**

- **What can it do to a team if a player is constantly pushing the envelope of bad behavior? How can the team members deal with this in a way that helps everyone?**

Chapter 24

Jenny picked Remington up from basketball practice that night. As he sat down in the front seat, he looked over at her. She had a huge smile on her face. "What's up?" he asked.

"I'm in!" said Jenny.

"What do you mean? You're in what?"

"Stanford! I got accepted!"

Remington's eyes lit up as he said, "Oh, my god, that's incredible! Congratulations!" He reached over and gave her a hug. "That is so cool. I knew you'd get in."

"I didn't," she said. "I was worried. Oh my gosh, I can't believe it."

In some ways, Remington couldn't believe it either. More than that, deep down, he didn't want to believe it. While his words had said, "That's incredible," his thoughts were, "Oh, crap. She's going to Stanford. What am I going to do? What's going to happen to us?"

Jenny was beaming, though. She had been looking forward to hearing this news for months. She always figured she would settle on U of M or MSU, but Stanford was her "dream school." Like Duke for Remington, Stanford was the place that Jenny had thought of for many years. Her family took a vacation to northern California when she was 12, and they drove down the northern coast on Highway 1. Jenny was captivated by the scenery she saw, with the ocean out one window and all kinds of different landscapes and cool oceanside towns out the other window. Jenny's older brother, Matt, was 17 at the time, and they were checking out colleges that he was interested in. He had always been attracted to biology, and while he had grown up in Montana, the ocean had always had an appeal and a draw for him. The more he read and watched nature shows on the Discovery Channel, the more marine biology became an interest for him, so he started focusing on schools in California. Stanford was one of the schools that he was interested in.

They drove down the coast hitting multiple schools along the way. They had set up tours at five different schools, and Stanford was one of them. Matt eventually settled on UC-Santa Barbara as his choice, but their visit to Stanford had a huge impact on Jenny. She fell in love with the place. As they walked through the campus, she kept staring at all the beautiful, classic-styled buildings and thought, "I want to be here someday." After they got home, when people asked her about her trip, she talked about Stanford most of all. As she made her way through her middle school and high school years, Stanford was always her top choice for college.

Now, she had been accepted. It was a very difficult school to get into, but she was ranked either one or two in her class throughout her first three years at Sacajawea. She had scored a 35 on her ACT test, and she scored high on all of the AP tests she had taken. While there was always some doubt about whether or not she would be accepted into Stanford, she had felt good about her chances. She was finally rewarded.

The problem was that now Jenny wasn't totally sure she wanted to go to Stanford. Of course, she loved everything about the place, and the idea of continuing her education at one of the finest schools in the country excited her. It was just that as her relationship with Remington had progressed, she wasn't sure she wanted to be split apart from him. They had talked about it over the course of the past year as they grew closer and closer. They both agreed that they should not make their decision about where to go for college based on their relationship. If there was a school that seemed like it was "the one" for them, they would go to it. They would just figure out how they would make their relationship work being split apart from each other—or if they would just end their relationship.

Neither of them liked thinking about the second option. The thought of not being with the other one tore each of them apart. They couldn't handle the idea of not being together. But in their rational thoughts, they knew that if they did go to different schools, they should break up with one another. It just wouldn't be fair to be young people on a college campus and not be able to date other people if they wanted to. And while rationally, that idea made total sense, emotionally it scared them.

"I don't want her going out with other guys," thought Remington. "What if she finds someone she likes more than me? It would be over. I don't want that."

"I don't want to go out with other guys," thought Jenny, "and I certainly don't want Remington going out with other girls. What if he finds someone he likes more than me? I couldn't stand that."

So as Jenny received her wonderful news about Stanford, both of them were struggling with it. While on the outside they each said all the right things about it being the greatest opportunity and how cool it would be for her to go there, inside they were each struggling to come to grips with the thought. Instead of discussing it, though, they avoided the topic. Neither of them said what they were really feeling for fear of hurting the other one.

The problem with that was that the more they said about how great it would be for her to go to Stanford and the more they didn't say about how they truly felt about how tough it would be, the more they each felt that the other one would be fine with it. They each started wondering if the other one actually wanted to stay together if they were at different schools. Jenny wondered how much Remington really liked her; Remington wondered if Jenny was looking forward to getting away from him.

As they both sat in her car contemplating this situation, neither one spoke for a few seconds. Finally, Jenny said, "Of course, I'm not 100% sure I want to go to Stanford."

Remington felt a tingle in his body and a surge of excitement at that. But his words did not follow that feeling. "What?!" he asked. "Are you kidding? How many times have you said to me that I need to go to Duke because it's my dream school? Well, Stanford is your dream school. You need to go to Stanford. At least you've gotten accepted to your dream school. All I have from mine are some text messages from an assistant coach. I haven't been accepted to mine yet."

Jenny was torn. Remington was right. It was her dream school, and now she was in. But the thought of leaving him was so hard right now. "Gosh, Rem, you make it sound like you want to get rid of me." She looked down at the steering wheel almost in tears.

"Whoa, whoa, whoa!" he said. "That's not it at all. I'm sitting over here dying thinking of you being there and me not being there with you. I can't stand the idea." Jenny looked up at Remington with a half-smile. "But Jen, this is what you have been thinking of since you were little. And now it's here. You *have* to go. If I got a letter from Coach K or from the Duke admissions office tomorrow saying that they want me and that I'm in, I would *have* to go, right? And you'd be the first person telling me that."

She was nodding as he continued. "And as hard as it would be for us to be on completely different sides of the country, we'd figure out what to do about it. We've said all along that we can't let our relationship determine our college choices. Well, here we are smack-dab in the middle of that exact situation. We've got to be smart and stick to our guns on this. As much as I hate to say it, you've got to go to Stanford."

Jenny nodded and said, "You're right. I'd kick myself for the rest of my life if I didn't give it a shot. A chance like this doesn't come around every day. I have to go."

She paused as Remington nodded and then she said with a laugh, "Listen to me. I just said, 'I *have* to go' to Stanford like that's a bad thing. What the heck is wrong with me? This is frickin' awesome! I *get* to go to Stanford!! I *want* to go!" She looked at Remington who continued to nod, and she added, "I just don't want to lose you."

Remington said, "I know. I don't want to lose you either. But Jen, it's Stanford. It's been your dream for all these years. You have to go. And maybe we'll decide to try to stay together while you're there and I'm wherever I'm at. Or maybe we'll do what we've said all along and break up and move on. I don't want to think about that right now, though. I just want to celebrate the fact that you're going to Stanford." He paused and said, "Did you hear that!? YOU'RE GOING TO STANFORD! That is so frickin' awesome! I am so proud of you and so happy for you." She smiled a big smile and leaned over, as Remington leaned over and gave her a big hug again.

And as much as it hurt him inside to admit it, he truly was happy for her. She had achieved her goal of getting into the school of her dreams. But it also added to his own doubts and fears. As he hugged her, he thought, "Now what about me? Where will I end up? Am I going to Duke? U of M? MSU? ASU?" His thoughts trailed off for a second and then another school popped into his head— "Stanford?" The possibility was intriguing.

Ideas to Consider:

- **Rationally, it's kind of a no-brainer for Jenny to go to Stanford. Then why is it so hard for her to commit to going there?**

- **Why is it important to make sure that we don't let emotions overrule rational thoughts with the big decisions of our lives? Why is it so hard to do this, though?**

- **What is Remington dealing with in his own mind in the last paragraph? What does he hint at as a possibility in the last sentence? Would that be a good idea? Why or why not?**

Chapter 25

The next month-and-a-half saw the Sacajawea team build something special. They lost only one game, a non-conference game against Colter. Colter was a class AA school, the largest classification in the state. They were three times the size of Sacajawea, so they always had more talent.

The game was a great test and a battle from start to finish. Remington showed what kind of a special player he was. Two kids on the Colter team were considered two of the best players in the state. They were projected as Division 1 prospects, with some people saying the guard, a junior named Ray Clark, could go to a big-time school of some sort. Three Pac-12 schools, Washington, Oregon, and Colorado, were already recruiting him, as well as all of the smaller D1, D2, and NAIA schools in the entire west.

Remington had played with and against Clark in summer tournaments and camps since they were little. They played together on one travel team through the years, and they played against each other for their school's summer teams. Remington enjoyed playing with Ray although Ray tended to dominate the ball a little too much. Remington really loved practicing and playing *against* Ray because it always helped Remington raise his own game. Ray was as good a player as Remington had played against in Montana, and their battles brought out the best in each of them. They had also become friendly because of it.

In the game against Colter, Remington outplayed Ray. Ray had no answers for any of Remington's attacks. He couldn't keep Remington in front of him. When he laid off, Remington buried 3-pointers. When Ray got up on him, Remington blew past him finishing at the rim or with a kick-out to a wing or a dish to Connor inside.

But it was on the defensive end where Remington really stepped up. While he was known as a great ball handler, passer, and shooter, people did not automatically think about defense when they thought about Remington. It's not that he wasn't a good defender. He was just so good on offense that people didn't think much about his defense. Remington hounded Ray wherever he went. He cut off dribble-drives, challenged every jump shot, and didn't allow him to get any easy looks. When Ray didn't have the ball, Remington made him go way out of the offensive set to receive a pass. At halftime, Ray only had three points and two assists. He also had four turnovers already.

On the other hand, Remington had 10 points, 4 assists, and 3 steals by half-time. He was putting together a really solid game, and he was doing it against what many considered the best team in the state. While Ray was not considered a "great" defender by many, he was no slouch, and when he played against Remington, he always raised his level. However, he had no answers for Remington.

People wondered if Remington could sustain his performance at both ends of the court in the second half. Even Del, Kevin, and Braden thought that there was no way he could shut Ray Clark down that way and keep his own offensive production up the way he did in the first half. Yet, the second half saw more of the same. In fact, Remington seemed to kick into a higher gear, and he rose to a new level. He ended the game with 26 points, 12 assists, 6 rebounds, and 5 steals. He held Ray Clark to 15 points and 6 assists. But Ray also had 7 turnovers compared to 3 for Remington.

For Connor, the night did not go nearly as well. The other D1 prospect that Colter had was a 6'6" senior post player named Daniel James. He was probably going to play in the Big Sky Conference, but with a great senior season, he could possibly go to a bigger school. Connor held his own against James early on. While James had about 15 pounds on him, Connor still banged with him. Connor had 9 points and 6 rebounds in the first half, 3 of which were on the offensive end.

Offensive rebounds are a very telling stat for a big man, for they are about the work you put in to get position on people. The harder you work, the more opportunity for offensive boards. Connor was working hard throughout the first half and it was paying off. However, James was also playing well, besting Connor by a slim margin. He had 12 points and 7 rebounds as they headed to the locker room at the half. Colter was clinging to a 1-point lead.

But it was in the second half where the proverbial man separated from the boy. Connor's lack of focus on conditioning throughout the year started taking its toll on him. His fatigue got the best of him, and he struggled to get down the floor and post up strong to receive passes. When he did get it thrown to him, he was slow-footed, and James was right there everywhere he turned. Connor couldn't get a shot off. If Remington hadn't drawn James over to him on dribble drives and then dished to Connor for open layups, Connor wouldn't have scored in the second half. He had only one offensive rebound in the half, and as he went to lay it back in, James quickly jumped up and swatted it away. Connor finished the game with 15 points and 9 rebounds. He had run out of gas physically, and he had been drained emotionally trying to keep up. He just didn't have the mental toughness to succeed against someone like Daniel James. Del hoped that this would be a good lesson to Connor.

The game itself was a barn-burner, with no team ever leading by more than seven points. The Colter gym was loud and raucous, with fans from both schools showing up in strong fashion. Back and forth the game went, with Remington leading the way for the Wolves and Ray Clark and Daniel James leading the way for the Hawks. It was everything people had hoped for and imagined.

The Wolves had a 1-point lead with fifteen seconds left. Ray Clark had the ball on the wing, and his coach called a set play. Clark tried to dribble it to the point to set the play, but Remington wouldn't let him turn to do so. Instead, Ray started to drive to the hoop. As he did so, Remington reached and poked the ball away cleanly. However, it bounced off the back of Nick's leg and right to another Colter player. He had a good look at a 15-footer, and he let it fly with eight seconds left.

Connor saw the shot go up, and he turned around to position himself for a rebound. However, he didn't do the most important thing—block out Daniel James. James slipped right around Connor's left side and then *he* blocked out Connor. The ball caromed off the rim then the backboard and James leaped up to grab it. He came down with it and immediately jumped right back up and laid it in off the backboard to put Colter up by 1.

Sacajawea had no timeouts left, and Brian Jackson was close to the ball as it fell through the hoop. As the Colter players were celebrating what they figured was the game-winning basket, Brian grabbed the ball and stepped out of bounds. With :03 on the clock, he turned and found Remington streaking toward the sideline. Remington caught Brian's pass on his run toward the sideline, turned as he took one dribble up the floor, picked the ball up as he took his allotted two steps, and heaved a shot about 70 feet towards the far hoop. The gym seemed to go silent as the ball floated through the air. The ball caught the front of the rim just enough that it pushed it straight ahead, hitting the back iron and careening up into the air and out to the free throw line. The buzzer went off, and the game was over. Colter had won by a point.

As devastated as they were, the Wolves showed everyone how good they were and how special this season could be. Of course, they wanted to win the game, but Sacajawea had just played one of the best AA teams in the state to a 1-point game, even without Connor playing his best. As they walked off the floor dejected, both the Sacajawea and Colter fans cheered their performance. There was no shame in the way the Wolves had played and battled against Colter. They showed everyone that the rest of this season looked extremely bright.

With Ray Clark, Daniel James, Remington, and the "rising prospect" from Oakland named Connor McDonald, this game created quite a bit of interest for college scouts to be there. Schools from around the west were there due to multiple D1 prospects playing in the game. Afterwards, while the scouts were still interested in Ray Clark, Daniel James, and to some degree Connor, Remington had now vaulted to the top of their lists of recruits.

As much as Remington was being contacted by schools before this game, it now became almost unbearable. All eight of the schools he was interested in either had someone there or had watched the game on the livestream the school had on its website. Of Remington's top schools, U of M, MSU, Gonzaga, and ASU all had scouts in attendance. Remington was glad it was Wylie Carson who came from ASU because he had maintained contact with Remington ever since the summer. Remington enjoyed talking with Wylie, and ASU continued to inch up the list of schools that Remington considered as his top choice. While his ultimate choice was still Duke, and Remington still held out hope that someday he would have more interest from them, the chances of that happening were sinking faster every week.

Ideas to Consider:

- **Remington is still not sure where he wants to go to school. This is a difficult decision for any student, let alone an athlete choosing where to play. Why is this especially difficult for Remington? What are the many factors that he (and any student) needs to consider in choosing a school?**

Chapter 26

For the final month of the season, the Wolves were unchallenged in any major way by all but one of their opponents. It was the third-to-last game of the regular season when they played a Saturday night non-conference game at Centennial on the western side of the state. The Pioneers were a perennial state championship contender. Their coach, Jerry White, was one of the best coaches in the state. His kids always played with great effort and great discipline. They were a class program through and through.

Centennial always drew a great crowd. While the student section usually didn't go over the line too much on what was and wasn't acceptable, they could push the envelope a bit with their cheers. They were getting on Connor McDonald in the first half, and Connor was not happy about it. They called him "Ronald McDonald," "Quarter Pounder" and "McChicken." He laughed those off, as did Connor's teammates. But they were constantly on him every time he was down in the end of the court where they were, and he grew tired of it.

Early in the fourth quarter, Grant Bolden, Centennial's best post player, blocked Connor's shot. It went off of Connor's forehead and out of bounds. It was what some people would call "a facial." The crowd exploded. As the Wolves trotted back down to their defensive end of the court, the gym quieted down. As Connor jogged past the Centennial student section, a student yelled out, "Is that why you ran away from California? Kept getting stuffed by *real* players." The students all laughed, and so did the players. Even the Sacajawea players chuckled.

Connor was not amused. He turned and flipped the kid off and started walking towards the bleachers. He said, "That's for you and your mother." One of the officials was standing about fifteen feet away from Connor, and he had heard the entire exchange. He stepped between Connor and the bleachers to keep Connor from going any further. Nick and Tim had also made their way over to Connor, and they escorted him out towards the middle of the court.

The referee blew his whistle, made his way to the scorer's table, made a "T" with his hands, and announced, "Technical foul on #44 in Red."

Del walked over to the referee and asked, "What happened?"

The referee said, "Some kid said, 'Is that why you ran away from California?' Your kid flipped him off and said, 'That's for you and your mother.'"

"Are you going to do anything to the kid?"

The referee had a shocked look on his face. "Seriously?! Are you kidding, Coach? Do you know how many things we hear that are far worse than that? I'm not gonna' do anything about it. You can talk to their AD if you want, but I'd be more worried about getting your kid under control if I were you."

Del said, "Well, you're not me. I'll worry about my kids the way I want to. You just worry about keeping control of the game."

"I think that's what I just did, Coach," the referee said as he walked back out onto the court.

Connor was still out at the half-line as a Centennial player was stepping to the free-throw line to shoot the technical foul shots. Nick, Tim, Brian, and Remington were all talking to him, trying to get him to calm down. Remington kept looking over at Del, waiting for him to sub someone in for Connor. Del had a rule about technical fouls in his Policy Sheet. Everyone knew the rule because it was one of the rules he always talked about at the Pre-Season Athlete/Parent Meeting. "If you get a technical foul for bad behavior, you're immediately coming out of the game. You might go back in after I talk with the official." The second part of the rule was that for a second behavior-related technical at any point in the season, you will sit for the remainder of that game and be suspended for the next game. If you received a third technical foul at any point in the season, you were off the team.

Del had gotten this rule directly from his dad, who had it in his Policy Sheet. Over the years, Mason Brooks instilled and enforced discipline in his program. His kids knew they better behave the right way, or they would pay for it. In twenty-five years of coaching, Mason Brooks only had a few kids who ever got a technical foul in a game, and he never had to enforce the rule for getting a second technical foul.

Del now had a decision to make. He was trying to figure out if he could afford to pull Connor out right now. As Leif Bjorkland, Centennial's All-Conference point guard, swished the first free throw, the score was tied. Del thought, "We need Connor. This is one of the best teams on this side of the state. We need to make a statement. If we win this game, our kids will know we can win the whole thing this year. But if we lose, who knows what it will do to us and the rest of the teams in the state who think they can beat us?"

All of these thoughts were racing around Del's head as Bjorkland hit the second free throw. Remington had moved towards the bench and said, "Coach. Are you getting someone in for Connor?"

Del snapped back, "Rem, you play; I'll coach."

Remington was shocked at the way Del spoke to him. It wasn't that he couldn't handle being talked to like that by a coach. It was the situation that shocked him. He backed away from Del and headed back to center court.

The referee was now getting the players over to where Centennial would throw the ball inbounds. Lost in his thoughts, Del realized that Remington was right. Del hadn't even talked to Connor about what had just happened. He hadn't taken him out of the game like his rule said he would. He hadn't addressed the behavior in any way. Del was paralyzed by his thoughts.

Now it was Kevin Nixon who said something. He stood up from his seat on the bench and moved right next to Del. He said, "Del, aren't you gonna' get Connor out of there? He had a technical foul for flipping a fan off. That's unacceptable in this program."

Del snapped at Kevin. "Coach, I determine what's acceptable in this program."

Just like Remington, Kevin was stunned. He held his tongue and sat down in his seat without saying anything else.

Kevin couldn't believe what just happened. "Are you kidding me?" he thought. "Did he really just say that? Is he really not taking Connor out? Is he afraid of him? This is Cade all over again. Is he so focused on winning that he has given up on all of his standards?"

Del, too, had all kinds of thoughts racing through his head. "Did I really just do that to Rem and Kevin? Who do they think they are telling me what to do and what's acceptable here? They're right, though. That is unacceptable. What was I thinking? Connor flipped a kid off and said 'That's for you and your mother,' and I'm not doing anything about it? Have I lost my mind?"

Ideas to Consider:

- **Did the fan at Centennial go too far with his comment? Should the fan be ejected or held accountable in some other way?**

- **Was Connor justified in his response? What could he have done differently? Should Coach Brooks take Connor out of the game? Why or why not?**

Chapter 27

Centennial inbounded the ball and set up their offense. Lost in his thoughts about what had just happened with Connor, Del had not said a word to his team or given them any instructions, so they set themselves up in their man-to-man defense. Del realized he needed to do something about Connor. He looked down the bench and told Jimmy Thompson to go in for Connor. Jimmy had only played a few minutes in the second quarter. He had looked overmatched and overwhelmed by Grant Bolden. This was a gamble for Del to take. But he needed to get Connor out of there.

Del turned to Kevin and said, "Sorry I snapped at you, Kev."

Kevin was gracious and said, "You're trying to win a game."

Del said, "I know, but you were right. I need to get him out of there and talk to him before he goes back in. I don't know what I was thinking."

Kevin started, "You're doing whatever you can to win." He paused and said, "But you still have standards that you want this program to operate under. You're not thinking you'll put him back in, will you? This is a meaningless Saturday night, non-conference game."

"Meaningless?" asked Del. "You think this is a meaningless game?!"

"It's meaningless in terms of our conference standings," replied Kevin.

Del said, "Well, sure. But it's not meaningless. We'll probably see these guys at state. We need to make a statement to them."

Kevin said, "What better statement could you make to them than beating them *without* Connor for the 4th quarter? And also, what kind of statement are you making to our guys, their parents, and everyone else if you put Connor back in after what he did?"

"Good point," said Del. "But what if we don't win?"

"That's okay, too," said Kevin. "It will give them a false sense of security. They won't know what hit them when they face us with Connor."

The referee blew the whistle as the ball went out of bounds off of a Centennial player. Jimmy Thompson reported in for Connor. As Connor came out, he asked, "Coach, why are you taking me out? We're right in this game."

Del said, "I'm taking you out like I should have done right after your technical. If you get a technical foul in this program, you come out of the game, so we can talk about it. You may go back in or you may not. But based on what that official told me, I don't think you're going back in. I'll give you a chance to explain what happened and then I'll make a determination."

Connor described what happened, just as the official had. Del said, "That's unacceptable on this team, Connor. That is not the standard we want to live up to. Go get some water, find a seat, and cheer on your teammates. I'm not sure if you're going back in. But I can guarantee you that you won't be going back in if I don't see you cheering on your teammates."

Connor headed to the water cooler, got a cup of water, and sat down. He took a drink, threw the cup under his chair, and put a towel over his head. After a minute he took the towel off and watched the game, occasionally yelling something out to his teammates.

Del sat and wondered what to do. "Do I put him back in or not? I know our standard is that we don't behave that way. I want to follow our standards, but we really need him right now to win this game. And my rule says I can put him back in. It's my choice. I'm the head coach. I can do what I want to do."

Del watched as Centennial extended their lead to four and then six points. He looked down the bench at Connor to see how into the game he was. Connor was watching the action intently enough. "He gets it, right?" thought Del. "He knows he screwed up. This would be his chance to redeem himself."

Jimmy Thompson had been playing much better than he did in the first half. He had scored on a nice drive and dish from Remington, and he got a big offensive rebound and kick out to Nick for a three-pointer. He was also defending against Bolden well. But with a little over 3:00 remaining, Jimmy fouled a Centennial player sending him to the free throw line with a chance to go up by eight points. Del asked Kevin, "Should we put Connor back in for Jimmy?"

"I don't think so," said Kevin. "This is really good for both of them. You might need Jimmy in the divisional and state tournaments, and the more reps he gets against good teams the better. He's holding his own out there, and his confidence is growing. Plus, it would be good for Connor to see that your standards and rules have value and aren't just words on a piece of paper." Del wondered if Kevin was telling him that he didn't really enforce the rules that he established. He realized that if that is what Kevin meant, he may be right.

"If I really mean what I say, I wouldn't think of putting Connor back in," Del thought. "If I put him back in now, what message would that be sending? That the rules are there, but there are ways around them? They really only apply when things are going well? They apply for the other players but not Connor?

That wouldn't be a good message."

Del turned and watched the action. Centennial was up by 8 points now with 2:45 left. Del called out a play, and the Wolves executed it perfectly. Jimmy received a bounce pass off of a pick & roll and laid it in the hoop. The Centennial lead was cut to 6.

On the ensuing possession, Jimmy had to switch out on Leif Bjorkland. Bjorkland blew past Jimmy, but Jimmy didn't give up on the play. As Bjorkland elevated to lay the ball in the basket, Jimmy chased him down, and with his long arms, got just enough of the ball to deflect it from its path to the basket. It bounced off the board, and Jimmy grabbed it. He outletted the ball to Remington to start the fast break. Remington found Nick sprinting up ahead on the left wing. Jimmy had started to sprint down the middle of the floor after his block, heading to the front of the rim. As Nick caught the ball, he saw Jimmy out of the corner of his eye. Nick started into his shot motion, and in one quick move, fired a pass to Jimmy as he entered the lane.

Jimmy caught the ball as he was turning towards the hoop. He took a 1–2 power step and elevated to the rim. He felt like a plane taking off from the runway. He had never felt like this before. In one motion he brought the ball over and a little behind his head with both hands, and then with all of his power, dunked the ball through the hoop. He hung on the rim for a split-second, amazed at what he had just done. He had thrown down dunks in practice and in JV games before but never like that. He dropped from the rim to the floor and started to run back to the defensive end of the floor.

The Wolves' bench and crowd were ecstatic. People were high-fiving each other all over the Wolves' side of the gym. With 2:20 remaining in the game now and his team up by only four points, Jerry White called a time out to settle the Centennial players down. The Wolves' players mobbed Jimmy as he came to the bench. Connor, though, couldn't bring himself to congratulate his replacement for what was an incredible play.

Kevin turned to Del and said, "You're not still thinking of putting Connor in, are you?"

"After that play?" Del replied. "Not a chance!"

Ideas to Consider:

- **Del finally realizes he needs to take Connor out. Why? What good did Kevin say might actually come from such a move?**

- **Jimmy Thompson makes some big plays after replacing Connor. How does Connor react while on the bench? Why is it important for players to "stay in the game" when they are on the bench?**

Chapter 28

Kevin hoped Del was getting it. Kevin liked Del a lot, but he also knew Del needed to grow as a coach. If Del was ever going to be the best coach he could be, he needed to behave more like his father. Mason Brooks was as good as it got when it came to coaching, and he had been very successful. But it wasn't the scoreboard success that Kevin was thinking of. It was the way he treated kids, the life lessons he taught them. That set Mason Brooks and all the other really good coaches apart from all the rest. They focused on character, integrity, hard work, discipline, and selflessness, and they created winning programs with those as their standards.

Del talked a good game when it came to those things. He discussed them with his teams, but when push came to shove, his actions didn't always follow his words. He would too often focus on winning first and the character pieces second. He would sacrifice a standard that was established to last for a long time in order to get the quick win in the moment. His dad would never do that. Kevin hoped that Del would figure it out and start focusing more on what his dad had tried to instill in him.

Del got into the huddle, congratulated Jimmy on how well he was playing and then turned his attention to everyone. He outlined what he wanted them to do defensively and offensively. He talked about staying together and continuing to push themselves. Unfortunately, Centennial had other plans. They too were playing to win the game and trying to make a statement. They wanted to beat this supposed super-team. As they came out of the timeout, the Centennial players had the same look of determination on their faces that the Sacajawea players had.

The final 2:20 of the game was back and forth, with both teams battling fiercely. With eight seconds left and the score tied, Centennial set up a pick & roll on the wing with Leif Bjorkland and one of the forwards. Remington was guarding Bjorkland, and Brian Jackson was guarding the forward. When Remington got caught up in the pick, they switched men. Bjorkland gave Brian a head fake and then blew past him. As Bjorkland attacked the basket, Jimmy rotated over to help. Bjorkland elevated for his layup and thought, "I'm not letting this kid block me again." As Jimmy elevated to block the shot, Bjorkland fired a pass to a teammate in the corner. The player shot a wide-open 3-pointer that found nothing but the bottom of the net. The buzzer went off as the ball swished through the net. The Pioneers had won 68–65.

The Centennial players, bench, and crowd exploded. The Wolves collapsed to the floor. Del tried to stay positive as he brought his players over to the bench to line up for the post-game handshake. They were all dejected, but Del was already thinking of a positive spin to put on it afterwards in the locker room. They went through the line and shook hands and high-fived the Centennial players. Del and Jerry White shook hands, and Del said, "Great game, Coach."

True to form, Jerry White said, "It really was, Coach. You guys played great without McDonald at the end. As hard as that had to be not playing him, I really respect a coach that lives by his standards like that. That's a great lesson for your kids and hopefully for McDonald. Your sophomore stepped up big for you, too. It's always nice when that happens."

Del was shocked. He didn't know what to say. Jerry White had just complimented him on the move he made to stay true to his standards, and Del hadn't even wanted to do it in the first place. It had taken Remington's and Kevin Nixon's words to get him to think about it, and even then, he wasn't sure he should do it. He was embarrassed. All he could muster was, "Thanks, Coach. Good luck the rest of the way."

They shook hands again, separated, and Del walked to the locker room, lost in his thoughts. He needed to quickly figure out what to say to a very dejected team waiting for him in the locker room. These were the moments that Del struggled with as much as any other. He walked into the locker room and saw the players scattered around, sitting quietly with their heads down. Some had towels over their heads. Some looked directly at him as he stepped in front of them. He gathered himself and started talking about how the outcome of this game and the way it played out was not the worst thing in the world.

"Boys, I hope you learned some things out there tonight. That's a really good team you just played down to the wire. And some would say we were a bit shorthanded down the stretch without Connor." Del looked at Connor, but Connor had his head down. Del wondered where Connor's mind was right now, but he couldn't concern himself with that. Turning toward Jimmy Thompson, Del said, "But I don't think we were shorthanded at all. I think we just watched a full-blown varsity post player explode before our eyes. Great job out there, Jimmy! You went into a hostile environment, played huge minutes, picked your team up when they needed it, and played like the player we all know that you can be." Del paused and then said, "Oh yeah... and you also had the dunk of the year!" Jimmy had a smile on his face.

Del then continued. "Now, of course, we can't be satisfied with a loss. But we can learn from it and gain something from it. We will come out better because of this. Centennial had every one of their players playing tonight. We didn't have Connor down the stretch. That won't happen again." Del paused, looked at Connor and said, "Will it, Connor?" in a fairly stern voice.

Connor looked up at Del and said, "No," in a quiet almost puppy-dog manner.

"No, it won't," repeated Del. "And as great as Jimmy played, with both him and Connor able to play the entire game, there is no way that team beats us. Hell, I don't think that team beats us again no matter what. We have too many players on this team with too much talent who play too well together for any team to beat us. I don't care who we put on the floor. Nobody in this state can beat us if we play the way we are capable of!"

The boys were nodding their heads at what he was saying. Del continued, "All right, let's learn from tonight, build on it, and not let it happen again. Get it?"

They all responded, "Got it!"

As they were getting dressed at their lockers, Remington, Nick, and Tim were talking together as usual. While most of the boys were fairly upbeat and talking about Jimmy, these three were talking about what Del had just said. Connor's locker was across the locker room, so he couldn't hear what they were saying.

"The big question is if Coach actually believes what he just said," said Remington.

"What do you mean?" asked Tim.

"He means that Coach just said he doesn't care who we put on the floor. We're still the best team in the state," said Nick. "Really? Then why didn't you want to take Connor out when he flipped that kid off? If he really thinks we're that good, that should have been a no-brainer. If that had been Jimmy or Mike or Cory, hell if that had been you or me," Nick said to Tim, "he would have pulled him out immediately like the rule says."

"Bingo," said Remington. "If any of us had done that, we would have been out of there immediately."

"Not so fast, my friend," said Nick. "I wasn't talking about you when I said that. There's no way he's taking you out if you do something stupid like that. Then again, you would never do something stupid like that. But the point is, you and Connor get treated different."

Remington was a bit hurt by this comment from his friend. He was about to say something when Nick held up his hand and said, "Don't be butt-hurt by it, dude. I'm not saying I have a problem with you. I'm saying you and Connor are so much better that Coach thinks twice with any decision he makes about you two. He feels he needs you both on the floor for us to win. I get it. Hell, there's times *I* feel we need both of you on the floor for us to win. But quite honestly, we only need you. Connor does good things, but he's not you, man. He doesn't make the rest of us better. He makes himself better. He scores and rebounds, but he does that for himself. Sure, we benefit from it, but he isn't doing it for us. He's doing it for himself."

Nick paused, saw Remington wanting to say something and then continued, "But your whole game is about us. And that has bled over to every other player on this team—except for Connor. All those workouts all off-season. All those open gyms. Everything we did as hard as we did was 'cuz you pushed us to do it. We didn't want to let you down. That's why we're so good. We are all really good players, and we CAN win state without Connor. Will it be easier with him? Of course. But we can do it without him. I just don't know if Coach thinks we can."

Remington said, "Thanks, Nick. I just knew how good we were and even more than that, how good we could be if we put our hearts, minds, and souls into it. And we all did." He paused and said, "Well, at least most of us did. You're right. I just hope Coach sees it." Remington paused and then added, "Actually, I think Coach sees it. I just don't know if he believes it."

Tim said, "Yeah, well hopefully we won't have to find out. Hopefully, Connor doesn't do any more stupid things between now and the end of the season."

Nick laughed a sarcastic laugh. "Are you kidding? You know he will. He can't help himself. The question is 'What will he do, and how stupid will it be?'"

Remington added, "And then the question will be, 'What is Coach going to do about it?'"

Ideas to Consider:
- **Did Coach Brooks do the right thing with Connor?**
- **What effect do you think Jerry White's words are having on Del right now?**
- **What does Coach Brooks say is a good thing to learn from their loss?**
- **Why are Remington, Nick, and Tim concerned that maybe Coach Brooks doesn't even believe his own words?**

Chapter 29

On the bus ride home from Centennial, Del asked Kevin and Braden what they thought he should do about Connor. Braden immediately said, "Coach, you already did it. You pulled him out of the game and sat him the rest of the game. Even though Jimmy played well, we lost because Connor wasn't in there."

Del looked at Braden, wondering if his 22-year-old freshman coach was criticizing him for pulling Connor out of the game, which in Braden's mind, led to them losing the game. Braden was like so many good players who got into coaching. They think only from a player's perspective and what was best for them as a player, not what was necessarily best for the team, the program, or the future. Braden was thinking only of that moment when Connor could have helped the team win *that* game. He was not thinking about the message it was sending to Connor or, more importantly, to the rest of that team, the younger players in the program, and the parents.

Ironically, Del hadn't done what he probably should have if he wanted to have the right impact on all of those people. Anyone watching who knew the team policy on technical fouls would have noticed that Del had not followed his policy at first. He hadn't pulled Connor out of the game right away after the technical foul as his rule stated.

Kevin, though, knew that right away. He knew that was the policy, and he agreed with that policy. It didn't mean a player couldn't go back into the game. But it did mean that if you got some type of technical foul, especially for some behavior issue, you came out of the game, so the coach could discuss it with you. The coach would then decide whether or not the behavior was such that you should or shouldn't go back into the game. But Del had not done that, and he now realized that a message was being sent one way or the other.

After Braden's response, Kevin said, "I don't know that you already did all that you need to do. You eventually pulled him out and sat him the rest of the game. That was a good thing. At the very least, you need to talk to him about it. The kid flipped off the crowd and said something about a kid's mom. That behavior is totally unacceptable on this team based on everything you say we stand for. So you need to address that."

Del said, "Absolutely."

Before Del could continue, Kevin said, "You also need to remind him of step two on the timeline for receiving technical fouls, that if he gets another one he's out of the rest of that game and sitting the next one."

Del had a look of shock on his face. Kevin said, "You do remember that is what your rule says, right?"

Del said, "Yeah, I remember. I mean, I remember now. I had forgotten that until you just said it. I've never had to use it, so I had forgotten that is what I had in there." Del paused, thought for a moment, then said, "Geez, now I wonder if I should have put that in there."

Kevin said, "Hell yes, you should have put that in there. Two reasons: One, you felt convicted about it when you adopted that rule from your dad. You had a good reason for feeling that way. You want kids to behave the right way on the court. Two, because you have a situation in front of you right now where you *need* it. Connor has not violated that rule for a second time yet. You will remind him that he sits the next game if he gets a second one. I think it's actually a great rule, and it puts you in the position to make sure he doesn't do anything stupid like that again."

Braden jumped in, saying, "I don't know, Coach. Anything can happen. Emotions run high in a game. He could do something or say something without thinking and then, Boom! You have to sit him because he had a moment where he couldn't control himself. I'm not sure you want to do that."

Del nodded his head and said, "Yeah, that's true."

Kevin didn't know whether to laugh or to jump across the aisle and slap them both upside the head. "Are you guys hearing yourselves? He might do something without thinking, and he couldn't control himself?! So we don't want a rule for kids who might do that?! That is exactly why you need the rule. We need to teach kids that this type of behavior is unacceptable. They need to have discipline, poise, and control over their emotions. This rule helps you instill that."

Del said, "Yeah, you're right. That's why I wanted it in the Policy Sheet in the first place. I just never thought I would need to use it." His thoughts trailed off behind his words as he looked at the floor of the bus.

Kevin could see Del was wrestling with what to do about this. This worried Kevin. The last couple of years, Del had allowed Cade Clemons to get away with way too much, and it destroyed the team's chemistry. Things had been really good this year, even with Connor acting the way he had. The rest of the team was too strong and too tight-knit to let anything happen to bring them apart.

But Kevin was worried that Del might not do what he needed to do with Connor. Kevin also knew he had to tread somewhat lightly around Del. He didn't want Del to feel he was trying to run everything. So he usually tried to make Del feel like Del was the one who was having the ideas that Kevin was offering. "Well, like you said earlier, at the very least, you need to talk to him about the behavior tonight and how wrong it was. And you need to let him know we can't see it again or there will be consequences. Personally, I'd tell him about the rule, but that's your call, Coach."

Del called back to Connor to come up to the front of the bus. Connor came forward and sat down in the seat that Braden had been sitting in as Braden slid toward the window. Del said, "Connor, I want to make sure we're on the same page going forward."

"What do you mean, Coach?" asked Connor.

Del leaned forward toward Connor a bit. "What you did in the game tonight was totally unacceptable, Connor."

"I know, Coach," said Connor, almost sounding a bit perturbed. "You told me that when you took me out of the game."

"I know I told you that then," said Del. "But I need to make sure you fully comprehend what I'm saying to you now. While flipping a kid off in the bleachers and saying a mean thing to him is nothing you've done before, think about how many times I have had to talk to you since last spring about things that you have done. Me having to address you in some fashion after you doing something you shouldn't have done is not a new thing."

Del paused, looking to see if his comment was registering. Of course, the bus was dark, so he was mainly seeing Connor's face from the lights of the dashboard and then the lights of oncoming traffic. But the two-lane road from Centennial up to I-90 didn't provide a lot of traffic at that time on a Saturday night, so he didn't see Connor's face as clearly as he would have liked.

Del continued. "But getting a technical foul is new territory. It is not something to be taken lightly. When you get one of those, you have stepped over a line that is bigger than just the confines of our team and program. Someone on the outside recognized your behavior as being inappropriate and had to punish you for it."

Connor nodded his understanding.

"Well, here's the problem with that," said Del. "It affects your team. The opponent shoots two free throws and gets the ball. It affects your program and your school because it paints us in a bad light. And it affects you. Of course, the immediate effect is you now have a technical foul which gets added to your personal foul total. But in our program, it also means you are coming out of the game, at least for a little while, so we can discuss it. We did that. As the game went on, I decided that you just needed to stay out the rest of the game. Jimmy was playing well, and quite honestly, I didn't want to reward you with playing after what you did."

Connor didn't say anything or indicate any kind of feeling. Del continued, "And now you have one technical chalked up to you. I don't know if you remember this from the Policy Sheet you signed at the beginning of the year, but if you get a second technical at any time the rest of the season, you're coming out of that game, and you're sitting out the next one after that. Do you understand that?"

"You mean a second technical at any time in the season?!"

"Yep, at any time," said Del.

"I thought it was a second technical in a game," said Connor. "A second technical at any time in the season seems a bit harsh. What if I get a bad call or the ref thinks he hears or sees something, but it didn't happen that way or something like that?"

"Yeah, that's a tough one, isn't it, Connor?" said Del. "I guess that means you better do everything you can to not let a ref think you have done anything wrong. You darn well better stay away from any kind of bad behavior."

"That just doesn't seem fair," said Connor. "I can't control the refs."

"No, but you can control yourself, and tonight you didn't do that," said Del. "In fact, about 99% of the technical fouls called are because people couldn't control themselves." He decided he should soften a bit for a moment, so he said, "Of course, if you were to get another one, we would look at it to see what you did and how bad it was. But just don't do anything that would even give an official an inkling of a thought that you deserve a technical, and it won't be a problem. Get it?"

Connor sighed as he said, "Got it," but he didn't seem happy about it.

Del said, "Okay, you can go back to your seat."

Connor got up and headed back to his seat. Del turned and looked out the front window of the bus. Kevin, sitting in the seat right behind him, leaned forward into the aisle, and said to Del's shoulder, "Good job, Coach. Good decision."

"Thanks," said Del. "I just hope he makes a good decision from now on."

Kevin chuckled sarcastically as he said, "Ha! He hasn't made many since we've known him. What makes you think he'll start?"

"That's the problem," said Del. "I don't have any reason to believe he will."

"Well," started Kevin, "the one thing that might is what you just told him. If he gets another T, he sits the rest of the game and then another one. If that isn't stuck in his head enough to make sure he behaves the right way, maybe he doesn't deserve to be out there playing."

"No 'maybe' about it," said Del. "If he can't figure it out, he doesn't deserve it."

Braden had slid back to the aisle seat after Connor had left. He was listening to Del and Kevin talk. He was kind of busting a gut wanting to say something, and he finally did. "I don't get it, guys. You just handcuffed your best or second-best player. You just set him up to fail. He's bound to do something or say something. That's just his nature. And who knows? All it will take is one weak ref who has rabbit ears, and it's over. He's done. Why would you do that?"

Del said, "Braden, I didn't handcuff him. He's the one who's handcuffed himself. If he can't control himself, he shouldn't be out there. You saw what happened after that T he got. Their kid made the two free throws, got the ball, and scored on that possession. That's 4 points. If he does something like that late in a tight 1-point game at Divisional or State, it could be over for us. He needs to know the consequences for his actions. So I'm giving him consequences for them ahead of time in hopes that he figures it out."

Braden looked as if he had just had a minor revelation. "Well, I hadn't thought about it like that before. I guess I see your point. I just don't like the thought of him not being on the floor when we need him."

Del said, "I don't like that thought either, Braden. But I don't like the thought of him acting like an idiot and hurting our team and our program even more than that."

Kevin was pleased to hear the way Del responded. Maybe he was getting it. Del had a lot to learn and a lot of growing to do as a coach, but how he was handling this situation with Connor was a good step in that direction. Kevin hoped Del would continue down this path following in his father's footsteps in this way. Kevin felt it would lead to a lot of great things for Del through the years if he kept it up.

Ideas to Consider:

- **Why does Braden Larson think the way he does about Connor and about coaching? Why does he need to grow more as a coach?**

- **Why is Del struggling with his own technical foul rule?**

- **Braden Larson and Connor think Del's technical foul rule is too harsh. Do you? Why or why not?**

Chapter 30

After Jenny's last talk with Remington about Stanford, she thought a lot about her future. She talked with her parents and her friends about all that was going on and all that she was struggling with. Every person she talked to said the same thing: "You have to go to Stanford. An opportunity like this doesn't come along every day." Then they would ask, "Why is there even a question in your mind? Is it the cost?"

She would tell them that, while the cost was high, she had already received a lot of scholarship money, and she was hoping to get more. Plus, her parents had set up a College Savings Plan when she was born. They had been putting money into that every month of her life. She would also be able to take out student loans to cover the rest of the costs. On top of all that, her parents both worked and made good money, so if they needed to help out, they could.

"Okay, then what is the problem?" her friends and family would ask.

"Remington," was the response.

Some of her friends immediately said, "He doesn't want you to go? Is he trying to control your decision? That doesn't sound like him. He doesn't—"

Jenny would cut them off and say, "No, no. Remington is not controlling me. He's totally on board with me going to Stanford."

"Well, then what the heck is it?" they would ask.

"I don't want to leave him," was always the reply. "I'm afraid if I go to Stanford, and he goes to Duke or ASU or wherever, that will be it. It will be over."

Jenny would then hear a variety of responses. Some completely understood how she felt and wondered how she could let him go. Others were more rational, saying that this is her future and that she can't give up on it now because of a boyfriend. While they all loved Remington, they also thought that the two of them needed to focus on their futures individually, without the other one. If they truly loved each other and were meant to be together, they would find their way back to each other. Then they would say, "If the two of you don't get back together, you will know that you were great friends growing up and that this was a great thing that you had during high school, but it wasn't meant to be for life."

Jenny would say, "Yeah, I get that. But I don't want to set him free. I don't want to find out it wasn't meant to be. I want it to be, period."

Some of her friends or family members would continue to try to help her think rationally and focus on her future. She would say she understood that, but it was hard. The response was often, "Well, you're going to have to make a decision soon. Stanford has their pick of the cream of the crop. If you don't let them know soon, you might not have a choice."

Jenny worried about that. Stanford was her top choice of a school since she was little. Now she was accepted there, yet she wasn't sure she wanted to go. "What the heck am I thinking? There is nothing wrong with feeling the way you do about Remington, but my gosh, he's a boy. There are other boys in the world that could be just as great as Remington. But there is only one Stanford. Do the right thing, register at Stanford, and start your future!"

Her dad had said something similar to that, too. His words slapped her into reality and then her own thoughts would echo her father's words. "I'm one of the luckiest kids in the country, getting an opportunity to go to Stanford. It's my dream school. It's awesome that it worked out this way. I can't wait to get there and get started." She would feel good about her decision, knowing it was the right decision. That would last until she thought about Remington, and then the doubt would start all over again.

It also worried her when she noticed the ease with which Remington had seemed to accept that she would be going to Stanford next year, and he would be going somewhere else. She thought, "Does he *want* to break up? Is he excited about meeting girls at whatever school he goes to?" She never said any of that to Remington, but it worried her. And the more he talked excitedly about her going to Stanford, the more worried she got.

The truth was that Remington was also hurting inside about Jenny going to Stanford. He didn't want to leave her. He wanted to stay with her forever. At least, that's what he thought. He was also smart enough to know that at seventeen, neither of them really knew what they wanted for the rest of their lives. He just knew that right now she was his favorite thing in the world. In fact, that scared him. Because ever since he could remember, his favorite thing in the world was basketball. It was pretty much all he thought about. And while he still loved basketball, a big part of who he was now had been taken over by his feelings for Jenny.

He would then think about his own dilemma with a college choice. Jenny's dilemma was different. She had been accepted into her dream school. She had the chance to fulfill a dream that she had since she was little. Remington, though, had not been accepted into his dream school, nor had he been offered a basketball scholarship or even a preferred walk-on type of situation from Duke. His chances of going there were limited. As a good student, he would get good academic scholarship money wherever he went. But to go to an expensive school like Duke, he would need a lot more financial help. While his parents had also set him up with a college fund when he was little, it was not going to cover *all* of the expenses he would have there. He would need to take out student loans if he went to Duke and wasn't on a basketball scholarship.

However, he had already been offered full rides to some of the other schools he was interested in, and things were looking good for him to be offered the same at the other ones. As he would scan his list of college choices, he would think about being on those campuses, playing basketball, and living what he thought the life of a college student would look like. With each of those thoughts for each of those schools, he got excited. He was especially excited about the basketball. He knew that wherever he went, he wanted to play. Basketball was such a big part of his life that he didn't want to stop it.

If he couldn't play at Duke, he wouldn't go there. In fact, he realized that, while it is one of the best schools in the country, the thing that had always attracted him to it was the basketball. All those years watching their games on TV, he wasn't focused on what their classes were like or their campus or the student experience. He was focused on playing at Cameron Indoor Stadium on national TV in front of thousands of screaming fans. He didn't want to be in the stands watching the players play. He wanted to be on that court playing in front of the *Cameron Crazies,* not sitting with them. If that wasn't going to happen, he wasn't going to go there.

And so, his mind would then drift off to the other schools on his list. At the top was Arizona State. He liked it there when he lived in Phoenix as a kid. Depending on traffic, it was about a half-hour ride from their home in north Phoenix. He and his dad went to a football game once. With Hayden Butte and its giant gold "A" on the side as the backdrop next to Sun Devil Stadium, Remington was blown away by the whole atmosphere of the place. Inside, the energy and excitement were amazing. While they weren't sitting in the student section, they were close enough to hear a lot of what the students were yelling and chanting. Those kids looked like they were having so much fun. Even at eight-years-old he thought, "I want to be a part of this."

As Remington thought back to those days, he would be flooded with mixed emotions. He loved living in Phoenix. He hated leaving there when they moved to Montana. While he had always liked Montana when they would go there on vacations, his home was Phoenix. It's where his friends were, and it's what felt right.

But because of the type of person he was, it didn't take him long to develop friendships in his new home in Discovery. He quickly became a popular kid in school because of how well he played basketball and how great of a team-mate and friend he was. Through the years, those friendships grew into the best he had. Unfortunately, he was drifting further away from his friends and connections in Phoenix. He stayed in touch with some of them on Instagram and Snapchat, but with each passing year, he was communicating less with many of them. By his senior year, two of his friends, Cruz Manjarrez and Darnell White, were the only ones he maintained any continuous contact with. For the most part, the Phoenix part of his life was a distant memory.

But now, with him considering going to college down there, those memories were coming back to him. He was thinking a lot more about "home" and about the possibility of being there for college. Cruz was going to go to ASU the next year, as were some of their other friends. When Remington told him that he was being recruited to play there, Cruz was ecstatic and said, "Dude, you've got to come play here. That would be so cool to see you ballin' here. I knew you would be good enough to play college ball."

Remington said, "Well, it would be cool to go there and hang with you and Darnell and any of the other guys if you all go there."

Remington was still thinking about the other schools on his list, too, so he had a hard decision in front of him. Adding to the difficulty of his decision was that Jenny had now been accepted to Stanford. While he hadn't really talked with Jenny about it, since she had been accepted there, he started thinking more about going there, too. It would satisfy a couple of his desires—playing for a major national program and not losing Jenny. With Jenny probably going to Stanford, he was now more torn about his college decision than ever before.

Ideas to Consider:

- **Why is Jenny not so sure about going to Stanford? How do Remington's words and feelings about her going to Stanford scare her?**

- **Why are they both struggling with each of their situations that are, ultimately, really good things for them?**

Chapter 31

The last few games of the regular season went according to plans for the Wolves. They were never really challenged again after the Centennial game. Their final game was Senior Night, when all the seniors and their parents were recognized before the game. This was always an emotional night. This year was especially that way, as this senior class had been so tight with one another, and they had had a lot of success in their years playing together. To see it all coming to a close was hard for all of them.

Because of the emotions of these nights, the home team often plays tight and struggles early on. Coaches will also often have seniors in the starting lineup who rarely play because this is their final home game, and it would be nice for them to have one chance to hear their name called as they get introduced before a loud, raucous crowd. For a team like the Wolves this year, this could be problematic. There were six seniors on the team, but only five players get introduced before the game. That meant that one of those seniors would not get to hear his name called and get to run out on the floor to the adoration of all the fans.

Remington had known for weeks that this would be the case. Barring an injury, sickness, or eligibility issue, one of them would not be able to be introduced. He met with Coach Brooks on the Monday of the final week and said, "Coach, I've been thinking a lot about senior night. I assume you're going to start all seniors, correct?"

"Yeah, that was my plan," said Del.

Remington said, "Well, we have six seniors, but there are only five guys who get introduced."

Del said, "Yeah, I know. That's been a tough one to figure out."

Remington said, "Well, don't worry about it, Coach. I don't need to start."

Del said, "Rem, you're the best player on the team. You've been a starter for the last two years, plus some games as a sophomore. You have done more for this program than any player since I've been here. If anyone deserves to start on senior night and hear his name called out and receive the cheers, it's you."

Remington dropped his head, a little bit embarrassed. He then looked up and said, "Thanks, Coach. That's nice of you to say. But I've had my name called out every game for the last, what 40-something games? But a couple of those guys have NEVER had their names called out, never got to go out and have the crowd cheer for them that way, while they high-five and chest-bump out at the free throw line. They've worked so hard for the program for the last four years, too, and they've never had that experience. It's so much fun. I want them to experience that one time."

"This kid is something," thought Del. "Even in one of the great moments in a high school athlete's life, he's thinking about his teammates."

Del said, "Are you sure about this, Rem?"

"Absolutely, Coach. Besides, I'll get to hear my name called out at Divisionals and at State." He paused and said, "That is, if I'm starting then."

Del smiled and said sarcastically, "Well, we'll have to see about that. You've really struggled with your production the last few weeks. You've only averaged 21 points and 10 assists. We might need to start someone else anyway. So maybe senior night will be a good chance to test some things out." He smiled and laughed as he clapped Remington on the shoulder.

Remington chuckled and with a big grin said, "Sorry, Coach. I'll try to do better on Friday."

"I sure hope so," said Del.

As Remington left the office Del thought, "He never ceases to amaze me."

Del immediately formed a plan to do something a little different with the introductions on Friday, and he went to Randy Watson the next day to okay it with him. It would be Remington's turn to be amazed.

On Friday, as the announcer was introducing each of the players, two of whom had never started before, the crowd was in a frenzy, cheering for each one. The ovations for the two who had never started seemed even louder than all the others. After the final senior, Nick Bertucci, had been introduced and received his ovation, the announcer said, "I have one more special announcement. As you notice, all five senior starters have been introduced. But this team has six seniors on it. Coach Brooks alerted us that early this week, Remington Roberts offered up his normal spot in the starting lineup, so that his teammates who had never started would have a chance to do so. Kinda' says it all about the type of person Remington is, huh? I think most of us would say that doesn't shock us at all."

The fans were clapping and cheering for Remington as they heard this. Remington did not know what to do, and he struggled knowing where to look or how to act, standing by the bench. He had spent his career with all eyes on him in amazement and wonder at how he played the game, but this was different. That was playing. He could get lost in the movement and the moment. Here, he had to just stand there and feel awkward.

The announcer continued, "How about we bring Remington out with the rest of his senior teammates? At guard, a 6'2" senior, number 4 REMINGTON ROBERTS!!!" The crowd exploded. Remington ran over and shook the opposing coach's hand. Del and Randy had alerted the coach and the officials as to what was happening, so they wouldn't be surprised by it. The coach grabbed Remington's hand, held it there for a second, and said, "Young man, in all my years of coaching, that's one of the classiest things I've ever seen a kid do. Good luck."

Remington said, "Thanks, Coach. Good luck to you, too." He turned and jogged over to where the rest of his team was waiting at the free throw line in front of their bench. The fans were cheering wildly for him. The entire team then mobbed the group for their last time on their home court.

As they headed back to the bench, Remington headed straight to Del. He opened his arms wide, and with tears in his eyes, he said, "Thanks, Coach," giving Del a huge hug.

Del said into his ear, "No, son. Thank you." Del had to fight back tears himself.

Del turned and stepped into the huddle of players standing there waiting for their final directions. He said, "Boys, go out there and have fun and make your school and your family and friends proud."

Remington nudged Mario Ravelli, one of the two seniors who was starting who had never done so and said to him, "Count us down, dude." This was normally Remington's job, and once again, he was passing it on to a teammate who had never gotten to do so.

Mario yelled out, "Wolves on three—1, 2, 3" and they all yelled, "Wolves!"

As often happens in Senior Night games, the home team struggles a bit early on. With players who don't normally play much playing the opening minutes and the emotions of all of the players running so high, things can be a little ugly. That was the case with the Wolves in the first few minutes of the game. Remington did his best to help from the bench by cheering on his teammates and yelling out instructions to the kids who were not normally out there. On dead balls, he offered pointers to Mario to try to calm him down a bit.

It could be a time of minor worry for coaches when this was happening on Senior Night. Trying to figure out how long to play the bench players, how far to let the opponent's lead rise was a balancing act. A coach had to consider how good his team was, how good the opponent was, and how important this final game was to the outcome of the final standings as he made his decisions.

Fortunately for Del, the Wolves already had first place in the conference locked up. The closest team to them, the Jefferson Bears, were two games behind them in the standings. No matter what happened tonight, they could not catch the Wolves. Also, their opponent tonight, the Windwalker Eagles, were in second-to-last place in the conference. Though the Eagles were ahead by eight points four minutes into the game, Del was not too worried.

On a dead ball with 3:48 left in the first half, Del turned, looked down the bench, and said, "Rem, go for Mario. Connor, go for Cory."

As the two of them stood up and headed to the scorer's table, Remington said to Connor, "Let's do this, Dude," and he fist-bumped him.

Connor said, "Absolutely. Let's finish the season off the right way."

That's exactly what happened. Once Remington and Connor were in the game, everything turned around and went the way people had figured it would go. Connor was an absolute animal inside. Windwalker had nobody who could handle him. By the time Del took him out thirty seconds into the fourth quarter, he had 24 points and 13 rebounds. Ten of his points came on five assists by Remington.

Remington played his usual stellar game. Along with the five assists to Connor, he had eight more to other players. Del left him in the game with the bench players a little longer, for he knew that Remington would do what he could to set them up to score. He ran pick & roll plays with Mario and Cory Wilson, the two seniors who had never started until tonight, and he was able to get them both layups. He loved that they both got to score in their final game.

Remington himself had 23 points, and as he came off the floor and gave Del another hug, he said, "I told you I'd do better tonight, Coach. Will you think about starting me next week now?" He smiled.

Del smiled and said, "Well, I'll have to think about it." They both laughed as Remington headed down the bench.

Remington hugged every player along the way down the bench and said, "That was fun. Now we get to work. State Championship!"

Ideas to Consider:

- **Why does Remington tell Del to start Mario instead of himself? What does that show about Remington as a person? Would you consider doing something like that if you were Remington?**

Chapter 32

There were two Divisional Tournaments for Class A schools in Montana—an Eastern and a Western tournament. There were four conferences in the state. The northwest played the southwest at the Western A Divisional Tournament in Butte, and the east and the mid-state conferences played at the Eastern A Divisional Tournament in Billings. Then the top four teams from each tournament met the following week at the state tournament in Great Falls.

Sacajawea was the heavy favorite to win the Eastern A Divisional. Their losses at Colter and Centennial were their only losses all year. Only two other teams—Longbow and Jefferson—had come within ten points of them. Every other game was a double-digit victory.

In their first game at the divisional, they faced a weak Badlands team from over on the Montana-North Dakota border and won by 32. They then faced Bighorn in the semi-finals. Bighorn was the team that they had lost to in the first summer tournament. It was the team whose coach, Jim Stilwell, only played eight players during that game. Del had told the boys that because Bighorn had not played all their players and the Wolves had done so all summer, Bighorn would not be as prepared later in the season as Sacajawea would be.

That is exactly what happened. While Bighorn's starters were a strong group and were able to hang with Sacajawea for a while, the Wolves' depth was too much for Bighorn. With Jimmy Thompson and Bob Bickford leading the way off the bench, the bench players for Bighorn were no match for the Wolves' bench players, and Sacajawea beat them handily this time by 18. After the game, Del reminded the boys of their summer game against Bighorn. He reminded Connor, too, of how he doubted the situation. Del felt good knowing that his summer strategy had paid off so well by preparing his reserve kids to play well against the better teams they would face.

The victory over Bighorn set up a re-match of last year's emotional divisional game with Longbow. Longbow had won their two games at this year's tournament by twenty-four and eight points, so it had all the makings to be a good battle. Longbow was an Indian team from the Crow Reservation. They played "Rez Ball," a classic Indian style of play that was a free-wheeling, run-and-gun game. You never knew where players would put shots up from, which meant you had to always be close enough to your man to get a hand up on a shot. You also had to always be sprinting back on defense, even if you had scored on your offensive end because the ball would be advanced as fast as possible, often with a baseball pass into the front court. If you didn't get back, you were giving up layups.

Critics said it was undisciplined, and there was some validity to that with some teams. Then again, there was some validity to that with non-reservation teams, too. If a coach allowed a lack of discipline, it didn't matter where you were from; the team would be undisciplined. But Longbow's coach, Ray Not Afraid, was not an undisciplined coach. He combined discipline in his teams with the ability to run and play loose and free. It was a deadly combination for most opponents. Most opponents couldn't sustain success with that level of running throughout an entire game.

Against a team like Longbow, if you were able to get a lead on them, you could not let up. No lead was ever safe against them because they could run and shoot their way right back into it in a matter of minutes. Unfortunately for them, though, no lead of their own was ever safe either, because they could run and shoot their way out of it, too. Del harped on this message with his team before the game. "If we get up, keep pushing. No let-ups. Don't give them any chance to get back into it. And if they get up, keep going. No let-ups. Keep attacking. They will shoot themselves right out of the lead."

Both teams played tight to begin the game, and at the end of the first quarter, Longbow was up 15–12. In the second quarter, though, Sacajawea settled in and got themselves going. Longbow did not have an answer for the 1-2 punch of Remington and Connor. They tried double-teaming Connor in the post, which left open shooters on the perimeter. They tried trapping Remington, which also left open shooters on the perimeter and Connor posted up on a kid who was 3 inches shorter and 30 pounds lighter than him.

Remington had seen his share of double-teams before. He knew how to handle them. While some kids crack under "Indian-pressure" defense, not Remington. He had played against these kids and others who played like them in tournaments around the state and around the western part of the country, so he knew exactly what was coming. He actually welcomed the double-teams, invited them to come trap him, for he knew that the moment someone came at him, someone else was open.

Teams would then try to cover for the player that had left his own man to go trap Remington. Remington's peripheral vision combined with his unselfishness made for a deadly combination against these teams. He would see the trap coming, see the rotation to the trapper's man happening, and fire bullet passes to the other open player for layups or for better angles to other open teammates.

Remington also knew how to split double-team traps before they occurred. He would see the trapper coming at him and take one hard dribble right at the man, freezing the man momentarily. He would then cross the ball in front of his body from one hand to the other or go behind his back or through his legs with it. He would split the two men just as they were about to trap him, and he would now have a clean drive into the free throw lane. Inevitably, another player would step over to help, and Remington had multiple options to choose from where he wanted to deliver the ball.

Most often, Connor was the recipient of the passes that Remington threw in these moments because it was Connor's man who would step off of him to help on Remington. By halftime Connor already had fourteen points, ten off of passes from Remington. Remington had eight assists to go with seven of his own points. The Wolves were now leading 34–26.

The second half saw Longbow come out and try to crank up the pressure and the speed of the game. Del had been ready for that. Most teams panic in those moments and put four players in the backcourt to try to break the press. This plays right into Longbow's hands with their superior quickness, speed, endurance, and athleticism. But Del had his players work on this during the week. He figured they would face Longbow in the championship, and he wanted his kids prepared.

Instead of keeping so many players in the backcourt, he kept only Connor and Remington back. Connor threw the ball inbounds to Remington as the other three players flew down the court. Because of Remington's superior vision, ballhandling, and passing skills, he easily found Nick, Tim, or Brian sprinting ahead of the Longbow defenders. They were constantly in 2-on-1 and 3-on-1 fast breaks. While the Longbow kids were fast and had great recovery speed, those three Wolves players were also fast, and the Longbow kids could not catch them. They got layup after layup against the back end of the press.

Ray Not Afraid called timeout with 2:45 left in the third quarter after yet another Wolves layup put Sacajawea up by 19. Not Afraid pulled the full-court press off, deciding to go to a half-court trap instead. But Del and Kevin were ready, and they told Remington and the boys what they would see.

Remington and Nick would bring the ball up to the half-line with each of them on opposite sides of the court from each other. Connor stood behind the zone a couple of steps outside the lane near the baseline. Brian and Mike Visteen were spotted up in the corners. Remington and Nick passed back and forth a couple of times, making the Longbow point guard run back and forth across the court as he followed the passes. Once Remington got near the half-line and the Longbow guard was still a few steps away, he exploded into his dribble towards the center of the court, splitting the coming trap.

He now had a defender standing in front of Connor and defenders covering the two shooters in the corners. Someone had to leave their spots to stop Remington's drive or to step to Nick who was wide open for a 3-point shot. Wherever the open man was, Remington found him for a wide-open shot. Much like in the first quarter, it was usually Connor for the first few minutes of the quarter. As his man stepped into the lane to stop Remington's drive, Remington would hit Connor with a no-look bounce pass or a lob to the rim.

One time, Remington was attacking the lane from the right side of the floor. Connor was on his side of the floor along the baseline. As his defender stepped up to stop his drive, Remington jump-stopped and looked toward Connor and then straight into the eyes of the defender. The defender landed with his feet about shoulder width apart. Remington then looked at Brian in the opposite corner and started into a passing motion as if to throw it that way. In one quick motion, he bounced a backhanded pass right through the defender's legs into Connor's hands as Connor was stepping into the lane. Connor gathered the ball as he made his final step, bounded off the floor, and threw down a thunderous two-handed dunk.

The Sacajawea crowd exploded at the play. The dunk was ferocious, and lit up the crowd. But the pass was what everyone was talking about after their initial cheering. "Did you see that?" "How did he do that?" "I've never seen anything like that!"

The Wolves were up by 27. Ray Not Afraid emptied his bench which allowed Del to do the same. The Wolves won the game 78–53. Connor ended the game with 22 points and 12 rebounds. Remington scored 16 points, and he set a divisional record with 17 assists!

Most important, they were Divisional Champions for the first time in many years, and they were headed to the state tournament. Del felt a huge relief knowing they had fulfilled one of their big goals and one of the monkeys on his back. He wished his dad could have been with him for this. His dad would have been so proud of him and the team for their accomplishment.

But now, he had to turn his attention to the other monkey on his back— a state championship. While nobody else necessarily put it there, Del felt pressure to win state. At the very least, they needed to bring home some kind of hardware—a second or third-place trophy. But with the team they had assembled this year and the way the season had gone so far, the expectations of a state championship were high. He wanted so badly to deliver one. Just one more week to go. "Can we all stay together and stay focused enough that we can finish this off?" he thought. One week from tonight, he would have his answer.

Ideas to Consider:

- How did Del's summer strategy pay off against Bighorn?
- What did the Wolves have to contend with from Longbow that they don't usually see from most other teams? How can that be a problem for a team?
- The Wolves are now headed to the state tournament. What must their mindset be this week to achieve the success they are seeking?

Chapter 33

There was a buzz around Sacajawea High School on Monday morning. Everyone seemed to be talking about the games over the weekend and then about the upcoming state tournament. They were excited at the possibilities of what lay ahead. Most people felt that with the way they steamrolled through the tournament with Remington and Connor leading the way, there was no way the Wolves could be stopped. Nobody else in the state had a 1-2 punch like those two.

Remington and Connor were named First-Team All-Conference players at the conference coaches' meeting they held at the Divisional Tournament. They were also both named to the All-State team, with Remington receiving the most votes and Connor receiving the second most votes. In the opinion of the coaches from the east side of the state, the two best players on that side of the state were two teammates from the same school.

Lost in all the hoopla over those two, though, was the fact that players three through six for the Wolves were some of the best in the state in those spots as well. Brian Jackson, Nick Bertucci, and Tim Nelson were all named 2nd Team All-Conference, and Mike Visteen was named to the Honorable Mention team. Six of their players were on one of the three All-Conference teams.

Unfortunately, not everything was a positive buzz, as Del was about to find out. At lunch, Connor's Spanish teacher, Lynne Gregson, pulled Del aside and said, "Coach, I need to talk to you a minute."

Del said, "Sure. What's up?"

"It's about Connor McDonald," she said.

"Oh crap," said Del. "What did he do now?"

"That's the problem," she said. "He hasn't done anything. For the last two weeks, he hasn't handed in any of his daily assignments. He was barely hanging on with a C a couple of weeks ago, but last week he dropped to an F. I reminded him a few times that he needed to get his make-up work in. I'm lenient with the athletes at the end of the season because I know what they are dealing with. But he has done nothing to fix this."

She continued, "And with him missing part of last week because of the tournament, I told him he had to get his work in before the tournament, or his grade would drop into the F range. I told him he could hand it in before you took off on Thursday morning, but he never did. Then this morning, when he came into class, I asked him for his work, and he said that since he hadn't turned it on Thursday, he figured it was too late to turn in."

She paused and had a look of anguish on her face. She said, "Coach, I don't want to keep him out this week. This is the state tournament! I know you guys have a really good chance to win it all. I want him to play. But he's not doing anything to help me help him stay eligible. I feel terrible."

Del tried to soothe her concern. He said, "It's not your fault, Lynne. He's the one that's screwing this up."

Lynne said, "Thanks for understanding. I told him he can turn it all in by this Wednesday, but if he doesn't, he will be ineligible. I'm sorry."

Del said, "Don't be sorry. It's his problem, not yours. You do what you need to do. I will talk with him tonight at practice."

Lynne said, "Okay, thanks for understanding. I really want you guys to win state, but I need Connor to do things the right way."

"So do I," said Del.

A little later on, during his afternoon prep period, Del walked down to the office to make some copies. When he walked out of the copy machine room, Jim Turner was walking into the school. Jim immediately walked toward Del and said, "Hey Del, congrats on a great weekend!"

"Thanks, Coach," said Del. "It was a lot of fun."

"Yeah, it sure was. You guys destroyed everybody. That championship game was amazing. Remington is so fun to watch. What a joy to coach, huh?"

"An absolute joy!" said Del.

"And Connor McDonald," said Jim. "It must be fun to coach him, too."

The look on Del's face said it all. Jim had watched a lot of the games and he had seen what a challenge Connor could be. As a coach himself, Jim saw things the average fan didn't see. Jim could tell that coaching Connor probably wasn't much fun.

Del said, "Connor is a different story, Jim. He is a constant struggle, a constant battle to behave the right way. With him, if it's not one thing, it's another."

Jim asked, "Like what?"

Ever since Del's dad died, Del had only two guys who he trusted to bounce ideas off of for guidance—Kevin Nixon and Jim. But he hadn't seen Jim all that much, so he hadn't been able to talk with him. He was glad to have a few minutes right now. "Oh," started Del, "there have been so many things with him this year, too many to go through. Unfortunately, I'm having to deal with one that just happened here at school today."

"Today?!" asked Jim. "It's Monday. It's state tournament week. What the heck is the kid doing today that you have to deal with?"

Del said, "He's failing Spanish."

"Geez, that's a bit harsh," said Jim. "It was Divisionals last week. Didn't the teacher give him any time to make it up?"

Del said, "Oh, she did. It's been happening for weeks. She's given him lots of chances. He just hasn't done anything. She's even giving him another chance this week, so he won't be ineligible. He's just being lazy."

Jim said, "Gosh, Del, sorry to hear that. This should be the time you're enjoying it the most. You're playing in the frickin' state tournament, and you're the favorite to win it all. This should be the best week of the year."

"I know," said Del. "It's sad, but I actually just can't wait for it all to be over."

"That *is* sad," said Jim. "So what are you gonna' do?"

"I'm not totally sure yet," said Del. "Any suggestions?"

Jim had tried to stay out of Del's way after Jim resigned and Del became the head coach. He wanted Del to be himself and not worry about trying to be like someone else. However, Jim also hoped that Del would take some of the things that Jim had worked to instill in the program and apply them, too, especially the character and team-building pieces. While winning was certainly a goal for Jim, he made sure that character, integrity, discipline, work habits, and selflessness were the identity of the Sacajawea boys' basketball program. Jim said, "Well, I would have done something about it earlier. I imagine you have had to deal with Connor more than just today."

Del nodded a "Yes" answer as Jim continued. "I would probably talk with him before practice tonight. I'd say, 'Look, you're not going to the state tournament on Wednesday if you don't have all of that work handed in.' If he balks at it, go without him. Hell, you might not have a choice. He'll be on the ineligible list, so it won't be in your hands. But if he does his work and isn't on the list, then of course he gets to go."

Del nodded his head in agreement. Jim then said, "But no matter what, I'd sit him for the first half of the first game against Grinnell Point. They aren't good enough to beat you. They're the weakest team in the west. You ultimately don't need Connor to beat them. But more importantly, the message you'll be sending to him, your program, and all the parents is, 'We're not going to accept that kind of behavior, no matter who it is or when it happens.'"

Del said, "I like that."

Jim said, "You'll be taking huge strides to curb these kinds of things from Connor and anyone else in the future. Your varsity team doesn't need any message like this anymore. You're at the state tournament now. You've got good kids who know what's at stake and how to behave. But all the young kids in your program will see that you mean business."

"You're right," said Del. "That will be a clear message as to what is and what isn't acceptable."

Jim then said, "You also won't lose your seniors."

Del looked at him quizzically. "What?" he asked. "What do you mean?"

What Jim wanted to say was, "Your seniors have watched you allow these kinds of behaviors every year. You've lost them already." But he didn't. Instead, he said, "Well, with what Connor has done and what I've heard from others, your seniors and juniors might be wondering, 'Why isn't Coach doing something about Connor? When is he going to stand up to him? When is he going to kick him off the team?'"

Jim paused to see if this was registering with Del. "Of course, I don't know for sure if that's how they're thinking, but those are good kids you've got there. They want things done the right way. It wouldn't shock me if that's how they're thinking. If you sit Connor out in the first game of the state tournament, they'll see you taking a stand like they have probably wanted to see you take with him before. They will be with you at that point."

Jim continued, "Del, I don't mean to hurt your feelings or anything. I just thought you might want to look at it from your kids' perspective." He paused, thought of something he wanted to say all along, and decided to just say it. "But Del here's a perspective that you probably should really consider. In fact, you've probably already considered it a whole lot more than any other."

Del looked intently at Jim and asked, "What's that?"

Jim said, "What would your dad do? How would your dad have handled Connor throughout the year? How would he handle this situation now?"

Del dropped his head. Jim was right. Del had thought all season long about how his dad would have handled Connor. Del had always had his dad there for counsel. But without him there anymore, he only had his own instincts, feelings, and memories of his dad's words, actions, and lessons.

Unfortunately, Del often didn't follow what he figured his dad would do. Part of it was that he wanted to make his own way, not just do what his dad would have done. But when Del was honest with himself, he knew he didn't want the confrontation, have the difficult conversation with Connor or his parents. He hated having to confront inappropriate behavior. He had been the same way with Cade Clemons last year, too. He just couldn't come down on Cade the way he needed to, and by not holding him accountable, Del let Cade ruin the team.

This year, he had basically done the same thing with Connor. He was just blinded to that fact because the team was winning so much. And Connor's behavior was not the same as Cade's. While some of it happened on the court with the team, Connor's issues were more while he was away from the team, so it wasn't right up in their faces. But it still affected the team in a big way. Del never fully realized how much of an impact it was having.

Jim Turner was still standing there looking at Del, wondering where his thoughts had taken him. It must not have been easy for Del to hear what Jim had said, but Jim felt he needed to say it. Del looked up at Jim and said, "Thanks a lot, Jim. I needed to hear that."

Jim said, "I know it's not easy, but I'm sure you'll do the right thing for your team. Good luck with it and good luck at the tournament."

"Thanks, Jim," said Del. "You going to make it up there?"

"Absolutely!" said Jim. "I wouldn't miss it."

"Good," said Del. "If you see anything that you think we need to do or just have any suggestions, come down at halftime or after games and talk to me outside the locker room. I can use all the help I can get!"

"Will do," said Jim and he walked out the door.

As Jim walked away, Del went back to his thoughts about Connor and what Jim and he had just discussed. Jim had given him the advice of sitting Connor for the first half of the first game. "That might be a good way to do it," he thought. "Then again, Connor hasn't actually *done* anything wrong that is punishable. He can still get his Spanish grade up. If he does, he'll be okay. I just need to let him know ahead of time what the consequences could be. That way he can fix the problem, and he can still play."

Del didn't realize it, but if he didn't hold Connor accountable again, he was setting himself up for a massive problem at the tournament.

Ideas to Consider:

- Once again, Coach Brooks has to deal with an issue from Connor. While none of the issues he has had to deal with have been so bad that he had to punish him in a major way, the incidents add up. Should Coach have handled Connor any differently before? What do you think he should do now?

- What does Jim Turner say to Del that gets Del really thinking about how he has handled Connor? How do you think Del will deal with Connor?

Chapter 34

As Connor walked into the locker room before practice, Del called him into the office. Connor sat down, and Del said, "Connor, I'm getting so tired of having to talk with you about some poor behavior of yours. Miss Gregson told me you're flunking Spanish."

Connor looked up with a startled expression on his face and blurted out, "That's not fair! I wasn't here last week because of the tournament."

"Right," said Del. "But that's not when your poor grade began. You haven't handed anything in for weeks. She said she has reminded you numerous times about it, yet you still haven't handed things in. She even gave you yet another chance to hand it in this morning, but you still didn't do it."

Del paused to see if the information seemed to be sinking in. He couldn't tell for sure, so he kept going. "Connor, if you don't have ALL of that homework handed in by Wednesday, you're ineligible for the tournament. After practice tonight, you have one mission—getting that homework done. And I don't mean just 'get it done.' It needs to be done well. You're already failing. If you hand it all in, but it is 'F' work, you'll still be failing. You've got two days to get it done, so GET IT DONE!"

The practice was about what one would expect for the first day of the week of the state tournament. There was excitement in the air, just like at school all day. Del addressed trying to keep it all in perspective and focusing on practice habits like every other week of the season. While it sounded good, he knew it was going to be tough to do. These were 16-, 17-, and 18-year-old boys he was dealing with. Getting them to stay focused on anything was difficult enough. Getting them to stay focused on habits and routines for four months was really tough. But getting them to do the same thing in the biggest few days of their entire athletic lives was going to be a gargantuan task.

Fortunately, Del had Remington Roberts on his team. Remington understood the importance of staying focused on the task at hand. Each night, whenever the boys started to let their effort, attention, or attitude slip in any way, he was right there to bring them back. "Guys, let's go. We're better than this. We've got two more days to be our best. Lock in!" The boys always got themselves redirected and refocused the moment he did that.

The only one who seemed to struggle getting back into focus was Connor.

About halfway through that night's practice, Del slid up next to Connor and quietly said, "Connor, are you giving this your best effort and attention today?"

Connor said, "I think so, Coach."

Del said, "Well, from my angle, you're practicing right now about as well as you're doing your Spanish homework. Both of those have to change immediately if you plan on doing anything at the state tournament."

After that, Del saw a noticeable difference in Connor's attitude, effort, and demeanor. He started working much harder, sprinting up and down the floor, diving for loose balls, and getting every rebound that was anywhere near him. He was even lifting other guys up, high-fiving them, and encouraging them.

Kevin Nixon said to Del, "What did you say to him?! I haven't seen him practice like this in... ever!"

Del quipped, "I spoke Spanish to him." Kevin laughed at Del's joke.

After practice, Connor was shooting at a side basket. Del went to him and said, "Great job the rest of practice, Connor. That's the best you've looked in a long time. You play like that at the tournament and nobody will beat us."

"Gracias," Connor joked.

Del laughed and thought, "Where has this kid been all year?" He then said, "I appreciate you wanting to get some shots up now, but don't you have something *mas importante* to go do now."

"Wow, Coach," said Connor. "*Muy bien* on the Spanish."

"Yeah, well I know a few words. But it doesn't matter if *I* know a few words. You're the one who needs to know them, so get home and get after it."

"Okay, Coach," said Connor. "I just have to hit a 3-pointer before I go."

Del joked, "I've seen you shoot 3s. You might never get to your Spanish work!"

Connor launched a 3-pointer that hit nothing but the bottom of the net. He smiled, looked at Del, and said, "Sorry, Coach. What were you saying? I couldn't hear you with all the rain that I was making!"

Del laughed and said, "Well, even a blind squirrel finds a nut every once in a while."

Connor headed towards the locker room and said, "*Adios,* Coach."

Again, Del thought, "Where has that kid been all year? He would be fun to coach. How come he isn't like that all the time? That's exactly how his teammates are. Why wouldn't he just fit that right into who he is?"

Later that evening, Remington and Jenny were at Jenny's kitchen table doing homework. They were both so excited, though, that homework was the last thing either of them felt like doing.

"I can't wait for the state tournament, Rem," Jenny said with a huge smile on her face. "This is going to be so much fun. You guys are going to win it all!"

Remington had a half-smile on his face. "I sure hope so, Jen, but I'm not sure. I mean, if we have Connor, I have no doubt that we can win it all. He's that good and that huge for us. But without him, we lose one really big piece to the puzzle."

"What about all that stuff you said last year when the season ended?" asked Jenny. "You were so confident that you could win it all with the guys you had. Well, they're all here now."

"I know," said Remington, "and I still feel that way. It's just that we haven't played without Connor much, so we don't have as many reps without him as we have had with him. I'm just not sure how we would react if he wasn't able to play."

"Well, why are you even worried about it? Connor hasn't done anything wrong, has he?"

"When *hasn't* he done anything wrong?" asked Remington sarcastically. "Yeah, now he's failing Spanish."

"Oh my gosh, seriously?!" said Jenny. "Is he on the ineligible list? Is he done for the week?"

"No, he can still play as of right now," said Remington. "He has to get in all of his makeup work that he was supposed to get in last week. It sounds like he hasn't done anything in there. Ms. Gregson is so easy to work with, you gotta' be a total moron to get her to come down on you."

Jenny thought for about ten seconds and then said, "Well, I guess I hope he stays eligible. I mean if you say you think you need him, then okay. But quite honestly, I'd love to see you guys win it all without him. That was your goal at the end of last year, and you felt like you could do it then. It would be so cool if that's exactly what you did."

Remington looked at Jenny and then got lost in his thoughts. She was right. That had been the goal, and he truly believed that with the guys they had coming back from last year, that they could get to state and win it all. Once Connor showed up, that just made it all the better in Remington's mind. He had a post player inside who he could throw it into who would be able to dominate, while he had perimeter players on the outside who he could pass to for open jump shots. It was a win-win.

After Connor had been there for a while, Remington got so used to it that he wondered how good they would be without him. Remington just liked how secure he felt having Connor there because he knew nobody could beat them. Without Connor there, though, there was doubt. Nothing was certain. But as he sat at Jenny's kitchen table thinking about what she had said, he realized that he wanted that challenge. He wanted to show everyone that they were a great team, with or without Connor.

In fact, in so many ways, they were a better *team* without Connor. Remington realized that, while Connor contributed so much more production to the team because there was no one else like him, he didn't contribute much at all to the *team*. He was a producer of points and rebounds. He was like a machine. Turn him on, put him in the post, and let him get points and rebounds. But when it came to any kind of team play and emotion and togetherness, he was fairly non-existent. It's what drove everyone nuts about him. But Remington was so focused on Connor's production that he often overlooked what Connor did—or didn't do—for the team.

Remington said, "Yeah, it would be cool to win the state championship without Connor. We're a great team without him. We could do it. I'm not saying I *want* anything to happen to Connor. I hope he can play. He's been a part of the team all year, and he deserves to finish things off with us. But you're right. He hasn't really been part of the team the way the rest of us have, and he wasn't there with us last year when we all committed to one another to make this happen. He hasn't really been all-in on it. It would be cool for those of us who were here last year and who put in all that work all these years to go out and win the whole thing without him."

Jenny smiled. "I totally agree."

Ideas to Consider:

- **How does Connor act differently near the end of tonight's practice than other nights? Have you known players who could be so different from one moment to the next? What does that do to your relationship with them? What does that do to the team?**

- **Why is Remington concerned about Connor not playing in the state tournament? What does Jenny remind him of how he thought at the end of last year? How does that affect him?**

Chapter 35

Before school on Wednesday morning, the day the team would be leaving for the tournament, Lynne Gregson showed up at Del's classroom to inform him that Connor had just turned in all of his makeup work. Del was relieved to hear that. She said, "I haven't looked at it yet, but it looked like all of it was there, so I thought I would let you know. I'll grade it on my prep period this morning and let you know if he's passing."

Del said, "Thanks, Lynne," as she turned to walk out of the room.

She said, "No problem, Coach. I want to see him play as much as you do. I just want to make sure we're doing things the right way."

Del said, "I couldn't agree more."

At lunchtime, Del was sitting in the teacher's lounge talking with Kevin Nixon. As they were talking about some final preparations for the short practice they would have after school before the bus left for the tournament that evening, Lynne Gregson walked into the room. As Del looked at her, he was trying to read the expression on her face. She looked very concerned. She said, "Coaches, can we talk for a minute?"

Del said, "Absolutely, have a seat."

She looked visibly shaken. She said, "I'm just so torn. I graded Connor's homework. Some of it was easy, and he breezed through it, but a bunch of it had some minor challenges, and when I say 'minor,' I mean minor. But he just flat-out didn't do it. I mean, he did the homework, but he didn't even try. Wherever something was the least bit challenging, he either left it blank, or he put down an answer that had nothing to do with the question."

Del's heart sank. He was stunned and upset, but he was even more upset over how Lynne Gregson was feeling about it. Here she was a teacher who just wanted her student to do his homework and to try his best, and when he hadn't, she was beating herself up over it.

She continued, "Coach, I just don't know what to do. I want him to play so badly for you at the tournament. But I'm struggling with how poorly he handled this whole thing. If school ended tomorrow, there is no way I could give him a passing grade with a clear conscience. But this is the state tournament. His actions are affecting a lot more than just him. If it were just the end of school, it would only be affecting him. But if he doesn't play because of this, it affects you and the team and the school and the community. I don't want to be the one who did that to all of you."

Del said, "Lynne, it's not you who did that to us; it's him. He's the one who didn't do the work."

She said, "I know that, and you know that. But everyone else won't know that. It will always be, 'Oh there's that mean Spanish teacher. She's the reason we didn't win the state championship.'"

Del reached out and put his hand on her forearm, "Lynne—two things: First of all, it's not your fault, and nor will it be your fault in anyone's eyes. He's failing a class. It happens to kids all the time. It's on him, not you. Secondly, don't sell the rest of the boys short. We can still win a state championship without Connor. It will be harder, but we're good enough to win without him."

Kevin looked at Del, wondering if Del believed his own words. Kevin had not seen Del's actions follow those words much before with regards to Connor and the rest of the team. Lynne's words snapped Kevin back. "Well, that's good to hear, Coach. I know the rest of the boys are really good, and I hope it's as you say. Still, I've decided that I am not putting Connor on the ineligible list. I am going to talk to him this afternoon and let him know what he did and where he stands and how he needs to keep working on this to get his grade up. But I am not going to be the one who keeps him from playing and possibly keeps you guys from winning the state championship."

Del said, "Are you sure? You don't have to do that for us."

Lynne said, "I'm sure. I'll keep working with him. I just hope he'll *start* working with me."

Del said, "Okay. Well, thanks for doing all that you're doing, Lynne. If there's anything more that I can do, let me know."

She said, "You can win the state championship, so all this will have been worth it!"

"We're gonna' give it our best shot," Del said. Lynne smiled and walked out the door.

Del turned to Kevin and said, "My God, what will that kid do next? I thought I had impressed upon him the importance of getting that work done before the tournament."

"Well," started Kevin, "he did get his work done. It's just that he didn't get it done satisfactorily. I imagine he thinks he did his work just fine." Del nodded in agreement. "Then again," Kevin continued, "maybe he knows exactly what he did and what he was doing, and he just didn't care."

"Could be that, too," said Del. "What do you think I should do?"

"It's a tough one," said Kevin. "She's not putting him on the 'F' list, so he's not suspended by the athletic department rule. But technically he has an 'F.' Maybe you do what you said Jim Turner suggested and sit him for the first half of game one."

"Yeah," said Del. "That might be good. Then again, I just don't know. How do I justify it when there actually hasn't been anything that he has done so blatantly wrong? I mean, even though it wasn't the best work, he did what he was asked to do."

Kevin was studying Del as Del was speaking. "Is he really believing what he's telling me?" thought Kevin. "Or is he trying to convince himself, so he can believe it?" Kevin then said, "Well, I think you would have a case either way that proves you are in the right if you suspend him for the half."

"Yeah, you're probably right," said Del. "I just worry that we won't get off on the right foot at the tournament and set the tone like we want. I also worry what it will do to Connor's psyche and confidence if we don't start him. This is the state tournament, after all. We can't be messing around with things now. We have a legit shot to win the whole thing, so I don't want to screw that up." Del paused, almost seeming to be talking with himself instead of Kevin. "Besides, it's the end of the season. There isn't anything more after this to deal with. We can write it off as a learning experience and start dealing with him for next year after this weekend."

Kevin struggled with what he was hearing. He was shocked to hear Del rationalizing what he was considering doing. Jim Turner was right. Grinnell Point probably couldn't beat them without Connor. This was the perfect time to sit him and have him deal with the consequences of his actions.

Del said, "Yeah, I've got to think about this and figure this out."

Kevin realized that there wasn't much that he was going to be able to say to Del that would make Del do what was the right thing to do. Del was going to "figure this out" by himself, so why bother? Kevin was concerned that whatever Del decided to do, it wouldn't be the last time they would have to deal with Connor for poor behavior. And he was worried that it wouldn't be the last time they would have to deal with him *this season.*

Ideas to Consider:

- **What is Del's dilemma with regards to Connor's Spanish class situation? What is the teacher's dilemma with it? What do you think Del should do?**

Chapter 36

The team bus was scheduled to leave for the state tournament in Great Falls at 5:00, right after their practice. Sacajawea was scheduled to play at 2:00 at the Great Falls Four Seasons arena against Grinnell Point the next day. Del wanted to get up to their hotel the night before and have some control over the boys that night and the next morning. The plan was to be in bed by 11:00 and up at 8:00 to get a good breakfast in them. Del was confident that the senior leaders on the team would make sure they followed the plan.

He was right. That night the boys all headed into their rooms before 11:00. They knew what was at stake, and nobody wanted to do anything to disrupt their chances at the success they were after. The next morning, they were all down to the breakfast room by 8:30. They looked excited to get the day going and get to the gym. Del knew the JV coach at Great Falls High School, and he had arranged a short shootaround there from 10:30-11:30. They then went back to the hotel where Del had light sandwiches ready for the boys to eat before heading to the gym at 12:15 to watch the first half of the game before theirs.

The girls' state tournament was also being played at the Four Seasons arena those days. Two girls' games kicked off the tournament at 9:00 and 10:30. The first game of the boys' tournament was at 12:30 between Two Medicine and Bighorn, followed by the Sacajawea/Grinnell Point game at 2:00. The team headed to the gym at 12:15 to watch the first half of the Two Medicine/Bighorn game before heading to the locker room to get ready for their game.

Finally, game one against Grinnell Point was here. In the locker room prior to the game, Del went through final preparations with the team. He had the starting lineups for both teams on the board, and he was going over their man-to-man matchups. Del had Connor listed in the starting lineup. He had talked to Connor about his Spanish situation during the game before theirs, and he let Connor know that even though the season ended this weekend, next week he would need to re-do his Spanish homework that was not done satisfactorily. Connor looked puzzled, but he just nodded his head and said, "Okay, Coach."

Kevin was disappointed in the way Del handled this. Del had the perfect opportunity to stand up for what was right, hold the kid accountable, and still come out victorious, while showing people the importance of doing things the right way. But Del was not doing that. By allowing Connor to start and play right from the beginning, he was sending the wrong message to Connor and to everyone else that "As long as you have talent, I'm not so concerned with your behavior."

Jim Turner had made the trip up from Discovery to watch the whole tournament. He loved to watch how teams played and coaches coached. Of course, as a lifelong resident of Discovery and the former coach of the Sacajawea team, he was more invested in them than any other team. He felt like he had mentored Del a bit in the years Del coached with him. He, too, was disappointed when he saw Connor in the starting lineup. He thought, "You have a perfect opportunity to stand up and say 'This is what is and isn't acceptable in my program.' You can teach that kid a lesson he needs to learn, while teaching the rest of the kids, parents, and community members that behavior matters in your program. But you're not doing the right thing, so none of them will get the right message."

The game started off as so many first games at tournaments do with both teams nervous, tentative, and afraid to make mistakes. There were turnovers and missed assignments. When the teams came to their benches at the end of the first quarter, the score was tied 10-10. Del said, "You just need to relax out there. You're going to be fine. You sat and watched Two Medicine and Bighorn in the first game play a crappy first quarter, too. It's time to get back to who we are and start playing our game. We're the better team, so go out and play. Quit worrying about the outcome. Just go have fun and play the way you're capable of playing. Just run your motion and use your skills and talents and take it to this team. On defense, give up no easy shots. Force everything to the outside. You're going to be just fine."

That's exactly what they did in the second quarter. Remington started attacking off the dribble better, which opened up his fellow guards on the outside and Connor on the inside. While the other players were still struggling to score from the outside, Connor was having a field day inside. He had 13 points at the half, as well as 8 rebounds, 4 on the offensive glass. As they headed to the locker room at halftime, Sacajawea held a 9-point lead.

In the locker room, Del said, "All right, that's a much better quarter. Just keep playing your game. You shooters will start hitting your shots, and we will be fine. We started to pull away from them a bit that quarter. Be ready for them to come at us a little harder this half. Be ready for some full-court pressure. Rem, you get it and distribute to the right people against any traps. They can't handle you. Everyone be ready for him to find you on that."

Grinnell Point never got closer the rest of the way. Sacajawea came out with a renewed focus, and their shots started falling. By the end of the third quarter, they were up by 19 points, and three minutes into the fourth quarter, they were up by 27. Del pulled the starters out, and the subs kept the lead in the 20s the rest of the way. Sacajawea won by a score of 67–45.

The boys were happy in the locker room, but not ecstatic. They expected to win the game. They also expected to play better than they had in the first quarter. Del did not want to dwell on the first quarter, though. "After a tough start, you settled down into who you really are and gave them everything you had and played your game after that. I don't foresee us having any problems from here on out. We know we deserve to be here, and we know that there is no one who can beat us if we just play our game.

"Tomorrow we play Two Medicine. They play a style very similar to Longbow. They're not as good as Longbow, but any of them can step up and have a big night. They will have no conscience putting up shots. And they will run and press and slap and harass you. You need to be rested, hydrated, and mentally prepared for what they will throw at you. They aren't as good as us, but they will come at us hard. We need to be ready." Del finished with comments about the schedule for the rest of the day and evening. After the boys showered, they went to eat and then hang out at the hotel before heading back to the arena to watch the games that night.

In the first game of the evening, Jefferson beat Bitterroot in a close game. In the other game Centennial, the team that had beaten Sacajawea when Connor got the technical foul, won fairly easily against Burlington. By far, Centennial was the toughest team on that side of the bracket. Del and the boys knew they could beat them on a neutral floor with Connor. It wouldn't be easy, but the boys knew they were better than how they played at Centennial. They also knew that Connor not playing down the stretch hurt them, too. Much as some of them hated to admit it, having him for the whole game would be huge.

But thinking about Centennial would have to wait. They had to be ready for Two Medicine. That was always one of the problems with tournament play. Too often kids—and sometimes coaches—would look past opponents. They knew they were better than an opponent they were about to face, and they started thinking about playing the next opponent who was much tougher. Unfortunately, sometimes they never got their opportunity to play that opponent because by overlooking the team they were playing, they weren't mentally prepared. All too often the immediate opponent was more focused and more determined in their quest, and they upset the supposed better team.

Del had to guard against this from happening with his boys. Back at the hotel, Del had a meeting with them in his room. He impressed upon them that they shouldn't be looking ahead to a potential re-match with Centennial. There would be no re-match and no state championship opportunity if they didn't beat Two Medicine, so they had to focus only on Two Medicine. He drew up some of their set plays, and he talked about some of their key individual players. He then said, "But boys, more than anything this game is going to come down to discipline. It's going to come down to who executes their own stuff properly, who will have the discipline to cut hard, block out, and do all the little things. You have handled the discipline elements well all year long. Tomorrow night you will need to handle them even more.

"Two Medicine does not play with discipline, and they will try to get you to do the same thing. They will try to get under your skin, get you off of your game. If you let them do that, you will be in for a battle. If you handle your business the right way and stay focused and disciplined, they can't beat you. It's really that simple. Keep your focus, keep your heads, and keep your cool, and you'll be playing for a state championship on Saturday night."

Del dismissed them, but before they started to move, Remington said, "Coach, can I say something?" The boys all stopped and turned around.

Del said, "Sure, Rem. Boys hang on."

Remington said, "Guys, Coach is absolutely right. We need to take care of our business tomorrow. That starts tonight. We need to get into our rooms, relax, and then get to bed. This is no time to be fooling around."

He looked around the room at his teammates. He liked the focus he was seeing from them. He continued, "Those of you who were on the bus ride home from our last game last year remember what we said about getting here and doing some damage this year. Well, we've got one down, but that's not the one we're after. I know this next one isn't the one we're after either. But we won't get a shot at the one we're after if we don't take care of this next one. We took care of today, and now we've got to take care of tomorrow. Put Centennial and put a state championship on Saturday out of your minds. Our state championship is tomorrow night. That is all we focus on—Two Medicine tomorrow night. Focus and discipline. Do the right thing, the right way, right now. That starts with getting our sleep tonight. Everybody in here."

The boys all stepped into a crowded huddle at the foot of Del's bed. Remington put his hand up, and all the boys put their hands in together. Remington said, "Focus on three—1, 2, 3," and they all said, "Focus!" Before they could break their hands away from each other Remington yelled, "Discipline on three—1, 2, 3," and they all yelled "Discipline!"

Ideas to Consider:

- **Why do you think Del played Connor in the first game? Do you think he trusts that the team can win without Connor?**
- **What is Remington's main message when he calls the boys back into the room before they head off to their own rooms?**

Chapter 37

Del was nervous, but excited, as he stood before the bench during warm-ups prior to the semi-final game with Two Medicine. He knew that he had the better team. He knew that if his kids played the right way and the way they were capable of, Two Medicine could not beat them. However, he also knew that if his boys came out tight, tried to do things they didn't normally do, and didn't play together, it could be a long night. Two Medicine could get into opponents' heads, and their style of play could take a team out of its game. Del had confidence that his kids would not let that happen, but it was still a concern.

His concerns were borne out right away. Two Medicine established a frenetic pace, pushing the ball, pressing, slapping, shoving underneath, and constantly pushing the Sacajawea players out of their comfort zones. Everything the Two Medicine players did got under the skin of the Wolves' players, and it started to creep into their mindset. It was like having mosquitoes or gnats flying around you. On their own, they weren't that big a deal. But multiples of them happening over and over again could wear you down and frustrate you. That was what Two Medicine did. Everything they did was working, and everything the Wolves did wasn't. The more things didn't work, the more the Wolves thought about it. The more they thought about it, the more things didn't work. They were caught in a vicious cycle.

Remington was playing his usual strong game, but he was the only one having any success. Connor struggled to get touches inside, and Nick, Tim, Brian, and Mike were all struggling to get comfortable on their shots because they were always worried that a Two Medicine player was going to be right in their face or sneaking up from behind to block their shot. None of them were especially confident handling the ball against Two Medicine's pressure either, so they had their share of turnovers.

Eventually, the Wolves settled down and started to turn things around. By the end of the first quarter, they had weathered the initial storm, and they were only down by a point, 16–15. In the huddle, Del said, "All right, those last three minutes were much better than the first five. I told you they were going to come at you. Once you settled down, though, and realized you're fine, things started to turn. Keep playing that way from now on. Del then gave some specific instructions on how to handle the Coyotes' pressure defense, and then they headed out to the floor.

The Wolves continued to play better, and they took a 6-point lead three minutes into the quarter. They were clicking for the most part. The only one who wasn't in sync was Connor. He struggled to get touches on offense. Two Medicine put a 6'6" lanky kid named Josiah Old Chief on him. While Old Chief matched him height-wise, Connor had 20 pounds on him. However, what he lacked in beef, Old Chief made up for in quickness and heart. As Connor posted up, Old Chief was out-maneuvering him for position. He used his quick feet and hands to get position on Connor, so it was hard for the guards to get the ball inside. Connor would yell, "Get me the ball!" at the guards after each possession down the floor that he didn't get it. They would yell back, "Quit standing there! Get open."

On the other end of the floor, it wasn't much better for Connor. Old Chief lured Connor away from the basket, shooting jump shots over his outstretched hand. He hit two shots from the free throw line area on two straight possessions. Being that far away from the basket meant Connor was not in good position to rebound, his strongest attribute. The other Coyote players all had an attack-the-basket mentality, and they crashed the offensive boards hard.

As the quarter was coming to a close, Old Chief caught the ball at the free throw line again. He started to elevate as if to shoot. Connor decided he'd had enough of Old Chief shooting over him, so he went up to block his shot. But Old Chief pulled the ball back down as Connor went flying by him. With the clock winding down, Old Chief took two dribbles into the lane and laid the ball in the basket. Connor turned and yelled at his teammates, "Where's the help?!" The rest of the guys just shook their heads as they ran off the floor to the locker room. The Wolves held a 3-point lead.

As they got into the locker room, Connor was fuming. He didn't say anything to anyone, but it was obvious, he was not happy as he sat down. Del said, "Connor, relax. Deep breaths. You're going to be fine." Connor scowled at Del, but he didn't say a word. Del continued, "You need to stay on your feet on Old Chief's shot and shot fakes. Get your hand up, but stay in a good stance. If they're going to beat us with him shooting from the perimeter, so be it."

Del paused and looked around at all of them. "But they're not going to beat us that way because he is not that good of a shooter. He hit two of them. So what? The bigger concern is that we all need to work to keep all of them in front of us, and then EVERY SINGLE ONE OF US needs to block out! If we don't block out, that is how they will beat us.

"We played a decent half, but we're much better than what we showed. Don't let them dictate the tempo. When you do that, you let them decide how you play. You've never done that all year long, not even against Colter, and

Colter is a far superior team to Two Medicine. You are all skilled players. You can all handle the ball well, and you're all good shooters. Trust your training, and go out there and do the things you do every day. When you did that, you were fine, and you will continue to be if you continue to do that.

Del talked about some strategy things, and then finished up. He asked Kevin and Braden if they had anything to add. Braden said he didn't. Kevin said, "Boys, believe. Believe in yourselves and believe in each other. Like Coach said, 'Trust your training.' You're all good players, and you're better players than they are. Believe that, and you're going to be fine."

As they headed back out to the floor, Del grabbed Remington by the arm and walking next to him said, "Rem, get the ball into Connor. He needs some touches."

Remington thought that was a bit odd, but he said, "Coach, I'm trying. Old Chief is all over him, though."

Del said, "Well, if he doesn't get some touches, he's going to come unglued out there. We need him if we want to win this game, Rem. Make sure he gets touches."

Remington couldn't believe what he was hearing. Coach had never said anything like that in the four years Remington knew him and played for him. He didn't even say that about Cade the last couple of years. He thought, "Does he not believe in the rest of us? Does he not see that we are really good without Connor?" He thought about mentioning it to Nick and Tim, but he knew that would just set them off, so he didn't say anything.

Ideas to Consider:

- **Why are the Sacajawea boys struggling with Two Medicine so much? What does Coach Brooks tell them they need to do?**

- **Why does Coach tell Remington he needs to make sure he gets the ball to Connor? What does that make Remington think?**

Chapter 38

Two Medicine got the ball to start the second half. The Wolves were defending hard on the perimeter, and the Coyotes couldn't get a good look for a shot. They eventually found Old Chief open inside when Connor had lost sight of him. Old Chief caught the ball down low as Connor recovered and got up behind him. Old Chief faked a pass across the lane that Connor leaned out to try to steal. Old Chief quickly wheeled the other way with the ball, and scored on a wide-open lay-up. Connor looked around for someone to yell at, but he was all alone. It was all on him, and he didn't like it.

Remington brought the ball up the floor. He called out play #2. It was a play involving Remington, Brian Jackson, and Connor up at the point. After he picked for Remington and rolled towards the basket, Brian was supposed to set a screen for Connor on the opposite side of the lane. The combination of the two screens led to confusion for Two Medicine, and Connor rolled right into a wide-open layup. Unfortunately, he was so shocked at how wide open he was, that he missed the easy layup. The ball rolled off the rim on the other side. Fortunately, Brian was there to grab it and lay it in the basket.

Connor was beside himself at his miss. He turned and yelled at Remington, "Get it to me where I can handle it!"

Running backwards down the floor, Remington said, "You mean right in your hands at your waist isn't where you can handle it? 'Cuz that's where it was when you caught it! I can't help it if you can't make a layup, dude."

On Two Medicine's ensuing possession, Old Chief flashed up to the free throw line to receive a pass just like in the second quarter. This time Connor came out hard. Old Chief rose up as if to shoot, Connor jumped, and then Old Chief jumped up to shoot it, making sure that he forced a foul on Connor coming down on him. The ref blew the whistle and headed to the scorer's table to indicate the foul. Old Chief said to Connor, "Nice try, dude."

Connor walked up to Old Chief and got chest-to-chest with him. "Shut up, Geronimo," he whispered into Old Chief's face. Old Chief went right back at Connor getting chest-to-chest with him, too, but players from both teams stepped between them.

Del yelled out, "Connor!" Connor turned and looked at Del. "Stay on your feet! That's exactly what I was talking about! We can't afford you to get into foul trouble."

It was Connor's second foul but they were only a minute-and-a-half into the second half. Del asked Kevin if he thought he should get him out of the game. Kevin said, "Well, yeah! Did you see how he started to go after Old Chief there? You need to get him out and calm him down."

Del said, "That was nothing. I mean because of getting his second foul."

Kevin thought, "Are you kidding? You're more worried about his second foul than the fact that he was about to go off on that kid?" But what he said was, "Yeah, get him out and talk to him a little to get his mind right."

Del thought about it. He looked down the bench and said, "Jimmy, go for Connor."

Jimmy Thompson hopped up off the bench and reported into the game. He jogged towards Connor, put his hand up for a high-five. Connor left Jimmy hanging, refusing to high-five him. As he came off the floor, Connor said to Del, "Coach, why are you taking me out? That's only my second foul. I can't do anything from the bench. Those guys need me."

Del said, "I don't want you to pick up a third foul early in the half. I need you to have your mind right when you go back out there. Jimmy is going to spell you for a couple minutes." Connor walked down to the end of the bench and sat down away from his teammates.

Jimmy did well against Old Chief, not going for his fakes. He also turned the tables on him at the offensive end with his own shot fake getting Old Chief in the air and blowing past him for a layup. Jimmy continued to play well throughout the third quarter. As the Wolves came to the bench at the end of the quarter, they were ahead 45–40. Del called Connor to go back in for Jimmy. Kevin leaned over to Del and said, "Coach, what are you doing? Jimmy's playing well."

"I know," said Del, "but I want to get Connor back in. We're going to need him to win this game, and I want him in there now." Del turned and got into the huddle with the boys. He talked about how they played well for the most part that quarter and how if they continue to play their game, good things will continue to happen. As the team huddled before going back on the floor, Remington yelled what he had yelled each time they huddled tonight— "Discipline on three. 1, 2, 3," and the team yelled, "Discipline."

On the second possession of the quarter for the Wolves, Connor posted up and gave Nick a good, open target. Nick fed a nice bounce pass into him. With his back to the basket, he took one hard dribble to his left. He was trying to set up a move to his right into the middle of the lane by getting Old Chief leaning the other way. He saw Old Chief lean the way he wanted him to, so he picked up his dribble and spun to his right, turning into the free throw lane.

However, Old Chief already knew what Connor was doing. He slid over into the lane in front of where Connor was going and planted his feet. As Connor gathered himself to jump up towards the basket, he lowered his shoulder and exploded into Old Chief, sending him sprawling. The official blew his whistle, put his left hand behind his head, punched straight out in front of him with his right hand, and yelled, "Offensive foul!"

Lying on the ground, Old Chief screamed in jubilation, and his teammates and their fans joined in the celebration. Connor threw the ball hard to the ground and yelled, "No way! That's terrible!" The ball went flying up higher than the rim.

Everything seemed to happen in slow-motion for Del. As the ball came back down, a Two Medicine player caught it. Meanwhile, Connor knew he couldn't take his action back, and he already realized what was about to happen. The official turned right back toward Connor, blew his whistle, and forcefully brought his hands together in the shape of a "T" in Connor's direction.

Del dropped his head, leaned over, and put both hands on his knees. "Now what?" he thought. "What is wrong with that kid? How could he do that?" Del stood up, looked out at the floor, as the official came to the scorer's table and announced, "Player control foul on #44 in white. Also, Technical Foul on #44 in white."

Del called out, "Connor, come here!"

Connor came over with a totally different demeanor than he had exhibited the entire game. "Coach, I'm so sorry. I didn't mean for that ball to go up that high. I tried to catch it on its way up, but I missed it. I know I should have controlled myself better, but I was upset with myself. I'm sorry."

Del was taken aback by Connor's words because he had never heard him speak like this. He didn't know how to react at first, but he said, "It's okay. I know you didn't mean to do it. You need to stay under control out there, all right? We need you to be able to stay in this game. That's your fourth foul now. One more and you're gone. We can't have that."

Connor said, "No, I only have three fouls."

Del said, "You have three fouls, but the technical counts as another one, so you now have four. You cannot get another foul, do you understand?"

"What?! A technical counts as a foul?" asked Connor.

"Yes," said Del. "I told you that the last time this happened."

Connor was stunned. "I didn't remember that." He paused and then said,

"Okay, I understand, Coach. Don't worry. I'm good. I won't get another one." Connor walked back out to the half line with the other players as the point guard for Two Medicine, Cal Davis, swished the second of his two technical foul free throws.

Remington looked over at Del, wondering why Connor was still out there. This same thing had happened at Centennial with Connor's first technical foul. The rule stated that a player getting his second technical foul at any point in the season meant he was automatically out for the rest of the game and then out for the next game. Remington thought, "Doesn't Coach even care to follow his own rules? How does he expect anyone else to follow them if he won't follow them himself?"

Kevin was thinking a similar thing, and he stood up and said, "Coach, you're getting Connor out now, right? That's it. That's his second technical of the year. He's done. You told him so yourself the last time."

"Not now, Kevin," said Del. "This is too important a time not to have him out there. You didn't hear how he was apologizing to me. He feels terrible about what he did. I've never heard him talk that way before. He knows he screwed up, and he just wants a chance to make it right."

Kevin said, "Well, that's nice and all, but you have your rule about this exact situation."

Del said, "That's right. *I* have that rule. And it's *my* rule. It's not the state's rule, or the league's rule, or the school's rule, or your rule. It's *my* rule, and I'll handle it the way *I* want to handle it."

"Some rule," Kevin thought, as he turned and sat back down on the bench.

Two Medicine took the ball out of bounds down by three points now. From that point on, Connor played completely under control. He did everything the way he was supposed to. He was talking positively to teammates, working hard on defense, and getting into good position so as not to pick up a foul. On offense, he worked hard to post up, but also set good, clean screens for teammates to get open on cuts. He got two offensive rebound put-back baskets two possessions in a row late in the game. The Two Medicine coach called timeout with 1:37 to go and the Wolves up 60–52.

As the Wolves came to the bench, Del said, "All right nice job. Way to work out there. Your defense is solid. Keep them in front of you and keep blocking out. Be ready for them to start jacking even more 3s than they have been already, and be ready for them to shoot from anywhere on the floor. Offensively, great job, Connor. You're setting great screens to get guys open, and I love your effort on the offensive glass."

Remington, Nick, and Tim all glanced at each other. They wondered if anyone else saw the irony in the fact that the one player who shouldn't even be on the floor because of his behavior was the only player that Coach was gushing over about how well he was playing. As much as they wanted to be excited about this moment and the fact that they were 1:37 away from going to the state championship game, they couldn't shake the feeling that the way it was happening was all wrong.

Del finished the timeout by saying, "All right. We are going to spread the floor out when we get it back. Make them come foul you. We shoot two free throws every foul now. Spread it out. No shots other than a wide-open layup. If you are challenged at all, kick it to a teammate. Be tough with the ball and take care of it." With Remington, Nick, and Brian all shooting their free throws at above 70%, the plan on the spread offense was to have them handle the ball up top, out high and wide and Connor and Tim be down in the corners to sneak behind the defense for a layup or to stay wide and be pressure-releases if the guards got into trouble.

Two Medicine hit a quick 3-pointer out of the timeout to cut the lead to five. They immediately set up their press. Remington got the ball in the back court. He faked a pass back to Brian who had thrown it in to him. He swept the ball across his body from left to right and started dribbling up the right sideline. Out of the corner of his eye, he saw Connor wide open across the court on the other side of the half-line. He fired a pass to Connor, as Nick was coming right up behind. All Connor had to do was toss the ball to the wide-open Nick, so they could all just take their places in their spread offense and kill some clock.

However, Connor had other plans. As he caught the ball about thirty feet from the basket, there was no Two Medicine player in his path. He immediately started to dribble to the basket, something he didn't do all that often. Del couldn't believe what he was seeing, and he jumped up and yelled, "NO!" But Connor never heard him, and he attacked the rim.

Old Chief had been sprinting back out of the press from the other side of the floor. He elevated at the same time that Connor elevated. Connor tried to dunk the ball, but Old Chief got enough of the ball that it hit the back of the iron and bounced out into the hands of another Two Medicine player. He immediately advanced the ball with a pass to an open teammate behind the three-point line in the corner. His shot hit nothing but net. Two Medicine was now down by only two points with 1:06 to go.

Nick quickly entered the ball to Remington. As Remington started up the floor with it, he was fouled. He calmly stepped to the line and hit two free throws to put the Wolves back up by four with a minute to go. On the Coyotes next possession, Old Chief got it on the low block. He turned to try to go around Connor, but Connor slid his feet and blocked him from his move. Old Chief turned to pass to a teammate, but Remington slid in and stole the ball.

He found Nick sprinting up the court and threw a baseball pass that landed softly in Nick's hands. Nick laid it in the basket to go up by 6.

Two Medicine had one more push in them. They hit a 3-pointer to cut the lead to 3 with twenty-one seconds left. As the Wolves were working the ball to break the Coyotes' press, Tim found Connor ahead of everybody and threw it to him. Old Chief fouled him with twelve seconds left. Connor could all but ice the game with both free throws.

Unfortunately, Connor missed both free throws in the pressure of the moment. Down by three with eleven seconds to go Two Medicine called time out to set up a play. Del told the team, "Switch on all screens. Challenge all 3s, but don't foul. If they tie it and we go into overtime, so be it. But do not give up an easy 3, and don't foul a 3-point shooter. Hand up, stay on your feet, and challenge. Watch for a quick 2. They are out of timeouts now, so if they score a 2, and it's under five seconds left, leave the ball alone. They can't stop the clock, and we win the game."

Two Medicine set up their play. Cal Davis passed the ball to the right-side wing. He started running through the lane and then down along the baseline. Two of his teammates started to set screens, one right after the other one, to get him open on the opposite wing. Davis stepped out to the 3-point line and caught a swing pass with five seconds left. Connor was guarding the first screener, and he saw it all happening. He left his man and headed out toward Davis. As Davis elevated to shoot the potential game-tying 3, Connor left the floor and reached as high as he could. He deflected Davis's shot a split-second after he released it and sent the ball flying back behind Davis's head towards the half-line. Nick, who had been guarding Davis, immediately sprinted to the ball, took two dribbles with it, and the buzzer went off. The Wolves had won the game. They were headed to the state championship game!

Ideas to Consider:

- **Why didn't Coach Brooks take Connor out of the game after his technical foul even though his rule said that he should have? How do you think the other players and coaches feel about Coach's actions? Do you think Coach should have taken him out?**

- **Coach will have another tough decision to make regarding Connor playing in the state championship game. What should he do? What would you do?**

Chapter 39

The Wolves' crowd erupted in jubilation. The players all started running after Nick as he had started running towards the bench. It was a mob scene for the players as they met right in front of the bench. Del, Kevin, and Braden had all been hugging each other, too. They quickly composed themselves and re-directed the boys' attention to getting lined up for the post-game handshake with the Two Medicine players.

Understandably so, the Coyotes were devastated. They had a chance to beat the best team in the state, and they came up just short. Their coach brought them together for a short huddle, and then they waited for the Sacajawea boys to line up to shake hands. After about fifteen seconds, both teams were walking past each other high-fiving, low-fiving, fist-bumping, and shaking hands.

As the first of the Wolves' players got to the end of the line, they immediately sprinted towards their students who had made their way down towards the floor and started hugging everyone they could find. A large congregation of players, parents, and other fans had formed right at the corner of the court. Security personnel started ushering the players out of that area so as to allow the Centennial and Jefferson players a lane to get to the court to begin their warmups for the next game.

Normally, Del, Kevin, and Braden would be moving the boys along to the locker room. However, Del wanted them to enjoy this moment with their friends and family. None of them had ever experienced winning a game to go to the state championship. While the biggest prize of all was waiting tomorrow night, there was no guarantee they would win it. He wanted them to be able to savor this moment and relish in the joy they were all feeling.

Truth be told, he wanted to enjoy it and bask in it, too. He had felt pressure building for the last few years to get back to state and to a state championship game. Of course, the ultimate prize was to win it all, but too often teams don't celebrate each hurdle they get over along the way. This was the final hurdle before trying to now cross the finish line, and Del wanted to drink it in fully.

He also had his share of naysayers in the back of his mind that he wanted to make sure knew that he had guided his team to the state championship game. He figured there were those who doubted him, those who felt he was too young, too soft on kids, too whatever they could come up with to explain why he hadn't gotten to the state championship. Now, they were no longer right. They couldn't take this moment away from him, and he wanted to be out there to see any of their faces and, if only in his mind, tell them to stick it.

Parents, community members, fans, and former players came up to him and offered their congratulations to him. It was all smiles and handshakes and hugs and laughter and tears of joy. This was a crowning achievement, and Del was basking in the glory.

Jim Turner made his way through the crowd, hugging kids, offering congratulations to everyone he knew on the team. He and Kevin Nixon spoke for a minute a few yards away from Del as Del was being mobbed by various people. The two of them did not have the same looks on their faces that everyone else seemed to have. They were in what one might guess was a serious conversation.

Finally, Del was alone, and Jim stepped over to him. Jim's demeanor changed to that of everyone else's and he smiled, spread his arms out wide, and said, "Coach! You did it!" as he gave Del a big bear hug. "Congratulations!"

"Thanks, Jim," said Del. "It feels so good to finally get there. This is what I have dreamed of for so long. I knew I could get here. I just didn't know how long it would take for me to finally experience this."

Jim was a bit taken aback by Del's use of "I" and "me." Jim was thinking, "Seriously? You're focused on *you* right now?" but he said nothing.

Del then said, "You were a huge part of this, too, Jim. You helped lay the foundation for me. I learned so much from you."

Jim said, "Well, thanks Del, but I think you're giving away too much credit. You're the one who has been in total control of this program for the last four years. It has your stamp on it now. I see a thing or two that you do that came from our time together, but most of what you do is all you. And quite honestly, much of what you got from me, I got from your dad. It's your dad who had a bigger impact on laying the foundation of the program."

Jim's words hit Del right in the heart. "Dad!" he thought. He hadn't even thought of his dad for the first five minutes of this celebration. "How could I forget about Dad? How could I not even think about him in this moment that he prepared me for? God, I wish he was here right now to see this."

Del felt himself starting get overcome with emotion, and he tried to push back tears. Jim leaned in and said in the most serious of tones, "How proud do you think your dad would be right now after watching you coach that game, coach your team to a state championship game, the way you handled everything that happened out there tonight?" He wasn't smiling and he stared into Del's eyes, his face about 10 inches away from Del's.

Del kind of leaned back from Jim, not knowing what to make of his comment and his look. But then in an instant, Jim's demeanor immediately changed. He had a big smile and said, "I'm sure he would be proud of you, knowing you had won that game by coaching your team and coaching your kids the same way he taught you. I'm sure he is right here with us, all around us, smiling and loving every minute of what he just saw his son do in the game he loved so much, the game he loved sharing with you so much."

Jim gave Del another big hug, stepped back from him and said, "I can't wait to see what you do tomorrow night. Good luck!"

Del was in a fog. He wasn't sure if he even said "Thanks" to Jim as Jim walked away. Del was so lost in his own thoughts about his dad and what Jim had said and what Jim had said about his dad and him and...

Del wondered if Jim had just called him out, if he was criticizing Del's coaching decisions tonight. There was almost a twinge of scolding in Jim's voice. *"How proud do you think your dad would be right now after watching you coach that game, coach your team to a state championship game, the way you handled everything that happened out there tonight?"*

Del wondered, "What was he talking about? Why wasn't he smiling? Of course, Dad would be proud of me. I just won a game that got us into the state championship game. What didn't I handle out there tonight the right way?"

As Del looked up and saw Connor talking to some friends, the answer came at him like being smacked in the face with a 2 x 4. Del felt like he might fall to the floor. "Oh, God. What have I done? Oh, my God." Del looked around and knew he had to get out of that crowd immediately. He needed space to think. He couldn't let anyone see him.

He turned and headed around the corner of the bleachers towards the locker room. People were congratulating him as he walked, and he tried to smile and say "Thanks" with a look of gratitude, but all he could think of was to get out of that place. He found a door to a storage room propped open.

He looked in the room. There were racks of basketballs and volleyballs and various pieces of different types of sports equipment. There were wrestling mats rolled up and stacked along the wall. There was nobody in the room. He went over to the mats and half-sat and half-stood on them.

He buried his head in his hands. "Oh God, Dad, I'm so sorry. I'm so sorry. How could I do that? How could I let Connor play? After all you taught me about doing things the right way, leading with character and integrity. After all the lessons I learned from you about never compromising your principles even for a victory, and I go and do that! My God, how could I?"

He looked up at the ceiling of the storeroom. "You would have never done that, Dad. When he got that technical, you would have had him out, no questions asked. I told Kevin it's *my* rule, but it was *your* rule to begin with. But you would have followed it. You wouldn't have sacrificed your standards just for a win. My God, what have I done? I'm so sorry, Dad." He looked at the floor again, tears streaming down his face.

Del tried to gather his thoughts. He needed to go talk to his team, but he didn't know how to face them yet. He looked up toward the ceiling again and said, "Now what, Dad? What do I do now to make this right?"

Kevin Nixon was out in the hallway looking for Del. He happened to be walking by that storage room when he heard a sound coming out of it. He poked his head in and saw Del. "Coach? I've been looking all over for you. The boys are all in the locker room. They're waiting for you to come talk to them. The other game's gonna' start in eight minutes."

As Del turned and looked at Kevin, Kevin could see that Del had been crying. Kevin was a little stunned and yet, he knew how emotional this moment was for all of them. For Del, it had to be even more so than it was for just about everyone else. Kevin smiled and said, "Pretty exciting, huh?"

Del wasn't smiling. He said, "Oh God, Kevin, I'm so sorry."

Kevin was taken aback. He asked, "What are you talking about?"

"I can't believe how I handled that whole situation with Connor," Del replied. Kevin nodded a look of recognition and understanding as Del continued. "I'm so sorry. There's no way he should have been playing. You were right again. But I was so consumed with winning that I snapped at you and then completely compromised any standards, any integrity that I have tried to live by and teach our kids. I'm so ashamed."

Kevin nodded and said, "You know, when you snapped at me about it being your rule, I thought, 'No, it's not. It's your dad's rule. But the difference is your dad would have actually followed his rules.' And then I thought, 'How proud do you think your dad would be right now?' I knew the answer, but I wondered if you would figure it out." Kevin paused, trying to find the right words to continue with. He then said, "Obviously, you have and that's good. But the question is, 'How are you going to handle it now?'"

"I don't know yet," said Del. "What do you think I should do?"

"Will my answer matter, Del?" asked Kevin. "Or will you just go and do what you think you need to do to win a game?"

"I'm so sorry it's come to this, Kevin. Please help me figure this out. After my dad died, you and Jim Turner have been about the only people who I trust, who really get what I'm going through. And I just shoved both of you away when you gave me the advice I needed to hear. I'm done doing that, Kev. I need your help. What should I do?"

Kevin smiled and said, "Well, the first thing you need to do is get in and talk to your team. We can talk about what the next steps for tomorrow need to be while we're watching the Centennial and Jefferson game. But I think right now, everything needs to be positive and upbeat with the boys. Let them enjoy this now, but then we also need to stress to them that the celebration ends in a couple of hours and then it's on to preparing for the championship."

"Should I say anything about Connor?" asked Del.

"No, I wouldn't yet because you don't know yet what you're going to do. I wouldn't single him out in any way right now, positively or negatively. Just focus on the team, and make it short and sweet. They won't be hearing much of what you say anyway 'cuz they're so sky-high right now. But let's get in there, talk, and get 'em out of there, so we can watch this game."

Del got up and walked towards Kevin and gave him a hug. "Thanks so much, Kev. I'm so sorry for how I handled things and how I treated you."

"Don't worry about it," said Kevin. "It's an emotional time in a very emotional game that we coach. Learn from it, move forward, and let's go win a state championship tomorrow." Kevin paused and then added, "The right way."

Ideas to Consider:

- **How did Jim Turner and Kevin help Del come to the realization of what he had done? Do you think Del will do what he should do, or will he just do the same thing again, like he always has?**

Chapter 40

Del and Kevin walked into the locker room. The kids were all talking and laughing with one another. As Del and Kevin walked in, they started clapping and cheering. Del was not ready for the kids' reaction, and he struggled with how to respond. He smiled, pumped his fist in the air, and remembered Kevin's advice about keeping it positive.

"Congratulations, boys! Guess what?" he said.

A few of the boys said, "What?" with anticipation and eagerness.

He leaned forward and yelled, "We're playing in the state championship game tomorrow!!" The boys erupted in hoots and hollers as if it just hit them that they were going to be playing in the state championship tomorrow.

Del put his hand up to calm them down. He said, "I can't believe it myself. Not that I didn't believe all along that we would be playing in the state championship. But I can't believe it's finally here. That was an amazing victory, boys. That was one of the most challenging games you have had. Two Medicine did everything we knew they would, and they pushed us to the brink. But you responded. You were ready, and you took care of business like we knew you would."

Del paused and looked around at their faces. As his eyes met Connor's, he quickly looked away. He felt awkward looking at him. He continued, "Here's the deal about winning a semi-final game to go to the state championship game. While I have never done it before, I know this: it is a strange mixture of absolute joy that has to be pretty much immediately shut down and replaced with absolute discipline and focus to turn around and get ready for the next night. Immature teams struggle with that concept. They get so sky-high from this game that they never recover and get prepared to play at an even higher level for the next game."

He looked around, saw Remington, Nick, and Tim nodding. "This team, though," he said pointing around the room at all of them, "is not an immature team. This is a team filed with seniors and juniors who totally get that the fun and joy of what we just went through needs to be enjoyed for an hour or two and then, Boom!—it's back to business." He paused, looked at each of them and said, "Do I make myself clear?"

Heads were nodding that they understood. "Get showered and go watch Centennial and Jefferson and see what you can learn. Everything you learn will help you tomorrow night. After their game, we will head to the hotel and discuss our game plan for tomorrow. Get it?"

They all said, "Got it," stood up, and circled around Remington. Remington said, "Guys, great job tonight. But winning the semis was not what we came here to do. The prize is tomorrow. We need to flush this game. Yeah, enjoy it, sure. But we need to start getting ready for tomorrow tonight. Our friends and families are going to talk about how great we are when we go out there. That's nice, but don't let it go to your head. Stay focused on the task at hand. We need to have the discipline to take care of business one last time." He raised his hand up, and they all put their hands together above their heads. He said, "Focus on three! 1, 2, 3," and they all yelled, "Focus," and he followed that with "Discipline on three! 1, 2, 3," and they said, "Discipline."

The Centennial-Jefferson game proved to be a fairly one-sided affair. By half-time Centennial led by 16. It was anti-climactic for the fans after the exciting barn-burner of a game that the first one was. It was also a much quieter arena. Two Medicine was only an hour away, and they always had a huge crowd everywhere they went. When their game was over, most of their crowd left the arena.

All of this was good for Del and Kevin. While it didn't help them that Centennial was so good, they discussed their own situation more than focusing on what Centennial and Jefferson were doing. The coaches took notes in the first half, focusing more on Centennial as they saw which way the game was going. Braden was diagramming plays, while Kevin and Del focused on individual players and coaching decisions that Jerry White made.

"Man, he's good," said Kevin. "His kids work so hard. They're always in the right spots. They do everything in textbook fashion. They're so disciplined. They never get rattled. And look at how they respond to him." Del agreed with Kevin.

At the half, Del turned to Kevin and said, "So what do you think we should do about Connor?"

Kevin said, "Well, not to be a jerk, but *we* shouldn't do anything to him. *You* are the one who needs to do it. I don't mean to say the classic, 'You got yourself into this mess, now you have to get yourself out of it,' but that's what it's like."

Del sighed. "I know. It's my responsibility, and I will be the one to handle it. I'm just asking what you think we—sorry, *I* should do about it."

"Well," started Kevin, "Connor has to sit out of tomorrow's game."

"For the whole game?!" asked Del, with a shocked tone to his voice.

Kevin looked at him in disbelief. "Del, didn't you hear yourself when you were talking to me in that storage room? You knew you screwed up. You knew he shouldn't have played the rest of the game. Why? Because it's 'your rule.'" Kevin made air-quotes with his fingers as he said it. "Well, *your rule* also says that when a kid gets a second technical, he sits out the entire next game."

Del sunk back in his chair and looked at the ceiling of the stadium. He was mentally reading the rule in his policy sheet. He finally said, "You're right. Why did I put that in there?"

Kevin could see Del was struggling. He said, "It's a good rule, Del. Also, *you* didn't put it in there. It was your dad's rule. Your dad wasn't an idiot. He was a man of character and integrity, and he wanted his players to be people of character and integrity, too. So, he had rules that helped them learn to behave the right way."

Kevin paused and then said, "No, Coach, the rule isn't the problem. You are. It's the way you handle your rules. You create rules to hold kids accountable and create the right culture, but when your rules might affect your ability to win a game, you abandon them. You start enforcing your rules only for certain players, but not for the players who need them the most. You're sending a terrible message to your players. 'I have one set of rules for the stars and one set of rules for everyone else.' Coach, you're losing your team because you've lost your way trying to win a championship. If you let Connor play tomorrow, you might win a championship, but you'll lose a whole lot more. You'll lose the respect of your team, your school, your community, and anyone else who knows what's really happening."

Del said, "You're right. I totally lost my way. I got so wrapped up in winning that I forgot who I was. I'm Del Brooks, son of Mason Brooks. We coach young men. My dad used to say, 'When you start coaching the sport first and the people second, it's time to get out because you've lost your way.' And that's exactly what I started to do."

Kevin said, "Del, I agree with your dad in one way, but I disagree with him in another way. It's not time for you to get *out*; it's time for you to get *up*. You were knocked down by the desire to win at all costs. Well, you may have been knocked down, but you haven't been knocked out. Stand up and do what is right. Follow your conscience, follow your standards, and follow your rule."

Del nodded and said, "How do you suggest I do that? I mean, I already blew it and didn't follow my rules a couple of times."

Kevin said, "Yeah, I know. It's kind of hard to all of a sudden live by the idea that you're going to do what you said you would all along. But I think I have a way to make it happen. Your rule states that when a kid gets a second technical, he has to sit for the next game. While it also says he has to sit for the rest of the game in which the technical happened, your rule for getting a 'T' the first time in a season says he *may* go back into the game later."

Del was nodding throughout Kevin's explanation, and Kevin continued. "You can tell Connor you mixed up your rule for getting a T for the first time and the second time, and that's why you left him in tonight. Then just go right to the concept that the rule clearly states, though, that a player getting a 2nd technical is suspended for the next game. Tell him that the rule is in place for a reason, that it's a good rule, and he violated it. You have to hold to the rule."

Del knew that's what he had to do. He also knew he would have to not only deal with Connor, but also Connor's parents. While they had been supportive of Del for the most part, they questioned him each time he had to punish Connor in some way. They had not been overly vocal or confrontational when this happened, but Del could tell they could get that way if push came to shove. And Del felt like push was about to come to shove.

"When do you think I should tell him?" asked Del.

"I would talk to Randy Watson," said Kevin. "He needs to be informed of it, and he'll have some ideas on what to do." Kevin looked around and spotted Randy down behind the Centennial bench talking to their athletic director. He pointed Randy out to Del and said, "I would go talk to him now and figure it out."

Del got up and started to walk away. He turned around and said, "Hey, Coach, thanks for everything. I don't know what I would do without you."

Kevin smiled and said, "No problem, Coach."

Del turned and headed to go talk to Randy and figure out how he was going to have one of the toughest conversations he ever had to have with a player... and probably his parents.

Ideas to Consider:

- **While Del and Randy Watson will decide what to do about Connor's situation, what does Kevin think he should do? Is that the right decision? What is Del most concerned with at this point?**

Chapter 41

Del and Randy sat down in the bleachers and talked. After Del explained what happened, Randy agreed that Connor needed to sit for the game. Del's rule stated that a second technical foul was an automatic suspension for the next game. Randy said it didn't matter how Del had handled it in tonight's game. It was there in black and white that tomorrow he couldn't play. Randy also reminded Del that Connor's behavior throughout the season had been anything but exemplary. If this were a kid who had done nothing wrong all season long, it might be a little tougher to feel the need to enforce this rule at this time. Yet, even in that instance, the final decision would still be that the player would have to sit.

"But with Connor's behavior throughout the year, this is kind of a no-brainer, isn't it?" asked Randy.

Del looked out toward the action on the court, scenes of Connor's misbehaviors all flashing through his head in milliseconds. He nodded his head and said, "Yeah, I guess it is."

Randy looked at Del with a bit of a sideways glance. "You guess it is?! You mean you're not convinced of it yet?"

"No," said Del. "I mean, yes, I'm convinced of it. It's just that I've been so blinded by my own desire to win, that I guess I overlooked his other transgressions. You know, none of them ever rose to a cut-and-dried, easy-to-see violation of a policy. He kept skating right above the line, sometimes dipping over it enough that it got our attention. But he never just rammed right through it, so I just never jumped to that level of punishment for him. But as I process through my head all the little things he did, they all add up."

Randy nodded and said, "Absolutely. Del, you have to sit him. There is no alternative. While I can't make you sit him from an athletic department policy standpoint, I am telling you as the AD that you have to sit him or else you will lose your team and probably lose your parents, other than his.

Del said, "So when do you think would be the best time to do it? Tonight or tomorrow? If tomorrow, would it be better in the morning, afternoon, or right before the game?"

Randy said, "That's a good question. What are you thinking?"

Del said, "I keep running through each scenario. Each has its own pros and cons. Tonight gets it out of the way and gets us moving forward immediately with everyone knowing what we need to do. But it also means Connor could do something stupid in the hotel tonight to cause a problem."

"True," said Randy. "But it would be done. You will probably also have a parent conversation that will follow, but that would also be done."

"Yeah, you're right," said Del. "Tomorrow morning is probably the only other good option. For that, the benefit is we have an evening of normalcy, whatever that is for the night before a state championship. But that one has me meeting with his parents on game day, when I want to be focused on getting ready for the game. It also means probably the worst night of my coaching life, playing all the scenarios in my head all night long. I get that I might not sleep all that well anyway. But it should be because I'm excited and nervous about the state championship game, not about talking to a kid and his parents."

"I think you may have just come up with your answer," said Randy. "You need to talk to him tonight."

Del asked, "Where and how do you think it would be best?"

"When are you headed back to the hotel?" asked Randy.

"Right after this game." Del was thinking through the schedule for the evening. "We've ordered pizzas to be delivered at 10:15. We're going to meet in the breakfast room and eat pizza and watch some film from our game with Centennial. I was going to let the boys stay up a little later tonight and sleep in a little longer tomorrow since we don't play until so late tomorrow."

"Yeah, that's a good idea," said Randy. "Well, maybe you better talk to Connor before you eat and meet with the team. That way you can let the team know, and you guys can begin the process of preparing for Centennial without him."

"Yeah, that sounds like a plan," said Del. "Will you be around the hotel?"

"Oh, yeah," said Randy. "I don't have any plans."

"Why don't you come join us for pizza? More importantly, though, I was hoping you'd be around once I tell Connor, in case I need some help with him or his parents," said Del. "I'm sure they will want to meet with me, and I might want you there when that happens."

"Absolutely," said Randy. "I'll be around."

"Thanks," said Del.

Randy said, "Sure. No problem."

Del continued, "And sorry for all that you've had to deal with and for how I've handled things through the years." He paused and said, "You know, I watched my dad coaching all those years, and while I saw and heard the BS that went with the job, I guess it never really registered with me as being such a big part of it. He just never seemed to let it get to him. I wonder if it was eating him up inside, and he just never let me see it."

"I imagine that was part of it," said Randy. "But he also didn't have a lot of this kind of stuff to deal with. I mean, sure he had to deal with inappropriate behaviors at times. But the key was that he dealt with them. He dealt with them right away, and he dealt with them the same way all the time. He had standards, he lived by the standards, and he made sure his teams lived by the standards. When they didn't, he held them accountable."

"I've got a lot of catching up to do if I want to be like him, don't I?" asked Del.

"Well, in some ways I would agree with that," said Randy. "But the other side of that is, quit trying to be your dad. You're not him. Take the good things he did, but apply them within the context of who you are. You're not *Mason* Brooks; you're *Del* Brooks. You have the same last name and the same blood in you. But other than that, you're you, not him. You be you. Just be the best you that you can be."

Del sat there absorbing everything that Randy had just said. He was right. Del was not his dad. He needed to forge his own path, while also staying true to the principles and standards that his dad had taught him. He needed to change and change quickly if he wanted to continue as a teacher and coach. His new journey needed to start tonight. It needed to start with how he would handle the situation with Connor. And while he knew it was going to be difficult, he couldn't wait to get to the hotel and meet with Connor and start down this new path. Where it would take him, he didn't know. He just knew it was where he needed to go.

Ideas to Consider:

- **Randy and Del come up with a plan for dealing with Connor. Does it appear Del is taking the right steps to improve?**

- **Why does it appear to Del that his dad didn't have to deal with all that Del has to deal with? What does Randy believe is the reason it looked that way?**

Chapter 42

On the bus ride back to the hotel, Del was lost in his thoughts. Suddenly, he felt a touch on his shoulder, turned and saw Remington standing in the aisle, with Nick and Tim behind him. Remington said, "Coach, can we talk to you?"

Del said, "Sure, sit down." Braden got up from his seat across the aisle from Del and moved to the seat behind. Remington sat down in the seat opposite Del. Nick was behind him, and Tim was directly behind Del. Brian Jackson had been sitting in the window seat behind Del and Kevin already, and he sat up straight when Tim stepped in to sit down in the seat next to him. Del leaned out into the aisle, and said, "What's up?"

Remington said, "Remember when we came up and sat like this on the bus ride home from our last game last year?"

Del said, "I do remember. You guys were excited about the possibilities of getting to state and doing some damage. You knew that if you put in the time and effort, you could win a state championship. And look at you now. You're playing for a state championship tomorrow night. It's a testament to working hard and sticking together and believing in one another. I'm so proud of you guys for all that you have done."

"Thanks, Coach," said Remington. "This is awesome. It feels good knowing that we accomplished what we set out to accomplish." Remington turned and looked back down the aisle of the bus. Del wondered what or who Remington was looking for. Remington turned back and said, "We want to talk about Connor, Coach."

Del said, "What about him?"

Nick piped in immediately with, "We don't think he should play tomorrow." Del turned his head towards Nick, and Nick continued, "Coach, your rule says if you get a second 'T', you sit out the rest of that game and then the entire next one."

Del winced a little bit as he heard one of his players quote his own rule, a rule that Del had not followed a few hours earlier in the semi-final game of the state tournament. Del tried to figure out how to respond. Remington said, "Coach, last year we came up here to talk to you about how we wanted to get to the tournament and how we were going to do it. Connor wasn't part of those plans back then. We didn't even know him. We knew we could do it with everyone we had coming back. Coach, every one of us who was here last year is still here. But we added guys into the mix that have really helped out. Of course, Connor is a big addition, and he can do things that no one else can. But he also does other things that no one else does and not in a good way. He doesn't follow any of your rules. He's a terrible teammate, especially to the young guys. He's all about himself. He hangs out with guys who are trouble both in and out of school. And he's got an F in Spanish, so he shouldn't even be playing."

"Where did you hear that?" asked Del, a bit shocked.

"From Connor!" said Tim. "He's been bragging about how he's failing Spanish, but because he's so good and we need him to win state, you let him play."

"I never said anything like that," said Del. "Ms. Gregson didn't put him on the eligibility list because he's working his way up, and she didn't want him to sit."

"That's not what he's telling everyone," said Nick. "He said you said we need him, so that's why he's still playing."

Del's mind flashed back to his own words. How many times had he told Connor, "We need you"? How many times had he told Kevin or other people that they needed Connor?

Remington said, "Coach, we don't need him. Like I was saying before, so many other guys have come along. Jimmy has been awesome. He's become a beast, and he fills in great for Connor. And Bickford has done a nice job when he's been in there. We knew Mike and Cory were going to do great this year, and they have."

Remington paused and then said, "Coach, I'm telling you—" Remington stopped and looked at Nick, Tim, and Brian and said, "Sorry, *we're* telling you. We don't need Connor. We'll be fine without him. We knew last year we were going to get here this year without him. With what he did tonight, how he's been all year, we're telling you, he shouldn't play tomorrow."

Del looked around at their faces. They weren't smiling now. There was an intensity about their looks that said they meant business. Del leaned into the aisle and motioned to Remington, Nick, and Tim to lean into the aisle, too. Brian leaned over Tim's shoulder to try to hear. Del spoke quietly. "I appreciate you guys telling me this. Coach Nixon and I talked about this earlier, and I met with Mr. Watson during the Centennial game. We had already decided that Connor is going to sit tomorrow. I will be telling him when we get back to the hotel."

The boys' demeanors seemed to change with Del's words. They looked relieved, almost happy. Del said, "I need each of you to give me your word that you are not going to say anything to him or to anyone else about it until I get to talk to Connor. He deserves to hear this from me, and not anyone else. Get it?"

Remington said, "Got it, Coach. Not a word."

Del said, "I also might need your help afterward in making sure everyone else understands why this had to be this way. They will need to be reassured, too, that we will be fine without him."

Nick said, "We got ya', Coach. We've already been telling them all that."

"Okay, good," said Del. "Now go back to your seats. We'll be back to the hotel in a few minutes. The pizzas will be here in about a half hour. We'll meet in the breakfast room at 10:15."

"Sounds good, Coach," said Remington.

Kevin turned to Del and said, "We're going to be just fine tomorrow. Those boys are ready. They've got something to prove. They didn't know who Connor was last year, and they planned on getting here. Now they want to prove that they didn't need him this year. While on paper we're not nearly as good without him, I wouldn't bet against us. Those kids are going to be out to show the state that they're pretty frickin' good, too."

"I think you're right," said Del. "I just hope they're ready to prove it tomorrow."

Ideas to Consider:

- **As good as Connor is, why do the boys want to play the state championship without him? Do you think they can win without Connor? Why or why not?**

Chapter 43

After they got back to their rooms, Del asked Kevin to get Connor and bring him to Del's room. When they got there, Del was sitting in the chair by the desk. Connor sat down on the end of the bed and asked, "What's up, Coach?"

Del said, "Connor, I owe you an apology." This immediately put Connor at ease. Del figured that would happen, and he wanted Connor to be in a better frame of mind to receive the news Del was about to deliver. "I did not handle you the right way in the game tonight when you got that technical."

Connor quickly realized that maybe this was not going to be a good thing he was going to hear. Del continued. "As you know from when you got your first technical at the Centennial game and I talked to you, our policy states that if you get a second technical at any point in the season, you are supposed to come out of the game for the rest of that game. Do you remember us talking about that that night?"

Connor nodded his head and said, "Yeah."

"The problem is," said Del, "I forgot that tonight. Well, that's not 100% accurate. I forgot it in the moment. Then I remembered it. What I forgot at that point is what's most important. I got so caught up in winning a game that I just blew off my own rule. I had done that the first time, too, at Centennial. I didn't take you out right away that night. Again, I was so caught up in winning the game that I just kept you out there. Then tonight, I did the same thing."

Connor dropped his head. He didn't like where this was going. Del continued. "Fortunately, I have good people around me who reminded me what this coaching thing is all about. Yeah, we want to win games and championships, but we want to win the right way. If I don't follow my own rules, what I end up teaching you, the rest of the players, and anyone who watches us is that our values and our standards only matter if they help us win. If they get in the way of winning, then I can look the other way and throw them out the window."

Del leaned forward and said, "Well, I just can't do that anymore. I can't live a lie like that. I need to be true to myself, my standards, and our team's standards. I let you, your teammates, our school, and our community down tonight when I didn't take you out of the game. And while you made some big plays down the stretch that helped us win the game and go to the state championship, it came at a high price. I lost my integrity. What kind of a leader, what kind of a person have I become that I am willing to throw those things away to win a darn basketball game? I realized I had sunk to a new low. Well, I'm done sinking to low levels just to try to win games. That's not who I want to be, and that's not the kind of lesson I want to teach you and all the young men I coach."

Del couldn't tell if any of this registered with Connor. He continued. "The other part of the rule says you're supposed to sit out the following game. If I'm going to regain any dignity and integrity, I have to uphold the rule and do what's right. Therefore, you're not playing in the game tomorrow night. You can still be with the team and sit on the bench, but you'll be in street clothes."

Connor said, "What?! You mean I don't get to play at all?"

Del responded, "That's right."

Connor was beside himself. "Why don't you just suspend me for a half or something, not the whole game? How can you do that? Coach, we don't stand a chance against Centennial without me? You saw what happened the last time, and that was only for a few minutes. Coach, I get that you're trying to act with integrity and all that kind of stuff, but this is the state championship. You don't get these kinds of opportunities every year, and until I showed up, you never made it this far. You need me. You've said so yourself."

"I know I have, Connor," said Del. "And there were times I believed it. But what I didn't realize was that while I was busy buying in to that belief, I was too blind to see the belief that I had at the end of last year and all summer long—the belief in the players that were here all last year, all spring, all summer, all fall, and all season long. At the end of last year, I believed in the boys that we had coming back. I knew we could get here and win a state championship with them. None of us knew you existed then. We just knew that we were good and if we worked hard enough, we could win it all this year. The more I watched them work all spring, the more I knew I was right."

Connor dropped his head. Del continued, "Then you showed up. You were unlike any player we had in the program with your size and talent. I started thinking that you were the missing link to our state championship dream. The problem was that I got blinded by your talent, so I didn't see all the other things that you brought, too—bad attitude, terrible work ethic, poor teammate, questionable behavior outside of school. All I saw was a 6'6" post player with strength and skills. The more I focused on that, the less I focused on doing what was right. Ultimately, I let you down. I let you continue to play even when you were not doing what you should have been doing. I'm sorry for that. I taught you the wrong lessons and in so doing, I taught everyone else the wrong lessons, too. Well, that ends tonight. I am doing what I should have done a long time ago."

Connor looked up. Del could see his eyes were filled with tears. He said, "So that's it? There's nothing I can do to change your mind?"

"No," said Del. "I can't do this anymore. Our team means too much to me to look the other way with regards to your behavior anymore."

Connor got up and walked past Kevin and out the door. After Connor was out of the room, Kevin said, "Nice job, Coach."

Del said, "I hated that. I hate coaching sometimes, and right now is one of those times. I don't want to have to tell a kid that kind of thing. I don't want to have to tell a kid he's done. There's nothing fun about that."

"You did the right thing, though," said Kevin. "You just taught him and your team a valuable lesson. But maybe even more importantly, you just taught yourself a lesson. This profession only matters when we do it the right way. It's about so much more than just winning. It's about teaching kids right and wrong and living up to our standards and values. When we don't teach that and don't do that ourselves, we've lost. But you just did the right thing."

"Thanks, Coach," said Del.

Kevin said, "Your dad would be proud of you right now."

Del dropped his head. His dad's smiling face flashed before his eyes. Kevin was right. This was how his dad would have wanted Del to handle this. He would be proud of Del for doing the right thing in a tough situation.

"Thanks," said Del. "Now if I could only have my dad here in a little while when I'm sure I'll get the call or visit from Connor's parents."

"He'll be here with you," said Kevin. "Just feel him inside your heart. He'll help you through it, help you say the right things. He was there with you a couple minutes ago helping you through it with Connor. He'll be there again when you talk with them." Kevin paused and said, "And so will I."

"Good," said Del, "'Cuz I'll need all the help I can get!"

Ideas to Consider:

- **Del finally did the right thing with regards to Connor. How does he feel? How does Kevin Nixon make him feel he did the right thing?**

- **Do you think he is doing the right thing, or is the state championship not the right time to start doing something like this?**

Chapter 44

As expected, Patrick McDonald called Del about ten minutes later. Patrick tried to sound calm and reasonable on the phone, but his voice continued to rise with each sentence. Del had been prepared for the call, and he said, "Mr. McDonald, I am about to go into a team meeting with the boys. We will be done around 11:00. Why don't we meet then?"

"Fine," said Patrick. "Where?"

Del had thought it would be best if they were in a somewhat public venue to help keep the meeting from getting too out of hand, but not too public that everyone heard them. He said, "We're meeting the boys for pizza in the breakfast room. We could meet in there afterwards."

"Pizza?!" asked Patrick. "Pizza is your big team meeting?! Pizza is more important than you talking to me about kicking my son off your team?"

Del said, "First of all, nobody kicked your son off the team. He's not playing tomorrow night. But I told him he can be on the bench with us. Secondly, we're eating pizza while going over the scouting report for tomorrow night's game. So, yeah, at the moment, it is more important. But I'm happy to meet with you right after that."

"11:00?" asked Patrick.

"Yeah, we should be done around 11:00," said Del.

"Fine," said Patrick, and he hung up the phone.

"Well, that went well," Del said sarcastically to Kevin.

Kevin said, "Why don't you let Braden and me handle the logistics of getting the pizzas set up, so you can get ready for meeting with him? Then you can come in at around 10:30 and go over the scouting report and cover what you want to cover."

"That sounds like a plan," said Del.

When Kevin left the room, Del turned around at the desk and started writing down a few notes on a pad of paper. He tried to remember every transgression that Connor had throughout the season and even back into the fall. He realized that he was filling up pages of notebook paper with all of the incidents Connor had been in. He said to himself, "Look at this list. Why didn't

I see this before?" Del wished he could turn back the clock and do what he was doing now about three or four months ago. Maybe then he would have handled things a bit differently, and he wouldn't be in this predicament now.

At 10:25, Del walked into the breakfast room where the team was laughing and enjoying pizzas together. The mood was light and fun, and everyone seemed to be getting along really well. As Del looked around the room, he didn't see Connor anywhere. Del walked over to Kevin and Braden and asked, "Was Connor down here at all?"

"Nope," said Kevin. "Haven't seen him."

Del walked over to Remington and nodded for him to follow Del. They stepped out of the room and Del asked, "Any idea where Connor is?"

"I think he's at his parents' room," said Remington. "Brian said that he came into their room about a half-hour ago, and he was pissed. Said you told him he's not playing tomorrow and that you're an idiot, and we need him to win and stuff like that. Brian said he packed up all of his stuff in his bag and left the room. Brian asked him where he was going and he said to his parents."

"Okay, thanks, Rem."

Remington said, "No, Coach. Thank you. That kid was trouble from the day he got here. I wanted to give him a chance, so I was slow to see it, too. But everyone else wanted him either dealt with or gone a long time ago."

"I know," said Del. "I just wrote down all the things that he has done over the year, and it just blew me away to see it all on paper and see how much I let go."

Remington was about to say something to Del, but he stopped.

Del said, "What is it?"

"Nothing," said Remington. "Not yet. You'll hear in a little bit."

Del was a bit puzzled, but he said, "Okay, now you've got me nervous."

"Don't be, Coach," he said. "You're gonna' like it."

"Well, now I'm intrigued," said Del while rubbing his hands together.

They stepped back into the breakfast room. Kevin, Braden, Nick, Tim, and Mike Visteen were all picking up trash and empty pizza boxes and putting them into garbage cans. That was one of the culture things that Kevin loved about this team. The older guys were the ones who did all the work, took care of all the responsibilities. Usually, it was Remington leading the way, but with him out of the room, Nick and Tim took over. While Kevin helped Del learn the value of teaching this servant mentality to the senior leaders and Del ran with it, Kevin knew that the credit for how well it worked went to those seniors who took on the responsibility and made it a core value of their program.

Del said, "All right guys, take a seat. Eyes and ears up here." He looked around and said, "First of all, when you see Mr. and Mrs. Swanson, you make sure you thank them for the pizzas. They bought those for us tonight." Charles and Jeanne Swanson had kids in the program when Del's dad was coaching, and they had been strong supporters of the basketball program ever since then.

"Next, we need to deal with the elephant in the room," said Del. Brian Jackson looked around like there might actually be an elephant in the room. Del said, "No, Brian, there's not an actual elephant in the room." The boys laughed. "What that means is that there is an issue that's kind of hanging in the air that no one wants to talk about but that needs to be discussed."

Brian smiled, nodded his head, and said, "Oh. Okay, Coach I get it."

Nick said, "Next time Coach will draw you a picture, Bri!" and the team erupted again.

"All right," Del said smiling. "That's enough. Let's deal with this issue. As you probably all heard by now, Connor is not playing tomorrow night."

Del looked around to see how the players were reacting. He saw a couple of head nods, and that was it. "As you know, our rule on technical fouls is that if you get a second 'T' during the season, you sit out the following game. Tonight, Connor got his second one. Therefore, he is sitting out tomorrow. I want to apologize to all of you. Not about sitting Connor out or the rule or anything like that. I want to apologize to you for how I handled it. Actually, I should apologize for how I handled a lot of things this year.

"But with regards to this situation, I want to apologize for not actually following my own rule. The rule also states that the first 'T' someone gets, they need to come out of the game right then. I didn't do that with Connor at Centennial. I eventually did after Coach Nixon reminded me. But the next part of the rule says that when a player gets their second 'T' of the season, they are to be removed from the game immediately, and they don't play again. I failed to follow that rule tonight. I was so wrapped up in winning the game, that I went against my own rule, my own standards, my own values in order to try to win a game.

"Boys, there is so much more to playing sports than just winning games and championships. There are so many life lessons that we can learn from sports. I try to set up moments for us to do just that. That rule can help teach a lesson. And I totally screwed it up. The only lesson I was teaching you is that if you have talent, and you can help us win, I'll look the other way on breaking a rule or on inappropriate behavior. And to tell you the truth, this was not the first time I've done this. I did it in past years, too."

Every player who had been in the program in the last couple years immediately saw Cade Clemons's face flash before their eyes. Del continued, "And quite honestly, I did it at other times this year with Connor. I just didn't do what I should have done because I didn't want to hurt our chances of winning. I knew we had a good team coming back from last year and that we could contend for a state championship long before Connor showed up. I just got blinded by what he brought to the team that we didn't have before, so I didn't handle him the way I should have. For that I am truly sorry."

Del looked around the room and said, "Boys, I hope you can forgive me. I hope you can see that I really do still believe in what we are capable of—this group, right here—what we can do tomorrow night. I hope you're as excited as I am about the opportunity before us tomorrow night." He then asked, "Any questions or comments from any of you?"

Brian Jackson asked, "So is Connor kicked off the team?"

Del said, "No, not at all. He is suspended for the game tomorrow. But he is still part of this team, and I told him to sit on the bench in his street clothes, which is what would have happened if this had been at any other time of the year. Also, you guys need to make sure he knows he is still part of this team. This is going to be difficult for him and a bit awkward, so he needs to know he has friends here and that you want him here."

Nick said, "Coach, not to be a jerk, but he doesn't have a lot of friends here, and quite honestly, not too many of us want him here."

Del said, "Well, Nick, tonight and tomorrow, that has to change. He needs our help. He helped us in some different ways this year. Now we need to help him. I'm counting on all of you to work to make that happen."

The boys nodded their heads in understanding. Del said, "Anyone else?"

Some of the boys just shook their heads while a few of them looked around to each other. Remington stood up and said, "I do, Coach." He half-faced the team and half-faced Del and said, "Coach, we're all ready."

Del asked, "What do you mean 'we're all ready'? Who?"

"Us. The guys. The team. We're all ready to win this thing tomorrow night. You won't regret this decision about Connor. I know it wasn't easy, and maybe it should have happened earlier. But it didn't and we're at this point now. But not only was it the right thing to do, Coach, it was also the best thing to do."

Remington looked around at his teammates and said, "We—this group right here—we get to be the team we planned on being since last year ended. We get to be the team we were meant to be. We get to show the entire state who we are and who we knew last year we were going to be this year. We get to do what we knew we could do all along the way we knew we could do it. we get to be our best tomorrow night when our best is needed. I can't wait to go out there tomorrow night and play with you guys."

Remington turned to Del and said, "I can't wait to go out tomorrow night and play with my brothers here, Coach. And to go to battle with you as the team we were supposed to be. Thanks for doing this for us, Coach. We are so ready for this moment. We won't let you down."

As Remington finished and started to sit down, the entire room exploded in cheers and clapping. The guys sitting around him were high-fiving him and patting him on the back. Del looked around, looked at Kevin, and said, "So I had this scouting report to go over with you now, but quite honestly, you don't need this. You're ready to give Centennial everything they can handle. Let's go kick Centennial's ass tomorrow night!" and Del ripped the sheet of paper in two and threw the pieces up in the air.

The boys jumped up out of their chairs and mobbed Del, chanting "Wolves! Wolves! Wolves!" Finally, Remington raised his hand in the air above his teammates. They all put their hands up with his, and just as he had been doing prior to the last few games, Remington yelled out, "Focus on three— 1, 2, 3," and they all yelled, "FOCUS!" He then followed that with "Discipline on three—1, 2, 3," and they responded with "DISCIPLINE!"

However, this time as the boys started to turn out of the huddle, Remington had kept his hand in the air and he yelled, "Not yet, boys." They all turned put their hands up with his, and he shouted, "Champions on three—1, 2, 3," and they all yelled even louder "CHAMPIONS!"

Ideas to Consider:

- **Del gets the call from Connor's dad that he was expecting. Do you think Del handled the call the right way?**

- **How does the team react to Del's news that Connor isn't playing? What does Remington say to the team that lets Del know they are ready?**

Chapter 45

The boys filed out of the breakfast room. Braden Larson went to chaperone them while Del and Kevin talked with Connor's parents. Del said to Kevin, "What a great group of kids. I can't wait for tomorrow night."

"Me, too," said Kevin. "I think they are so ready to show people who they really are. It's going to be fun."

"Yeah, well, now I get to prepare for some other fun, huh?" Del asked.

Kevin said, "You'll be fine. Do you have anything written down?"

"Oh yeah," Del said. "I wrote down each incident from the year that Connor did. Look at this," Del said opening up his notebook. "These pages are filled with just incidents that I could remember in about ten minutes."

"Wow!" said Kevin. "Really makes you wonder what we were thinking."

"Thanks, Kev," said Del, "but I'm the idiot who let him keep playing."

"I get that," said Kevin, "but still, we should have all seen it clearer than we did. I guess when you're down in the weeds with things happening and all that is swirling around, you kind of don't see it all that clearly."

Randy Watson walked in the room. "Did I miss the pizza?" he asked.

"We saved you a few slices," said Kevin. "And let me tell you, keeping twelve teenage boys from eating those wasn't easy!"

Randy smiled and said, "No, I imagine not. That was probably the toughest coaching decision you guys have had to make all weekend."

Del half-smiled and said, "I wish that was the toughest decision I had to make all weekend."

Randy said, "Yeah, no kidding. Well, you've made the right decision with Connor. How did it go when you told him?"

"Not great, but I guess it could have been worse," said Del. "He couldn't understand why I was doing it, asked if my decision was final, and when I told him it was, he walked out of the room."

"Did you tell him he can sit on the bench tomorrow night?"

"Yeah," said Del.

"And?" asked Randy, before taking a bite of pizza.

"Nothing," said Del. "I don't think he cares one bit to sit on that bench if he's not playing." Just then, there was a knock on the half-opened door to the breakfast room, and Del said, "Come on in."

Patrick and Debra McDonald walked in. Del said an awkward, "Hello. How are you doing?" and immediately regretted asking that.

"How do you think I'm doing, Coach?" asked Patrick.

Debra tapped him on the arm and said, "Pat," in a mildly scolding tone.

Patrick looked at her and then back at Del and said, "Sorry. It's just that this really caught us by surprise." They all sat down around a table.

Del said, "Well, I can see how that could happen. But I assume Connor didn't remind you after the Centennial game about the rule on technical fouls that he and I discussed and that you all signed off on in our Policy Sheet."

"No, he hadn't until he came to our room tonight," said Patrick. "I don't have the Policy Sheet with me, but I don't remember that rule."

"I have one here," said Del, and he handed it over to Patrick. Del pointed to where the rule was in the Policy Sheet and said, "It's right here." Patrick held the sheet so he and Debra could both read it.

After reading the rule, Patrick said, "Coach, I see that the rule says that he sits the following game after his second technical. But it also says he's supposed to sit out the rest of the game immediately after receiving the second technical. You didn't sit him out tonight, and he ended up winning that game for you."

Thoughts raced through Del's mind on how to respond, but he stayed focused on the main point. "You're right it does say that. And quite honestly, I got caught up in the moment. I put the desire to win a game ahead of doing the right thing and living by our standards. I let winning cloud my judgment. One of the best things about youth and school sports is that they teach kids great lessons about life. The best lessons happen when we intentionally work to teach them. And in that moment, I taught the absolute worst lesson I could teach—that it's okay to throw away your standards and values and rules if it will help you win. It took some very smart people in my life to point it out to me after the game what I had done."

Del continued, "I realized then and there, that I had let the team down, let myself down, and even let Connor down, by not doing the right thing. I realized that I needed to do the right thing at that moment, what I should have done originally, and follow my own rule. Otherwise, I would be continuing to live a lie, and not following a standard that is very important to me."

"Yeah, see that's something I don't get," said Patrick. "Why is this so important? Come on now. Kids will be kids. They make mistakes. They do stupid things sometimes. You point it out, let 'em know it was wrong, maybe give 'em a small punishment and then allow them the chance to prove themselves again and handle themselves the right way. Why can't you do that here?"

"You're absolutely right," said Del. "And that is exactly what I am doing. That's how the rule is written. The first time he got a technical was at Centennial. I pulled him out and talked to him. The rule states that I will then decide if he can go back in. That night, I chose not to have him go back in. When Jimmy Thompson went in for him, it gave us a chance to see what he could do, and he responded well. I felt that could really help our team down the stretch, and it has. But even more important than that, what Connor did, flipping off the crowd and making a lewd comment, was enough for me to decide that he shouldn't go back in. I couldn't reward that behavior with letting him play again."

"Yeah, and look what it got you," said Patrick. "You lost the game. If Connor was playing, you would have won."

"Maybe," said Del. "But we would have lost in a much bigger way. We would have lost our own self-respect. We would have maybe lost our team believing that any of our rules and standards mean anything. So, I'm okay with the fact that we lost a non-conference game against a really good opponent with a kid who behaved that way not playing at the end of the game."

Patrick tried a different tactic. "Coach, look. Connor's a good kid. He made one mistake. Well, okay, two mistakes. My God he's 16-years-old. What 16-year-old doesn't make mistakes? You gonna' tell me you didn't make mistakes at 16?"

"No, I'm not gonna' tell you that," said Del. "Of course, I made mistakes. And when I did, *my dad* punished me. He tried to teach me the lessons that I am now trying to teach my players." Del paused to see if Patrick McDonald got his point that Patrick should have been the one holding Connor accountable, that *he* should be right there with Del saying this was what Connor needed.

Del continued, "My dad was my coach. I got a technical foul my junior year in our first game against Jefferson. Three minutes to go, we're down by 2, and I got mad at a referee's call. I yelled out, 'Oh come on! No way!' Boom! I get hit with a 'T.' My dad had a sub at the scorer's table faster than that referee could get there to report the technical. When I came off the floor, he said to me, 'I don't care who you are. You will never behave that way on a floor for this team again if you intend to stay out there playing. Do you understand?' I nodded, walked to the end of the bench, and watched my team lose by 3. So, yeah, I made mistakes, and I know a little bit about what Connor's going through."

Debra asked, "Did you ever get a second technical?"

"No way," said Del. "I knew my dad meant every word he said. I loved playing for him, and he loved coaching me. But I also knew that I was just another player on the team when we got between the lines. And if my dad had a rule, it didn't matter who you were. You followed it, or you paid the price."

Del paused as Debra McDonald nodded her head, seemingly understanding and agreeing with Del and his father's handling of that situation. Patrick said, "Yeah, I remember your dad. I graduated from Sacajawea in '95. He was a good coach. Some of my friends played for him, and they loved him. But he sure seemed hard on them at times. I don't know if I could have handled it."

Del said, "Yeah, he was tough, but he was fair. You knew exactly where you stood with him. You also knew that even though he was tough, he loved you. My friends would tell me that they felt like he was their second dad. In fact, one of my friends said he felt like my dad was more like a dad to him than his own dad."

Del continued, "Ever since those days, I wanted to be a basketball coach. And I wanted to be a basketball coach just like my dad. I've tried to model myself after him, while still being myself, too. But the last couple of years, I have fallen short too many times. While my dad's shoes were big shoes to fill, I wanted to try to do right by him, make him proud of me. Tonight, after I left Connor in the game, I realized that there was no way he would have been proud of me the way I handled that. I knew then I had to do the right thing. I had to follow the standard that I had established and sit Connor out tomorrow night. Two wrongs could not make this right. The only thing that can make this right is doing the right thing. Sorry if you don't agree with me on this, but that's how it has to be."

Debra was nodding her head in agreement and understanding. But Patrick couldn't let it go. "But it's the state championship, Coach! How many chances does a kid get to play in the state championship? You're denying my kid that opportunity. And you're also hurting your chances of winning it."

"Well," said Del, "to tell you the truth, I still like our chances. And if Connor does the right things next year, and starts turning things around, I like our chances of him leading us back here next year."

"But you're so close now," said Patrick. "How can you risk that by not having your best player out there?"

Del paused, trying to figure out how best to address Patrick's comment. Finally, he said, "Our best player will be playing tomorrow night. Remington Roberts is the best player I have ever coached, and he may be the best player I've ever seen in person. And many other coaches have told me the same thing. Connor is an excellent player with a lot of skills, and he has the potential to be great, too. But he's going to have to figure some things out before that happens."

Patrick was a bit taken aback, and his demeanor changed as he said, "Like what? He's got all the tools."

"Yeah, he's got tools," said Del. "But tools are only as good as the person using them. Connor has a lot of work to do in a variety of areas. First, he doesn't like to work very hard. Second, he isn't all that committed to his teammates. Third, he isn't committed to his classes. The only reason he is even playing in this tournament is that he has the nicest Spanish teacher ever, and she didn't put him on the 'F' list even though, technically, he is failing Spanish. And finally, his behavior outside of the team is going to need to get cleaned up."

"What the hell are you talking about?" asked Patrick.

Debra said, "Pat, calm down."

Patrick said, "No, Debra I won't calm down. I don't know where all this is coming from. Where do you come off saying those things about his behavior?"

Del opened up his notebook and flipped through the pages of notes he had written on Connor's behavior. "These are some of the incidents that Connor has had happen since you guys moved here. Heck, not even since you moved here I guess, but at least since I have known him. He skates right on the edge. He pushes the envelope with teachers and rules and the law."

Patrick and Debra were reading through the list that Del had put together while Del was speaking. Reading the list of Connor's behavior, Debra's eyes started welling up with tears. Del reached over and grabbed the napkin holder and slid it to her. She whispered, "Thank you."

Patrick said, "Well, I knew about some of these things but not all of them. Why didn't you tell me about these? Why didn't I hear about them?"

Del said, "Some of them would have been from the school, not from me. Some of them were things that we addressed with Connor individually. As you look at that list, you realize that any one of them is not the worst thing that could happen. Maybe his grades would be the one problem that is big on its own. And the potential of what could have happened at that party if he had gotten there earlier. But for a lot of these, you might just blow off as a boy being a boy. But when you look at that list in its entirety, you see that Connor is doing a lot of things he shouldn't be doing."

Del looked at Debra. She had her head down and was wiping her eyes. "That's what I mean when I say he needs to clean up his behavior. Your son has a ton of potential. He could definitely go to college somewhere to play basketball, maybe even a Division 1 school. But there is no way any D1 school is going to take a chance on him with that list right there. He's going to have to change if he wants that to happen. But if he does make those changes, he will be better, our team next year will be better, and he will have a better chance to go to a better school. But it all has to start with him. He has to decide that he wants to do that. If he does, the sky's the limit for him."

Patrick looked like a defeated man. He kept looking at the sheets of paper with the things that Connor had done, then at Del, then at Debra. He was searching for something more to argue. Finally, he said, "But. . ." He dropped his head then looked up again and said, "But what about . . ."

He let the thought trail off. Debra reached out, took his hand, and said, "Come on Pat. Connor's back in the room, and Coach should be with his team."

She turned to Del and said, "Coach, can Connor still be with you guys tomorrow if he stays with us tonight? I don't know if he feels comfortable being back with the boys right now."

Del said, "Absolutely. Whenever he's ready, we'd love to have him back."

She said, "Okay. Thank you." She stood up and said, "Come on, Pat."

Patrick McDonald stood up and nodded his head but didn't say a word. They turned around and walked out the door.

Del turned to Kevin and Randy, and said sarcastically, "Well, that was fun."

Randy said, "You did a nice job with them. You maintained your composure, said some things that he needed to hear, but you weren't mean about it. That was really good."

Del said, "Thanks. I hated having to do that, but I know I had to."

Kevin said, "Once again, your dad would have been proud watching you handle that."

Del fought back a tear, and said, "Thanks. I sure hope so."

Ideas to Consider:

- **What is Patrick McDonald most upset about? Do you think he has a legitimate point, or should he be worried more about something else?**
- **How do you think Del handled the meeting?**

Chapter 46

"No way," said Jenny. "I'll believe it when I see it." She and Remington were sitting in the hallway outside of his room talking before he had to go in to go to bed.

"I know. That's what I thought, too" said Remington. "But Coach seems serious this time. I've never seen him open up like that, talking about how he totally let us down and himself down and his dad down. He was about to get pretty emotional."

"You really think that he won't let Connor play? Come on, Rem. You've heard this kind of thing so many times from him."

"I know, but I'm telling you, there was something totally different about him tonight. And when I talked with him about us wanting to do this without Connor, he was totally on board with it. It's like he had forgotten all that we talked about last year on the bus ride home, and all that we did throughout the spring and summer to make it happen. But now, he remembers, and he knows we're ready to win it all, with or without Connor."

Jenny looked down at the paisley pattern in the hotel carpeting, not sure if she should say what was on her mind. "Rem, do you really think you can win without him?"

"Absolutely!" he replied. "I'm sure of it. Connor's great in terms of his skills, but we're a much better *team* without him. And every one of us wants to show the state how good we are. Remember, we didn't know Connor when we all made the plan to get here and win the whole thing. We didn't know him when we started our workouts. Once he was here, we got even more excited. Then we saw how he didn't show up, didn't work that hard, didn't want to join in with us. So we basically said, 'Screw him. We can do this without him.' And we just kept working as if he wasn't going to be with us anyway."

"Yeah, but you've played with him all year long," said Jenny. "Are you sure you can just flip a switch and play without him?"

"I think so," said Remington. "Nick, Tim, Brian, Mike, Cory and a couple of the younger guys were all in on this from day one. And the way Jimmy Thompson and Bob Bickford have continued to get better all year long, yeah, we're ready."

"I sure hope so," said Jenny. "I would love to see you guys holding that state championship trophy tomorrow night. That would be so cool."

"It's all I can think about," said Remington. "This is what I've waited for my whole life playing basketball. When I would watch my dad's teams play down in Phoenix, I would think how much I wanted to play high school basketball. And then, the year they won the state championship there, and I got to be on the bench with them for the games and then out on the floor with them afterwards, I thought, 'I can't wait to do this when I'm in high school.' And now here I am one game away from it. I can't believe it's finally happened."

"It is so cool," said Jenny. "I'm so proud of you." She paused, looked over at him and said, "Do you remember the day we met?"

"Grizzly Park," he said. "One of the greatest days of my life. How could I forget that?"

She smiled and said, "I remember thinking how cute you were the moment I saw you. I hadn't really ever felt that way about boys. But there was something about you that was different. Then you started talking to me, and you were so nice that I realized that was it. Your niceness just kind of showed through you, and it made you cute, too."

"Huh?" said Remington. "That doesn't make sense."

"I know," said Jenny. "Even as I'm saying it, I don't understand what I'm saying. But I know exactly how I felt and how I still feel. You were a combination of cute and nice and friendly, and then pretty soon, you were also helping me with basketball and soccer and anything else I needed help with. And you treated me different than anyone else I ever met. And when you talked about basketball—which was *all the time*—I could tell you were going to be really good. You talked about your dad's state championship and how you wanted to win one, too, I knew right then that this would happen."

"Well, we haven't won it yet, Jen," said Remington. "While I totally believe we can win it, Centennial is really good. They're the only Class A team that's beaten us. They're legit. And I have to admit, not having Connor will make it a lot harder, no doubt. But I just have this strong belief that we will get it done. I just know in my heart that we're going to do it."

"I know it, too," said Jenny, not totally convinced, but at least believing that it could happen.

"Well," said Remington, "I need to get to bed. I don't think I'm going to sleep all that well tonight because I'm so excited, but I at least need to try."

"Okay, Rem," said Jenny. They both stood up and Jenny reached over to him and put her hands around his waist and gave him a kiss. He wanted so badly to kiss her back even more, but he also knew that they were standing in the hall right outside all of the players' and coaches' rooms and that players and coaches were stepping in and out of rooms the whole time they were talking. He was a bit embarrassed that she kissed him there, but he also loved it.

Jenny pulled her face away from his and said, "I hope you can get a good night's rest."

Remington smiled and said, "I'll try." He pulled away from her. "Good night, Jen. See you tomorrow."

"Can't wait, Rem. Good night." Jenny turned and walked down the hall to the elevators to take her up to the room that she and her parents were staying in. Remington turned and opened the door to his room and walked in.

He was rooming with Nick, Tim, and Mike. They were each in their beds watching ESPN's SportsCenter. Nick said, "Did you get Jenny all tucked into bed, Sweetie-Pie?" Tim and Mike laughed.

"No," said Remington. "Just sitting out there talking about Connor and the game tomorrow."

"I can't wait," said Nick. "Centennial doesn't know what's about to hit them."

Remington said, "I sure hope so."

Nick had a puzzled look on his face. "There you go again. Don't you think we can win?"

Remington was struggling with what he really thought, and he tried to save face. "No, it's not that at all. It's just that we've played *with* Connor all year long. We're used to him being on the floor with us for so much of the game. I just hope we aren't looking for him or thinking that he will come up with a big board or bucket for us when we need one."

Tim said, "No way. We can't let that happen. It's up to all of us to step up and fill that gap that's left without him. I'm as glad as anyone that he's not playing, but I'm also smart enough to know that he does a lot of good things for us when he's out there. We need to be the ones to fill that void."

Mike said, "Yeah, but none of us is a big post player."

Tim said, "True. But we all still need to commit to getting boards and attacking the inside. And let's face it—Jimmy has played really well the last month when he's been in there. We just have to really encourage him and pick him up and help him do what he has been doing."

All three boys nodded their agreement with Tim. Remington said, "I hope Jimmy is not too nervous. I mean, I'm sure he is just like all of us. But I hope he feels ready to go. You're right, Tim. He has done well the last month. I think he's ready. I just hope he thinks he is."

"We need to pick him up all day long," said Nick. "Make sure he knows we believe in him and that he's ready for this. Remind him about how good he played against Centennial last time."

"Absolutely," said Remington. "We also need to do the same for Bickford and the rest of the young guys. They're going to be so nervous. Hell, I'm so nervous, and I play all the time. We need to help them stay calm and focused on doing what they do best if they get in. This is truly going to have to be a team effort."

"No doubt," said Nick. "It ain't gonna' be the Rem and Connor Show."

"It never has been," said Remington, a little hurt that Nick would single him out with Connor that way.

"Yeah? Well, tell that to Coach," said Nick.

Remington looked at Nick, looked at the other two and said, "I've got a better idea. Let's all show him."

They all smiled, high-fived each other, and Nick said, "Now you're talking. This is gonna' be so much fun. I can't wait."

Ideas to Consider:

- **Why is Jenny worried about the state championship the next night? What memory does she have that helps her realize that it's going to be okay?**

- **How are Remington and his roommates feeling about the game? Why is belief such an important ingredient to success?**

Chapter 47

State championship Saturday is unlike any other experience for a team. For many players and coaches, it is the first time they are playing in the state championship game. That means it is uncharted territory on how to handle it. Also, it is the ultimate prize that they have been working towards all year long. There is no more after this. They know that today is the last time they will be competing that year and maybe forever. So it carries a different kind of weight and emotion.

This was what Del and the rest of the Sacajawea team were navigating as the night of the game approached. Add to that the fact that their second-leading scorer, best rebounder, and strongest inside presence was not going to be playing, and it made for an even more challenging day and evening.

They were able to get into Great Falls High's gym again in the late morning to do some shooting, walk through some of the things they wanted to do that night, and go over some of the things they expected Centennial would do. Coaches like their kids to have every advantage they can get, so showing their players the opponents' plays and tendencies can be beneficial. The problem is finding the right balance. Give them too much, and it becomes information overload, and the players can start to overthink things.

This is especially important on the offensive end. Players need to play without thinking too much. Of course, they need to be thinking, but their thoughts should be natural extensions of what they do. They shouldn't have to process so much that they don't just use their natural abilities to execute. Del tried not to pile too much on his kids. However, he also knew that without Connor, they were going to need to be prepared for some things that they hadn't had to deal with throughout the season.

Del was especially concerned for Jimmy Thompson. While Jimmy had played well in his backup role to Connor by coming in and giving the team great minutes when needed, tonight would be a whole different experience. Not only would he be asked to shoulder a much bigger load of minutes and responsibilities, but it was the state championship game! There were so many added pressures and emotions for everyone in this game. But for a player who didn't play as much on a consistent basis, it could prove to be overwhelming.

Therefore, Del and Kevin gave Jimmy only some basic ideas and concepts to focus on—some of his best go-to moves, a few of the plays that they had run all season, playing man-to-man defense against one of Centennial's big men or playing the middle in a 2-3 zone defense, and playing in the back of the press. These were all things that Jimmy had done well during the year, and Del was confident he could do them well tonight.

Del and Kevin also made sure they told him that, too. "You are so ready for this, Jimmy," said Del at the walk-through. "You have played well all year long, you have grown every week, and you continue to excel. You also had a lot of success against this team the first time we played them, so I am really confident you're going to shine tonight." Jimmy smiled, nodded, and thanked Del, but his tone and demeanor didn't exude the same level of confidence that Del's words did.

The rest of the day was a blur for most of the team. There was a trip to Subway for lunch after the walkthrough, followed by a few hours of sitting around the hotel, trying to rest and relax before the game. A couple of the players took naps, but most were too excited to really get any sleep. Dinner was at 4:30 at Applebee's, and then it was off to the arena to watch the 3rd and 4th place game between Jefferson and Two Medicine.

At halftime of that game, the Wolves went into their locker room to get ready. After getting dressed, the boys went out and stretched and got some shots up in a small auxiliary gym in the back of the stadium. While they were gone, Del wrote some things on the whiteboard in the locker room. He heard the locker room door open, and as he turned around, he saw Connor.

Connor had not been around for any of the events of the day—breakfast, walkthrough, lunch, hotel, dinner, or ride to the gym. Del texted him to alert him about each event, but he never got any response. Del didn't push it one way or the other. He knew Connor was struggling, so he just let him be.

Connor said to Del, "Hey, Coach."

"Hey, Connor," said Del. "How are you doing?"

"Okay, I guess." He paused. Del didn't know what to say. Connor then said, "Sorry I wasn't around today."

Del said, "It's okay, Connor. I understand."

Connor said, "If it's okay with you, I'd like to sit on the bench like you offered."

"Absolutely," said Del. "I wouldn't want it any other way."

"Okay, thanks Coach." He nodded back toward the door and said, "I'm gonna' go out and see the guys."

Del said, "Okay, Connor. I'm gonna' get them in here in a few minutes. I want you to be in here with us then, too, okay?"

"Yeah, sure," said Connor. "I'd like that."

Connor walked out of the locker room and headed into the auxiliary gym to see the guys. He was a little embarrassed being in his street clothes while they were all in their uniforms and warmups shooting. Brian Jackson went right over to him and high-fived him and said, "What's up, dude?"

Connor said, "Not much. Just thought I'd watch you guys win a state championship, that's all."

"You mean 'us guys' win a state championship, Connor," said Brian. "You're still part of the team, dude."

Connor said, "Glad to hear at least one of you feels that way."

"Dude, we all feel that way. You were a huge part of us getting here." Connor smiled, and Brian grabbed the ball, took a 3-point shot at the side basket Connor was standing under. It hit nothing but net.

Connor grabbed the ball, passed it back out to Brian, and said, "You need to be wet like that all night, Bri!"

Remington had made his way over to Connor and Brian. Remington said, "What's up?" as he extended his hand for a high-five with Connor.

Connor smiled a sheepish grin and said, "Not much. Figured I'd come coach you up on how to throw sick passes."

"Good," said Remington, "cuz I'll need all the help I can get!"

It felt good to Remington that Connor was there. He always wanted Connor to be there with the rest of his teammates, but Connor rarely joined in. Even though the two of them would not play together again, Remington thought that if they could be this way now, maybe Connor would see the value in being this way with his teammates next year.

Del walked into the gym and watched the boys shooting. He was glad Connor was there. He knew that it would be good for Connor next year to be there today, to be a part of this and see how it all played out. Del called out to the boys and told them to head back into the locker room. It was time for his final pre-game speech of the year.

"Well, this is it," Del started. "Our last game. Our last time together sitting like this. And while that may create all kinds of emotion in you—I know it certainly is in me—I want you to do a few things. First, I want you to think about where you have gotten to. The State Championship Game. That's no small feat. It is the one major goal every team in the state, heck every team in every state, has at the beginning of the year. And you are one of only two teams who made it here in our classification. No matter the outcome tonight, boys, no one will ever be able to take that away from you. You'll always be able to say that you played in a state championship game.

"I also want you to consider what it took to get here. You worked your tails off from day one. Actually, you worked your tails off a lot longer than that. Some of you," Del looked around and found the eyes of Remington, Nick, Tim, and Brian, "came to me on the bus ride home from our final game last year and told me you wanted to play in this game this year. Well, everyone wants to play in this game. But not everyone has a plan and is willing to execute that plan. But you did. You said you were going to do it, and then you went out and worked to make it happen. You truly deserve to be here.

"Finally, I want you to think about this. *Look who you've become.* Look at the team you have become this year. Look at the individual players you have become this year. But most important, look at the person you have each become this year. Your growth as a team, as players, and as people has been incredible. Your accomplishment of getting to this game in some ways is merely a by-product of who you have become. You set out to achieve something great, and along the way, you yourselves became something great.

"Whatever happens tonight, win or lose, don't let that define you. You have defined yourselves in all that you did to get to this point. You have become better versions of yourselves, both individually and collectively. Take that with you on your journey and let that define you, shape you, and push you to the achievements, outcomes, and successes you seek in life.

"But how about we start with tonight?" asked Del with a smile. "Let's have tonight's game be the first success on the new journey that we are all on!"

The boys all smiled along with Del. He then outlined some basic game plan things, some things that Centennial did and some things that the Wolves needed to do. More than anything, though, he focused on enjoying this moment. He told them that they would be nervous and that the Pioneer players were feeling the same way, but that pretty soon, they would just be doing something they have loved to do for a long time—playing basketball. The sooner they could get to that feeling of the joy of playing and living in the moment, the sooner things would feel normal again, and the better they would play.

Braden Larsen had stepped out the door, and he now stepped back in and said, "Three minutes, Coach."

Del said, "Thanks, Coach." He turned back to the team and said, "Boys, I want to thank you for all that you have done this year. All that you have done for our program, our school, and our community. But personally, and maybe selfishly, I want to thank you for all that you have done for me. You brought me some of my greatest highs in this sport. You have provided me some of my favorite moments and so many fun times. But I think most importantly, you taught me things about myself that I needed to learn. Unfortunately, I ain't the sharpest tool in the shed sometimes, and I need to learn the hard way." Del chuckled as he said this, and the team chuckled with him.

He said, "You taught me the lessons that I have been trying to teach you—things like hard work, discipline, mental toughness, selflessness, and integrity. I wanted to teach those traits that help make you people of character. But you taught me those lessons, too. And for that, I am so grateful to you."

Del paused as he looked around the room at heads nodding, some eyes looking at him, others looking at the floor lost in his words or in their own thoughts. "I am so proud of you, so proud of all that you have become. I know I'm not alone. Your parents, your friends, the school, and the community are all proud of you, too. Let's go out and give them one more thing to be proud of." Del paused, looked around, and then said, "Get it?"

The boys yelled, "Got it!" They stood up and gathered around Del, putting their hands up on his. He had tears in his eyes. He said, "It's all yours, Rem."

Remington said, "Boys, this is it. This is what we worked so hard for all year long. Let's go out and do what we set out to do last year. Let's finish what we started. Hold nothing back. We're the better team, and we know it. Now, let's go out and show it! 'Focus' on three—1, 2, 3," and they all yelled, "Focus." He then said, "'Discipline' on three—1, 2, 3," and they all yelled, "Discipline." He then yelled, "'Together' on three—1, 2, 3," and they all yelled, "Together," as they all pulled their hands down in one fell swoop and headed out of the locker room.

Ideas to Consider:

- **Why is it important to try to treat your pre-game habits for a big game like any other game? Why is that so hard to do, though?**

- **What does Del's main focus in his pre-game talk seem to be? Why do you think he chose to focus on those things?**

Chapter 48

The state championship is unlike any other game that a team plays all year long, with its own unique pageantry, excitement, and nerves. As both teams stood for the extra-long introductions of everyone associated with the teams, thoughts raced through Del's head. "We made it! Those boys told me last year they wanted to get here this year, and we did it. Are we ready for this moment? Have I prepared them well enough? Can we do this without Connor? Did I do the right thing by not allowing Connor to play? I wish Dad was here to see this."

Del looked down the line at all of his players. An overwhelming sense of pride overcame him. Of course, he was proud of getting to the state championship. But more than anything, he was proud of the young men he got to work with every day. They were all that a coach would want a team to be. As his seniors were being introduced, he thought back to when they came into the program as freshmen. There was such great promise of who they could become. A lot of people pointed towards this night and this game as the ultimate outcome of what this team could become.

Without diminishing the importance of a state championship, Del thought, "These kids are so much more than just state championship game players. That title is not nearly enough to define them. They are so much bigger and better than any game. I am the luckiest coach in the world to get to coach these kids in this game. Win or lose, it doesn't matter. I can't fathom that it could get any better than this."

Centennial's coach, Jerry White, was the kind of coach Del aspired to be like. Del looked at the Centennial players while they were meeting his players for handshakes at half-court. He thought, "His kids always handle themselves the right way. I bet he's thinking of his kids in a lot of the same ways I'm thinking of mine right now."

Del and Jerry were the last two people to be introduced. As they met at half-court and shook hands Jerry said to Del, "Congrats on getting here, Coach. You've done an incredible job with your boys. I also want you to know something. I always loved coaching against your dad. He was a class act, and his teams always played the right way. In fact, I stole a lot of what I do from him. I see a lot of him in you, Del. Keep up the great work."

Del was stunned at Jerry White's words. He stumbled for a second and finally said, "Thanks, Coach. That means a whole lot to me coming from you. I've always loved how your kids handle themselves and how you guys play. Just try not to play that way tonight, okay?"

They both chuckled and Jerry said, "We'll see about that. Good luck!"

Del said, "Good luck to you, too!" They shook hands again and headed to their benches to give last-minute instructions to their teams. It was finally time to play.

Del started his smaller, older lineup. With Connor out, Mike Visteen started at one of the guard spots, something he rarely did. That meant Brian Jackson was playing inside, a place he was not nearly as comfortable playing. It had also been a long time since he had played there very much, and he hadn't been prepared to do so when they left for the tournament. At the shootaround in the morning was the first time in a long time that he got some work in that position. Kevin Nixon helped him out by offering some pointers on some things he needed to do, but he did not look comfortable at all in the walk-through, and he looked even worse in the first two minutes of the game.

Both teams played a bit tight and nervous to start. With Sacajawea's players not in their usual places, they were struggling to find themselves. Four minutes into the game, Centennial was up 10-6, and Brian already had two turnovers and one of his shots blocked. Del turned to Kevin and said, "We've got to get Brian out of there. He's really struggling. Do you think Jimmy's ready?"

Kevin said, "Yeah, I do. But don't take Brian out. Put him on the perimeter. Let him get his confidence back by being where he is comfortable."

Del agreed. He looked down the bench and said, "Jimmy, go for Mike."

Jimmy Thompson reported into the game. The look of relief on Brian's face was obvious when Jimmy told him to move to the four-spot. Almost immediately, Jimmy made an impact. On Centennial's first shot, he blocked out Grant Bolden, their 6'6" All-Conference post player, jumped up, and snatched the rebound. He kicked it out to Remington on the wing and then sprinted down the middle of the floor ahead of Bolden.

Seeing Jimmy out of the corner of his eye, Remington looked ahead to Nick in the corner in front of him. Another Pioneer defender was running toward the basket ahead of Jimmy. As he saw Remington look at Nick, the defender stepped out towards the corner. As the ball bounced off the floor into Remington's right hand, he continued looking at Nick. This pulled the defender one more step out, giving Remington the space he needed. Without putting his left hand up on the ball or taking his eyes off of Nick, he fired a one-hand pass to Jimmy in mid-stride as Jimmy crossed the free throw line. Jimmy caught it, took two steps, and laid it in the basket. This was the Sacajawea style of play that everyone was accustomed to, and that one play set everything back on the right track. The Wolves started clicking.

Brian became the player he had been all season. A few possessions later, he was spotted up in the corner. Remington saw him open but couldn't get it to him from his angle. However, he saw that Tim could get it to him. Remington passed the ball to Tim, and Tim quickly swung it to Brian in the corner. Brian swished a 3-pointer. The Wolves were ahead by 2. Both teams traded baskets, and when the buzzer sounded to end the first quarter, the Wolves led 18–16.

Connor had been fairly quiet on the bench. He was not accustomed to sitting on the bench in any way, let alone in his street clothes. He felt like all the eyes in the gym were on him, so he stayed fairly still at the far end of the bench. When Jimmy went into the game, though, he started studying what was happening inside. He watched how Grant Bolden was posting Jimmy up and how Jimmy worked to stop him. At the other end, Connor watched Jimmy struggle with Bolden's size. While Jimmy was 6'5" himself, Bolden had a 20-pound advantage over Jimmy. There was no way Jimmy was going to be able to bang inside and muscle Bolden around. As the players came off the floor at the end of the quarter, Connor greeted Jimmy and said, "Dude, you're doing great. That guy's a stud, but you can take him. Keep it up."

Jimmy was a bit startled. Connor had never been this positive with him before. He would talk to him, but usually to criticize him in some way. They were often guarding each other, and all Connor wanted to do was intimidate him. Jimmy had gotten numb to it as the year went on. As Jimmy improved throughout the season, Connor was not beating him as much, and there were many times Jimmy made Connor look foolish by executing moves and fakes on him. This would make Connor more upset, causing him to talk more trash. That just made Jimmy play harder and made him want to beat Connor even more. By the end of the season, Jimmy was beating Connor a lot in practice. This caused Connor to talk less to Jimmy. So it was shocking to Jimmy when Connor was not only talking to him, but talking nicely to him.

Del talked to the team about their jitters being over and how they were themselves again. He talked about a few specifics with regards to things Centennial was doing and what the Wolves needed to do this quarter. As they broke the huddle, Connor again went to Jimmy and said, "You got this, dude," and patted him on the rear end as Jimmy headed to the floor.

The second quarter, though, saw a change in Jimmy's play. Grant Bolden started to show why he was an All-Conference player. He used his size and strength to muscle his way through and around Jimmy. Jimmy tried to use his footwork, but Bolden just pushed him out of the way. As the quarter continued, his confidence level sunk. Fortunately, Bolden got his second foul midway through the quarter, and Jerry White sat him out for a bit. The post player who subbed in for him did not have the same kind of strength and skill as Bolden, and Jimmy started playing well. Remington started looking for Jimmy more, trying to get him the ball in good spots, so he could have success. It was working. Remington found him in the lane for a drop step layup and on the baseline for a short jumper. Jimmy's confidence level was back up.

With Jimmy's two quick buckets, the Centennial defense was collapsing on Remington's drives and Jimmy's inside play. That left Nick, Brian, Tim, or Mike open on the wings and corners. As Remington penetrated and Centennial defenders stepped in to help on Remington and Jimmy, Remington found open shooters on the perimeter. Each of the four shooters got good, open looks at the basket over the last three minutes of the half, and their shots were falling.

At the half, the Wolves were up 38–32.

In the locker room, Del told them that things were looking good. He talked about how Remington was getting into the lane and finding his own shot, Jimmy inside, or the shooters on the perimeter. He talked about how the shooters were getting the looks they liked and knocking them down because they weren't just standing around waiting. Del said that defensively, he liked how well they were switching between their man-to-man and zone defenses. He mentioned that they had not had to press and that they might press at times in the second half to see how Centennial handled it. He then did a quick review of the rotations of their White, Black, and Red presses.

Finally, he tried to boost Jimmy's confidence by talking about how well he played, talking about some of his good moves and his strong rebounding. Del reminded him that Bolden would be back in the second half. He said, "Everything you did out there against the back-ups you can do against Bolden. You just have to believe it and believe in yourself. He's a good player, but you are, too. Trust in yourself. You'll be fine." Jimmy nodded his head as everyone was echoing Del's words of encouragement.

Ideas to Consider:

- **Confidence is tricky, and it can come and go in an instant. What are the coaches and players doing to try to help Jimmy Thompson have the confidence he needs for this moment? Have you done that type of thing for any of your teammates before? Has anyone ever done that type of thing for you? How did that make you feel?**

Chapter 49

With Bolden back in the lineup to start the second half, Centennial's game plan was to re-establish him inside, and it was working. Once again, Jimmy struggled with Bolden's strength. Whether he was posting up or going to the offensive boards, Bolden was having his way, and Jimmy got down on himself. The Pioneers took an early lead, and Del called timeout. Once again, Connor tried to pick Jimmy up and offer encouragement and advice to Jimmy. "Dude, you're going to be fine. You need to relax but also be aggressive. Get after it hard and aggressively with no fear, but relax and just play. You'll be fine."

Connor wished so badly that he could be out there himself. He knew he had screwed up big-time, and he felt terrible about it. He started realizing how much he loved playing basketball. He also realized how much he wanted to contribute to the team. It was tearing him up inside that he couldn't be on the floor tonight. He decided he could contribute in another way, encouraging and supporting them, and offering advice and suggestions based on what he was seeing from the bench. "If I can't play *in* the game, I can at least *be into* the game," he thought.

Jimmy continued to struggle with Bolden. With three minutes left in the quarter and Centennial up 56–48, a Pioneer guard took a jump shot from the free throw line. Jimmy turned to block Bolden out. Bolden executed a "swim move," throwing his right arm and hand straight up and over Jimmy's right shoulder. He pushed his left hand against Jimmy's arm and then pulled his own right arm down in front of Jimmy's body, thereby getting in front of Jimmy. As the ball came off the rim, Bolden jumped up, grabbed it, and slammed it through the rim. The Centennial crowd exploded, and Jimmy dropped his head.

Kevin said to Del, "I think we need to press, Coach. Bolden is killing us inside. I think we need to make him get up and down the floor and get him a little tired. He picked up his third foul a little bit ago. Let's see if we can't get him tired and maybe pick up his fourth."

"Should we leave Jimmy in?" asked Del.

"No," said Kevin "Put Cory in. He's our best big man in our press, and he runs the floor well."

Cory Wilson, a 6'4" forward with long arms, ran like a gazelle and played the back of the press well. Unfortunately, he had been inconsistent in his play all season long. One game he played like he was All-Conference, and the next game he disappeared. He had put in a lot of time since last year, and Del felt terrible that he didn't get much playing time this year. Del looked down the bench, and said, "Cory, go for Jimmy. We're going to go to our White press. You'll be in the back of it. Play that centerfield spot like you do so well. Be aggressive and run the floor."

The Wolves were down by ten when Cory subbed in for Jimmy. Kevin saw how dejected Jimmy was when he came off the floor and Jimmy sat down next to Connor. Kevin walked down the bench and sat next to him. He said, "Hey, don't worry about it. That kid's really good, but you're doing fine." Jimmy did not look like he was buying it at all. He looked shell-shocked. Kevin said, "Jimmy, you've got to trust your training."

"Coach, I know, but nothing I try is working," Jimmy said desperately.

Connor said, "Dude, you're fine, but you can't just bang with that guy. You've got to finesse him. You're a lot quicker than he is. Use your footwork like you do on me in practice. And use those fakes you're so good at. Not to be cocky, but he's not better than I am, and you destroy me with those every night. Give him everything you've got. You'll be fine."

Kevin said, "Connor's right. His strength is his strength. Your strength is your footwork and quickness. He's used his strength against you, but you haven't tried to use yours on him. Slide your feet and cut him off. Beat him to his spots. On offense, catch and go. Use your spin moves. Use your two-dribble drop step. Use your up and under. They will be there, but you need to trust them."

Connor said, "Just do what you do to me in practice. You'll tear him up."

Del set the boys up in their White press, and Centennial set up their press break. When the official handed the ball to the Centennial player standing out of bounds on the baseline, Leif Bjorkland, their All-Conference point guard, broke to the corner to receive the inbounds pass. As he caught the ball, the first trap of the press was already upon him. Bjorkland passed it back to the inbounder who was under the basket. As he started to dribble to the other side of the floor, Tim ran hard at him, forcing him to pick up his dribble and start to make a pass to Bolden up the sideline. Cory was ready. In three long, loping strides, he stepped in front of Bolden and intercepted the pass. He landed with his feet just inside the sideline and fired a pass to Remington at the point. Remington saw Brian cutting from the back side toward the rim and hit him for a layup.

With that one play, the Wolves had a new energy. They immediately got into their press again. Bjorkland was ready for it, and he weaved his way through the press. As he attacked the basket on a 2-on-1 with Bolden, Cory was the only Wolves' defender to beat. Bjorkland looked as if he was going to drive, but he deftly fired a pass across the lane towards Bolden. However, playing against Remington Roberts every day, Cory had seen that kind of play hundreds of times. But Leif Bjorkland's passes were not like Remington's. Cory reached out his long arm and deflected the ball out in front of him. Cory saw a Centennial player running toward the ball, so he dove, laying himself prone in the air. He tipped the ball ahead to Nick before the Centennial player could grab it. Nick turned and found Tim ahead of everyone and lofted a pass to him for an easy layup. The Pioneer lead was now six, and Jerry White called timeout.

As the Wolves came to the bench, the entire team mobbed Cory for his effort on those two plays. Their energy level was completely different. Del told them to keep that pressure up. He talked about adjustments that he expected Jerry White to go to. "He's drawing up what he wants to do against full-court pressure, so we're going to go to our Red Half-Court Trap for the rest of this quarter. He won't be preparing them for that, and he won't want to burn another timeout to discuss it after we attack them with it. Stay aggressive, and get out in those passing lanes. Offensively, just play and attack. I want Bolden tired in the fourth, so let's just run him and attack them from here on out. No letting down!"

As the teams lined up for the inbounds pass, the Centennial players were all in the backcourt expecting the Wolves players to be up there with them. But all of the Wolves players stayed back inside the three-point line in the half-court, as if they were waiting to pick up the Pioneers in their half court man-to-man defense. The Centennial players looked relieved, and they turned and jogged down to their normal spots on offense.

As Leif Bjorkland crossed the half-line with the ball, the Wolves sprang into action in a frenzied blitz. Remington and Nick ran right at Bjorkland to apply a hard trap. Bjorkland immediately picked up his dribble. However, the Centennial wings were slow to react. Tim and Brian picked up the two wings, leaving Cory in the lane with two Centennial post men on either side of the lane. Bjorkland saw the two open post players, but with Remington and Nick draped all over him, he was struggling to get a pass off. He jumped up, and Remington and Nick jumped up with him, mirroring the ball with their hands. Bjorkland threw a pass to Grant Bolden, the bigger target and closer of the two post players. Remington tipped the ball, changing its direction and slowing its speed.

Cory was already anticipating exactly what was happening. As he saw the deflection, he adjusted his movement and beat Bolden to the ball. As he grabbed the ball, Bolden ran into him and knocked him to the floor. Bolden had picked up his fourth foul. Jerry White had to sub him out. The Wolves and Pioneers traded baskets and stops, until the end of the third quarter, and Centennial held a 5-point lead. As the Wolves headed to the bench, there was a feeling of confidence that had not been there earlier in the quarter.

Del stepped into the huddle. "Great job out there, boys. But understand that we've got at least eight minutes left to play. Stay energized, but maintain your focus, discipline, and composure. Be ready for them to come out and throw some things at you like you did to them that quarter. I don't know if Coach White will put Bolden in right away, but you know he's coming back at some point. However, with four fouls, he can't be as aggressive as he usually is. Take advantage of that. And if he is aggressive, by all means, go after him and see if we can get him to foul out."

Del then turned his attention to strategy. "They've seen the half-court trap for the last couple of minutes, so I'm sure he's drawing some things up for that. Let's go to our Black 1-3-1 three-quarter-court press for a bit and see how they handle it. Again, the more we can get them in a fatigued state the better. We have rotated in some fresh bodies, so we should be good to go. Let's keep the pressure on both offensively and defensively. Let's go."

As they stood up to break the huddle, Remington pulled the guys in and said, "This is it, boys! This is what we put in all those hours of work for. It's the fourth quarter of the state championship! Leave nothing in you. Everything you've got! 'Focus' on three—1, 2, 3," and they all yelled, "Focus." He then said, "'Discipline' on three—1, 2, 3," and they all yelled, "Discipline." He then yelled, "'Together' on three—1, 2, 3," and they all yelled, "Together."

Ideas to Consider:

- **What does Connor mean when he thinks, "If I can't play *in* the game, I can at least *be into* the game."? How does he do that? Why is that an important step for him?**

- **What does Kevin Nixon mean when he tells Jimmy Thompson, "You've got to trust your training"? How does Connor echo that thought in trying to boost Jimmy's confidence?**

Chapter 50

Cory Wilson started the fourth quarter the way he finished the third. Del switched the defense for the first possession, putting Cory out front at the top of a 1-3-1 defense. Leif Bjorkland tried to pass the ball across the court to the other guard, but once again, he misjudged the length of Cory's arms. Cory deflected the pass into the backcourt, picked it up, and found Remington cutting toward the middle of the floor. He received the pass from Cory and drove to the middle of the lane. Grant Bolden had run back as fast as he could to try to stop Remington. Even though it was the first possession of the quarter, Bolden already showed signs of being tired.

Remington went straight at Bolden, and he elevated in an attack towards the basket. Brian Jackson cut to the basket behind Bolden. The other Centennial defenders had not gotten back quickly enough to be in good position, and Brian was ahead of them. Remington "shot" a one-handed floater over Bolden's outstretched arm. But he was not shooting the ball; he was passing it to Brian up near the rim. Brian elevated, caught the pass in mid-air, and laid it in off the backboard.

The Wolves were now down three. They went back to their full-court press. This time Centennial was ready, and they were able to break the press with relative ease. However, they were tentative with Cory in the back line, and rather than go right at him, Leif Bjorkland peeled out and set up their offense. For the next three minutes, Centennial and Sacajawea traded makes and misses. Bolden was getting tired, but he was still playing well. Cory looked tired trying to defend him. He had played more minutes tonight than he had played in any other game in the last two weekends.

With 5:12 left in the game, Leif Bjorkland drove the lane and pulled up for a jump shot. Cory slid over to help out on Bjorkland. As Bjorkland shot the ball, Cory tried to slide back to block Bolden out, but he got there too late. Bolden had inside position. As the ball caromed off the rim, Cory leaped to grab it, but he was tired. He banged into Bolden as Bolden was reaching for the rebound. The referee whistled the foul on Cory, sending Bolden to the free throw line for a 1-and-1 opportunity.

Kevin leaned over towards Del and said, "Coach, it's time to get Jimmy back in there."

Del asked, "Do you think he's ready for this moment?"

"Yeah, he's good. I talked with him, and so did Connor. He's good to go."

Del called Jimmy and told him to report in for Cory. The Sacajawea crowd gave Cory a standing ovation as he came off the floor. He had given the boys the spark they needed to get themselves back into the game.

While the players were lining up for Bolden's free throw, Connor stood up and called Remington over to the bench. "This is odd," thought Remington, but he jogged over to where Connor was standing in front of his seat. While Connor was not completely comfortable talking with all the seniors, he respected Remington. He knew Remington was an excellent player, so his estimation of him was high. Remington also threw him enough passes for easy buckets, that he liked that aspect of him a lot.

When Remington got to Connor, Connor said, "Dude, you know how you put the ball either down low in my hip pocket or up at the rim for me?"

Remington was looking down to the other end of the floor watching Bolden make his first free throw. He turned to Connor and said, "Yeah."

"Do that for Jimmy," said Connor. "He likes when you get it to him in those spots, too, and he is so tough to stop when he gets it there. Also, get it to him on his inside hand, so he can set up his two-dribble drop step. That move is killer. Bolden's footwork isn't good enough to stop how quick Jimmy is with his moves, especially that one. He kills me with it every day."

"All right, cool," Remington said.

Connor sat back down in his seat. Del and Kevin looked at each other, a bit dumbfounded. "Where was that kid all year?" asked Kevin.

"I don't know," said Del, "but I sure would have liked to have him on our team!"

Kevin said, "Well, maybe he just showed up at the right time. And he's absolutely right. Jimmy does kill him when he gets the ball in his spot."

Bolden missed his second free throw. Jimmy grabbed the rebound and turned to look for an outlet man. He threw it to Nick, who fired a pass up the floor to Remington on the right wing in front of the Wolves' bench. Jimmy was on the other side of the lane. He flashed across the lane to the side where Remington was. Bolden followed him. Remington delivered a bounce pass to Jimmy's inside hand, just like Connor suggested. Jimmy caught it and made a quick spin move to the middle of the lane. Bolden had overcorrected his positioning, and now Jimmy had a step on him. Jimmy got to the other side of the basket before Bolden could recover, and Jimmy shot a reverse layup with his left hand. The ball kissed off the backboard and fell through the net. Connor jumped to his feet, threw his fist in the air, and yelled, "Yeah!!" Remington looked over at him and gave him a thumbs-up. The Wolves were down by two.

At the other end of the floor, Bjorkland immediately worked to get the ball inside to Bolden. However, Bolden was tired and Jimmy was fresh. Also, after his quick move and score on Bolden, Jimmy was energized with confidence. As Bjorkland tried to get it to Bolden, Jimmy outworked Bolden to get to his spot, and he took the passing lane away. Bjorkland swung the ball to a teammate on the perimeter. Bolden yelled at him, "Get me the ball!"

Bjorkland yelled back at him, "Move your feet and get open!"

Jimmy heard the exchange, and it energized him even more. "No way he gets an easy touch the rest of the game," Jimmy thought. On the shot by Centennial, Bolden tried the same swim move he had used earlier on Jimmy. However, Jimmy had already worked himself into better position, and he slid his feet to where Bolden was trying to get around him and blocked him out. Bolden didn't even try to go around him this time.

Jimmy leaped and grabbed the rebound. He found Nick again in the outlet spot. As soon as his pass left his hands, Jimmy quickly stepped past Bolden and took off on a dead-sprint down the middle of the floor. Bolden was now behind him and trying to catch up. Remington cut towards the middle of the floor, and Nick found him. Remington caught the pass and took two dribbles toward the left wing. Out of the corner of his eye, he saw Jimmy sprinting to the rim. Remington turned, stopped, and threw a two-handed alley-oop toward the front of the rim. Jimmy leaped, caught the ball, and slammed it through the rim. The score was tied. Bolden never made it to 3-point line.

The Wolves' crowd exploded. As Jimmy turned to head back down court, Connor had jumped up with everyone else on the bench hooting and hollering. He cupped his hands around his mouth and yelled, "You've got him, Jimmy! He's tired. Keep attacking him! He can't stay with you!"

Ideas to Consider:

• **What does Connor do that shocks Remington and the coaches? How did his idea have an impact right away?**

Chapter 51

The next three minutes saw both teams giving everything they had. Neither team could pull away from the other, and the largest lead had only been four points. With 1:27 to go, Jerry White called timeout with the score tied, 70-70. Del pulled his team into the huddle. "I'm not sure if he plans on attacking right away or if he is going to have them hold the ball. 1:27 is a long time to hold it. Stay patient out there if that's what they do. Stay up in them, but don't foul. Someone will make a mistake. When they do, pounce on it!"

Del paused for a quick second and said, "But if they attack at any moment, you need to be ready. You need to all be communicating with one another. Depending on when we get the ball back, either attack, or look to me and we'll set something up. We have one timeout left if we need it. Any questions?"

Remington said, "Coach, should we trap Bjorkland to get it out of his hands? I don't think their other guys are that good at getting them set up."

Del looked up at Kevin to see what he thought. "I like it," said Kevin. "Make Rooney play the point if you can. He would rather catch and shoot it on the wing than get other guys set up to score."

The horn sounded, and everyone stood up. Del reiterated, "Be patient. They will make a mistake." He put his hand up, and the boys put theirs up to meet his. Del said, "Wolves on three—1, 2, 3," and they all shouted "Wolves!"

Del's inkling proved to be true. Centennial spread the floor out, and played a version of "keep away" from the Wolves. The Wolves defended the Centennial players well. With 1:00 remaining, Jerry White yelled out, "Iso!" Leif Bjorkland had the ball at the point. He turned and made sure everyone was in the proper spot. As Bjorkland started a hard dribble drive, Tim slid over to help Remington trap Bjorkland just outside of the lane. Bjorkland found Thad Rooney on the wing, though, who was open for a 3-pointer. He caught it and shot it quickly as Tim was sliding back to challenge his shot. The shot hit the front of the rim, then the backboard, then the side of the rim, and Jimmy snared the rebound.

Jimmy outletted the ball to Remington, who dribbled it up the right side of the court. As Remington started up the floor with the ball, Del yelled out, "Spread!" It was the Wolves turn to play a little keep away now. Remington,

Nick, and Brian were up on top, with Tim and Jimmy in the corners. The three guards each took turns handling the ball on dribble attacks toward the lane from the point and corners near the half-line. But Centennial's help defenders kept cutting off their drives. That was fine with Del. He just wanted to get the clock down to 0:20, so he could call time out and set up the play he wanted.

In the timeout, Del said, "We're going to run 'Special.' I know we haven't run it much in games, but we worked on it earlier today specifically for a moment like this." Del quickly drew up the play again on the whiteboard. "This play takes a little bit of time to develop. After we inbound the ball, get to your spots right away. Rem, hold it out front until 0:14 left. Then yell 'Go!' Jimmy, that's when you will turn and start your screen action for Nick. Brian, that's when you will cut to the corner. Nick, be strong with the ball before you hand it to Rem." Nick nodded.

"Rem, when you get it back from Nick, look at all your options. "You should get it back at around 0:08. That's an eternity, boys. We want to shoot it with two or three seconds left. That's enough time for an offensive rebound and shot, but not enough for them to get a rebound and go the length of the floor. If we miss, DO NOT FOUL THEM OVER THE BACK GOING FOR THE BALL! We will just go into overtime. Get it?"

They all yelled, "Got it!" They broke the huddle and went to their spots for the inbounds pass. Amazingly, the Centennial players were not out pressuring the inbounds pass. Remington got the ball on Nick's inbound pass. He took it to the point and stood there dribbling as the clock ticked down. At 0:14 he yelled, "Go!" Jimmy was at the free throw line and he turned and cut towards Nick in the right corner to set a screen for him. Nick faked like he was cutting to the basket, and then he cut off of Jimmy's screen out to the right wing. Jimmy rolled to the right block. Brian cut from the left block to the right corner replacing Nick. Tim popped from the left corner up to the left wing.

Remington passed the ball to Nick on the right wing. He then followed his pass to receive a handoff from Nick. Nick turned his back to his defender and protected the ball as he handed it to Remington. Nick then turned and cut to the far corner on the left side of the floor. Remington was holding the ball on the right wing waiting for Nick to get to the far corner. Brian was now in the corner to his right, and Jimmy was posted up on the block in front of Remington. Tim was on the left wing and Nick was in the far-left corner.

Remington saw the clock read 0:07 as he swept the ball down hard from his right to his left and began his dribble attack into the lane. Jimmy was posted up against Bolden. Bolden was on the top side of Jimmy with both feet in the lane. He didn't want to leave Jimmy alone, but he also had to help on Remington's drive. Brian was back behind Remington in the right corner being guarded by Thad Rooney. As Remington drove, Jimmy sealed Bolden off, so

Remington could toss a lob pass towards the corner of the backboard. There was no way Bolden could get it if Remington put it up there.

Thad Rooney, guarding Brian in the corner, saw all this happening. He knew he was supposed to help on Jimmy on any drive into the lane. He started to slide down the baseline away from Brian to take the pass to Jimmy away. Remington caught a glimpse of him sliding down to help on Jimmy. Brian recognized what was happening, and he slid up the three-point line a few steps toward the wing where Remington had just been.

Somehow Remington knew exactly where everyone was. He looked up towards where he would toss the ball to Jimmy near the backboard. This lured Bjorkland, Bolden, and Rooney to each try to take that lob pass away. But Remington had other plans. As he looked up to where he would throw the lob pass, he instead flipped a one-hand underhanded pass off the dribble with his left hand behind his back to where he figured Brian was now standing.

People say it all the time, but it was as if Remington had eyes in the back of his head. The ball came to Brian in perfect position to catch it and shoot it. He stepped into the catch, elevated, and shot a three-pointer. It was as if the entire play had been put into slow-motion as everyone in the stadium followed the flight of the ball. The clock ticked down—0:03, 0:02, 0:01—as the ball fell through the air and swished through the bottom of the net. The arena exploded, and Jerry White made a "T" with his hands above his head while yelling "Timeout." But as he was doing so, the buzzer sounded, and the clock read 0:00. The game was over. The Wolves were state champions!

The Wolves' players were jumping up and down in total jubilation. They mobbed Brian after his game-winning shot, and the players on the bench sprinted onto the floor and joined the mob. The Wolves' fans were jumping up and down and screaming. Some tried to get out on the floor with the team, but security people held them back. The fans lined up around the court, waiting to get a chance to join in the celebration with the players.

Crushed by their defeat, the Centennial players stood in front of their own bench consoling each other. They started to line up for the post-game hand-shake line. Many were in tears. They had fought so hard, only to come up short in the last seconds. Even though they were a perennial state championship contender, it never got old playing there. Winning always felt great, and losing felt like someone had just ripped their hearts out.

As Del was hugging his players, he pulled all of the boys into a quick huddle and said, "Line up to shake hands. Understand what they're going through and be respectful, boys. They just pushed you to the absolute limit." He then put his hand in the air, the boys joined him, and he said, "Centennial on three-1, 2, 3," and the boys yelled, "Centennial."

They made their way through the handshake line. Del and Jerry White were each at the back of their respective lines. As the Wolves' players each finished with the line, they immediately sprinted to their fans, who were still not being allowed out on the court, as the tournament committee was setting up for the trophy presentation at center court. When Jerry White met Remington and shook his hand, he said, "Young man, I've seen some amazing players in all my years doing this. But you're at the top of the list. Congratulations!"

Remington said, "Thank you, Coach. I really appreciate that. You've got a great team. I loved having the opportunity to play against them tonight."

When he got to Del at the end of the line, Jerry White said, "Congratulations, Coach! I know what it feels like to win your first one. You deserve it. You've done an amazing job. I'm sure your dad would be real proud."

Del choked back a tear and said, "Thanks, Coach. That means a lot."

Jerry said, "You're going to miss that Roberts kid a whole lot. I don't think I've ever seen anyone like him. That kid is the complete package. He does it all—scores, handles it, defends, and leads. And he's the best passer I've ever seen. I've never seen a pass like that in the most crucial moment of any game, let alone a state championship. Yet he not only had skill to pull it off, but he had the guts to throw it. Where is he going next year?"

"Not sure yet," said Del. "He has some D1 offers and lots of D2 and NAIA schools. But he has just wanted to focus on finishing this off first."

"Well, if there's anything I can do, anyone you want me to talk to, let me know. He's good enough that we could be watching him on TV in the future!"

"I think so, too, Coach. Thanks for the offer."

The two men split up and headed to their respective areas on the court, as the Montana High School Association director was about to begin the trophy presentation for both teams.

Ideas to Consider:

- **Why is it fitting that for the final play of the game, Remington throws a pass instead of taking the final shot?**
- **What does Coach White say about Remington to both Remington and Del?**

Chapter 52

After Matt Blake, the Director of the Montana High School Association, handed the second-place trophy to Leif Bjorkland and Grant Bolden of Centennial, he turned his attention to the Sacajawea team. He commented that it was the first time in a long time that Sacajawea had been back to the state championship and how under Mason Brooks, Sacajawea had been regulars at the tournament. He said how proud he felt Mason Brooks would be to see his son Del carry on the tradition and bring home a state championship to Discovery. The Sacajawea crowd erupted in applause at that comment, and Matt Blake handed the trophy to Del. The two men exchanged a handshake, and Del said, "Thank you, sir." Del then thrust the trophy in the air, looked toward the ceiling, and quietly said, "Thanks, Dad."

Del turned and handed the trophy to Remington who was standing next to him. Remington took the trophy in his hands and raised it high above his head. He had just set a state tournament record for assists in a single game at the tournament, handing out 17 of them! He had also set the record for the entire tournament with 41 assists over three games.

But none was more amazing than the last one. People were still talking about that final pass that set up Brian Jackson's game-winning shot. Many still could not believe it. People who had not watched Remington play before wondered, "How did that kid see his teammate behind him? How did he know where to throw it?" Even those who had seen him play were shocked. The passes and dribble-drives he had made through the years had made people numb to how skilled he was. But even that pass had them in awe.

Remington turned and pulled all of his teammates around him and held the trophy above his head for them all to reach out and touch for a team picture with it. He then handed it to Nick, who handed it to Tim, and so on down the line of all the players. They each got to hold the state championship trophy in their own hands for a few seconds before passing it on to a teammate.

They all then were escorted to the free throw lane in front of their own bench, where a stadium custodial staff member had set up a ladder for the ceremonial net-cutting celebration. The fans were now allowed to be out on the court with the team, and people were hugging everywhere they turned.

Beginning with the managers, then the bench players, and working their way up to the starters, each of them went up the ladder to cut off a little piece of the net. Brian Jackson was the player who they had go up the ladder to make the last cut off the first basket. After he cut his little piece, he pulled the net off of the rim. This was the net that 25 minutes ago his jump shot had swished through, securing the state championship for Sacajawea. He looked out at the cheering crowd around him, swung the net over his head a few times, and placed it around his neck.

After Brian came down off of the ladder, Kevin Nixon carried the ladder down to the other basket. It was the seniors' turn. Mike Visteen went first, followed by Cory Wilson. As each senior finished and came down the ladder, the next one went up. Remington's teammates told him he should cut the last loop. He was the heart and soul of this team. He was always focused on all of them. They told him it was his turn to take the spotlight.

He was a little embarrassed by it all, and he said, "No, Coach should cut the last loop. He's the one who led us here."

Del was standing with the other seniors as they were discussing this. He heard Remington's comment and said, "No, Rem, your teammates are right. You led us here. You were the leader of this team. You go up and get that net on the last cut. You've earned it, son."

Nick went next, followed by Braden Larson and Kevin Nixon, and Del. Del cut his piece of net and looked to the ceiling again, as the crowd was chanting, "Coach Brooks! Coach Brooks! Coach Brooks!" It was an amazing feeling to Del. Standing there on that ladder looking out at everyone, he felt a bit like he had reached a pinnacle. He had worked so hard to get his team to this point, and he wanted to savor the moment.

Kevin Nixon noticed that there were two loops left to cut, but only Remington was left. Kevin yelled up to Del, "Coach! There's one extra loop. I think you need to cut that one, too. That one is for your dad."

Del looked down at Kevin, stunned at the thought. He looked at the crowd. Those who heard Kevin's comment started yelling, "That's right, Coach."

"Cut that piece for your dad."

Nick yelled out, "He was here with us the whole way too, Coach."

Some of the fans who were there had played for Del's dad. One of them yelled out, "Cut it for Mason!" Others echoed his comment, and the crowd started chanting, "Ma-son Brooks! Ma-son Brooks! Ma-son Brooks!"

Del could barely see what he was cutting through the tears in his eyes. He made the cut and took the piece of net and thrust it above his head. He looked to the ceiling and said, "That's for you, Dad." The crowd was cheering and chanting "Ma-son Brooks!" the entire time.

Del gathered himself, wiped his eyes, and headed down the ladder. As he stepped off the ladder, Remington was there to meet him. They hugged a big bear-hug. Remington spoke into Del's ear, "We did it, Coach. Thanks for everything you did to get us here."

Del pulled away from Remington a bit, and with tears still in his eyes and more on the way, said, "Once again, Rem, the thanks goes to you, buddy. You got us here a lot more than I did."

Del handed Remington the scissors and Remington started up the ladder. Suddenly, he stopped. The crowd was chanting his name. But he had just realized something wasn't right. As he stood on the second rung of the ladder, he could see out over the heads of everyone. He found who he was looking for. As he stepped off the ladder, he said, "Just a minute."

People started yelling, "Hey! Where are you going?"

Remington made his way through to the edge of the crowd where Connor was standing with Jimmy Thompson. Connor had not felt comfortable being inside of the crowd with all of the players going up the ladder and cutting the net. It was too much for him to take, so he stayed out of the way. He watched and he cheered as each player and coach went up the ladder, but he couldn't be that close. It just hurt too much. Jimmy had his little piece of the net tied around the strap of his uniform by his shoulder. Remington got to Connor and said, "Dude, what are you doing out here? You deserve one of these," pointing to Jimmy's piece of the net, "as much as anyone else."

Connor looked stunned. He started to say something, but Remington just said, "Come on. I want you up on that ladder with me to split the last loop." Remington grabbed Connor by the arm and started pulling him with him.

Connor and Remington walked through the crowd, and everyone started cheering again. They started chanting, "Connor! Connor! Connor!"

As the two boys stood at the bottom of the ladder, Connor said, "How the heck are we gonna' get up that ladder together?"

Remington said, "Yeah, good point. I guess I didn't think this all the way through. You go first."

Connor said, "Are you sure?"

"Absolutely," said Remington.

Connor climbed the ladder to more chants of his name. He cut the final loop, but left it attached to the rim. He cut his own small piece of the loop and waved it above his head as the crowd cheered. He came down the ladder, handed Remington the scissors, and said, "Thanks, Rem."

Remington smiled and said, "Dude, you deserved it. You were a huge key to us getting here, and quite honestly, even on the bench tonight, you were a huge help. Thanks for all you did to help us get here, man." They bro-hugged, and Remington turned toward the ladder.

Remington then climbed the ladder to chants of "Rem-ing-ton! Rem-ing-ton! Rem-ing-ton!" He cut the final piece of net from the last loop, grabbed the net, and held it high in the air. Like Brian Jackson, he then swung it around his head, yelled a yell of total jubilation, and placed the net around his neck.

Remington looked out at the crowd cheering him on. He had a huge smile on his face. He looked out at all the fans and friends of his. Suddenly, Remington was overcome with emotion as he thought about all the years of playing while growing up in Phoenix and then in Discovery. He thought of all the years of getting in the gym to do skill work, the weight room workouts, the open gyms, playing in Grizzly Park, practices, games, locker room talks, and road trips.

He then saw Nick, Tim, and Brian standing below him. As he looked at his three closest teammates, he thought about them walking to the front of the bus last year to tell Coach about their goal to get here. "This is what I wanted," he thought. "This is what I was thinking of when we talked with coach. I wanted to feel this feeling so bad. It's even better than I imagined."

As he was about to step off the ladder, his gaze caught Jenny out on the perimeter of the crowd with tears streaming down her face, smiling and waving at him. He hadn't gotten to spend much time with her during the post-game celebration, as he had been with his teammates and coaches more than anyone else. He had briefly spent a moment with her, and she gave him a huge hug. Now, seeing her smiling and waving at him, he smiled and pointed back at her.

Just then she was mouthing words to him slowly. He tried to read her lips, and then it hit him what she said—"I... love... you."

"Oh my gosh!" thought Remington. His eyes widened at her and he mouthed back to her, "WHAT?"

Once again, she mouthed, "I... love... you," and this time she pointed at him when she said, "you."

He didn't know what to do, so he did what seemed the most natural thing to do in the moment—he mouthed back to her, "I love you, too!"

Her smile widened. Tears seemed to gush down her face now, and Remington was a little embarrassed by the moment. He wanted to get off that ladder fast, go hug her, and hear her say it for real.

He finished waving to the crowd and quickly climbed down the ladder. He made a beeline for Jenny. As she saw Remington coming off the ladder towards her, she drifted a little further away from the back of the crowd so as to be alone. When he got to her, he threw his arms around her for a giant hug. He then pulled his head away from the side of her head, looked into her eyes, and said, "What did you mouth to me when I was on that ladder?"

She said, "You know what it was because you mouthed it right back to me."

"I want to hear you say it," he said.

She whispered into his ear, "I love you, Remington."

He pulled his head away from hers again and looked into her eyes, smiling from ear-to-ear. "Oh my gosh, you said it! You really said it." He then leaned his head back next to hers and whispered in her ear, "I love you, too, Jen!" As he pulled back away from her ear, he looked into her eyes, seeing the tears flowing out of them. "I've been wanting to say that to you for months, but I didn't know if I should. I didn't know if you felt that way about me."

She said, "I didn't know you felt that way about me either, Rem."

They were so glad to finally say it to the other, and they were so glad to hear it from the other. They had felt it for the longest time, but they didn't dare bring it up to the other one, for fear of ruining their whole relationship by laying something so heavy like that on the other one. One minute they were both worried about if the other one felt the same way about them; the next minute they were on Cloud Nine, and all the world seemed so right.

They now realized that they were standing out on the court at the Four Seasons Arena somewhat surrounded by a throng of people who wanted to congratulate Remington on leading his team to the state championship. They pulled away from each other as friends and fans came up and patted him on the back, offering him congratulations. Remington thanked everyone who congratulated him, but he kept his left arm around Jenny's shoulders.

As he was thanking people who were congratulating him, over the tops of heads he saw his dad. His dad had been the one who had introduced him to this game that he loved so much and that he had become so good at. His dad had been the one who started him down the path towards a dream of winning a state championship. And now that Remington's dream had just come true, he needed to go share this moment with his dad. He pulled his arm off of Jenny's shoulder and said, "I've got to go see my dad."

She said, "You mean you haven't seen him yet?"

"No," he said. "With all the excitement and everything going on right after the game, I haven't gotten over to be with him and mom yet."

"Rem, get your butt over there now. You need to share this with him. He's the whole reason this thing ever started, isn't he?"

"Absolutely," he said. Remington gave her a quick kiss and headed towards where he saw his mom and dad. They had just shaken hands with Kevin Nixon, who was now walking away from them.

As Remington approached his mom and dad, they all had giant smiles on their faces. He held his arms wide as he approached his mom. She said to him, "Congratulations, Honey! I'm so proud of you!"

Remington threw his arms around his mom in a big hug and said, "Thanks, Mom." He pulled away from her and said, "That was so fun!"

She said, "It was fun for us, too. You played fantastic!"

Remington turned to his dad. His dad had tears in his eyes, and immediately, Remington's eyes teared up, too. He reached out for a giant hug. His dad said, "Congratulations, Son. I'm so proud of you and so happy for you."

Remington buried his head in his dad's shoulder and said, "Thanks, Dad. I couldn't have done it without you."

Steve said, "Oh, I don't know about that."

Remington pulled away from his dad and said, "No, seriously, Dad. You're the whole reason I ever started playing this game. You're the whole reason I fell in love with basketball. Watching your teams growing up, being on the floor with them, you taking me to your gym to shoot and work on my game, coaching me on my AAU teams down in Phoenix and up here. If it hadn't been for you, I would have never gotten here."

"Thanks, Son. I may have had a little bit to do with it. But what you did, what you've accomplished, that's all you, Buddy. I may have helped lay a foundation and helped you find your love of the game, but you took it and ran with it, and became the player you became because of what *you* did, not what I did." He paused and then said, "And now look at yourself. You're a state champion!"

Remington smiled and said, "I love the sound of that!"

Marie said, "All those years dreaming of this moment, and now here it is. Way to go, Rem."

Remington said, "Thanks, Mom. I still can't believe it."

Steve said, "You played an amazing game, Bud. That final pass was unlike anything I've ever seen in a game. I never worked on something like that with you. How did you throw that? How did you know Brian was behind you there?"

Remington smiled and said, "I just took the things you taught me and kind of worked on them at a little different level and at different angles through the years. I had practiced that one before, but I never tried it in a game before. I was also a little worried what Coach would say or do if I tried it, so I never did. But in that moment, it was the perfect pass for that spot. It just felt like the most natural thing to do."

"Well, it was simply amazing," said Marie.

"It was," said Steve. "But you know what was just as amazing and what I was even more proud of?"

"What?" asked Remington.

"When you got off that ladder, walked over to Connor, and pulled him up there with you to get a piece of that net."

Remington dropped his head, embarrassed a bit by the compliment his dad was giving him. "Well, he was a key to us getting here. He was a part of it all season. Even though he was a butt-head at times, he deserved a piece of that net as much as anyone. I just thought he shouldn't be left out."

"That's so you, Son," said Steve. "It's also what I love most about you and what makes you the player you are. You're always thinking of others, always thinking of your teammates. I couldn't be prouder of you."

"Thanks, Dad," said Remington. He looked around the gym and said, "Well, I want to talk to some other people and then get in and get a shower and get ready to head back to Discovery."

Marie said, "Are you riding with us?"

Remington looked torn about how to answer her. Before he could say anything, Steve said, "Marie, this is the last bus trip he'll ever take with these teammates, and they're carrying home the state championship trophy. I think he should probably go with them. It will be the best bus ride he's ever taken."

Remington smiled as Marie said, "Oh, of course. Sorry. I hadn't even thought about that."

"It's okay, Mom," said Remington.

He turned to Steve, gave him another hug, and said, "Thanks, Dad. Love you."

Steve said, "Love you, too, Son. Have fun."

Remington hugged his mom and said, "Love you, Mom."

"Love you, too, Rem," said Marie.

Remington made his way around to other friends and groups of people who were all offering their congratulations to him. After a while, he made his way back to Jenny. She said, "How was it talking to your mom and dad?"

"It was the best," said Remington. "I know we're supposed to struggle with our parents when we're our age, but I've got the best parents ever."

"I don't know about that," said Jenny. "I think mine are pretty cool, too."

"Yeah, they are," said Remington. "God, we're a couple of nerds, aren't we?"

"I wouldn't have it any other way," said Jenny, and they both laughed.

Remington said, "I'm going to go get a shower, and then the bus is headed home. It'll be really late when we get home. Can I see you tomorrow?"

"Of course," said Jenny. "How about we meet at the Elkhorn for lunch at noon? My treat for the state champion!"

"That sounds awesome, Jen!" said Remington. "I'll see you then."

He gave her a hug. She whispered in his ear, "I love you, Rem."

"Love you, too, Jen," he said. He gave her a quick kiss and headed towards the locker room. It felt so good to say that and to hear her say it, too.

He headed towards the gap between the bleachers that led to the locker room. As he was about to step off the court for the last time as a high school basketball player, Remington paused for a moment, turned around, and looked at the crowd milling about and talking with one another. He looked around the giant stadium, the bleachers, the banners in the rafters, the baskets, scorer's table, and benches. He thought about the end of the game and the last forty minutes celebrating their championship and thought, "I'm not sure how or where I'm going to get it, but I want more of this feeling... for a long, long time."

Ideas to Consider:

- **What makes the net-cutting especially emotional for Coach Brooks?**

- **What does Remington do during the net-cutting that, once again, shows him to be the "ultimate team player"? Why did he do that?**

- **Jenny and Remington finally say, "I love you," to each other. Why did they wait so long? Why should people in an intimate relationship be careful about how early they say this? How might it affect their relationship? How do you think it will affect Jenny and Remington?**

~ ~ ~ *EPILOGUE* ~ ~ ~

Remington and Jenny finally said it. Now what? Did that affect them and their college decisions and their futures?

Where did Remington decide to go to school? Did he fulfill his lifelong dream and go to Duke? Or did he choose ASU and go back home to where he started his basketball playing career? Or did he choose another D1 school elsewhere in the country? Or did he stay in Montana and play for the University of Montana or Montana State?

What about Jenny? Did she choose Stanford? Or did she stay in-state? Did the two of them end up together at the same school?

Sorry, but you're going to have to wait to find out. The answers to these questions and so much more await you in Book #3 of the series.

Stay tuned at <u>SlamDunkSuccess.com</u> to hear more about when Book #3 in the *Remington Roberts Series* is released. Until then, check out Book #1 in the series, *Ultimate Team Player: Remington Reunites the Team*, if you haven't read that yet. Also, check out the next page for information on how to get the **FREE prequel** to the series, *Discovery Calls: Remington Relocates.*

Who is Remington Roberts?

Where did he come from?

How did he become
such a great basketball player?

Find out in the prequel to the Remington Roberts Series—just released—*Discovery Calls: Remington Relocates.* You can get this prequel in digital format for FREE! Just go to the SlamDunk Success website and sign up to receive Scott's newsletter.

You will receive a link to download the eBook (PDF format). You will learn where Remington came from, where he grew up, how he started down the road to becoming a great basketball player, and how he ended up in Discovery, Montana, which is over 1,100 miles away from his home.

Visit <u>SlamDunkSuccess.com</u>
and sign up for our newsletter
to get the prequel now!

Other Books by Scott Rosberg

Ultimate Team Player
Remington Reunites the Team

Discovery Calls
Remington Relocates (eBook)

Time Out!
How We Can Fix the Problems in Kids' Sports Today

The Responsibilities of Coaching

A Head Coach's Guide for Working with Assistants

The Assistant Coach's Guide to Coaching

Playing Time:
A Guide for Coaches, Athletes, and Parents

Establishing Your Coaching Philosophy

Team and Program Policies: Elements to Consider

The Sportsmanship Dilemma:
Guidelines for Coaches, Athletes, and Parents

Building Your Coaching Staff Chemistry (eBook)

Senior Salute
Gift Booklet for Senior Athletes

Inspiration for the Graduate
Gift Book for Graduates

You can find each of these titles at
SlamDunkSuccess.com

You can also join the SlamDunk Success
community to start receiving Scott's newsletter,
blog, and any new updated materials.

Email Scott with any questions at
scott@slamdunksuccess.com

About the Author

Scott Rosberg has served in the roles of English teacher, coach, and athletic director for over 35 years. In addition to the *Remington Roberts Series*, Scott has published multiple non-fiction books on character-based coaching and athletics, team-building, and leadership, all of which can be found on his **SlamDunk Success** website, SlamDunkSuccess.com. He has also published two books of inspirational messages and quotes—one for senior athletes and one for graduates. Scott has published numerous articles, blogs, and videos. He does workshops, classes, and presentations at schools, conferences, and businesses. He hosts a podcast called, *Great Quotes for Coaches*, available wherever you listen to podcasts. Finally, check out the **SlamDunk Success Facebook page.**

Scott is also a member of the **Proactive Coaching** team of speakers. Proactive Coaching is dedicated to helping organizations create character-based team cultures, while providing a blueprint for team leadership by helping develop confident, tough-minded, fearless competitors and train coaches and leaders for excellence and significance. Proactive Coaching can be found on the web at www.ProactiveCoaching.info and on the Proactive Coaching Facebook page at Facebook.com/proactivecoach.

www.ingramcontent.com/pod-product-compliance
Lightning Source LLC
Chambersburg PA
CBHW071153260626
47162CB00003B/1040